Acclaim for A. L. Kennedy's

DAY

Winner of the Costa Book Award

"Few historical novels wear their research so lightly and integrate it so well, with a flawless instinct for the telling detail. But *Day* is much more than a triumphant marriage of research and storytelling." —*The San Diego Union-Tribune*

"A novel of minute particulars, of the ticking silence of time just creeping on. After the war is over, Kennedy seems to say, life— whether one wants it to or not—goes on, and sometimes it's a pale imitation of what came before, especially if what came before was hell." —*Milwaukee Journal Sentinel*

"A remarkable performance." —*The Sunday Telegraph* (London)

"Evocative. . . . Kennedy's war scenes show a depth of research into technical matters as well as the psychological responses of people caught in the maelstrom of war." —*Rocky Mountain News*

"*Day* confirms, if confirmation were needed, that Kennedy is a singular, superlative author." —*Scotland on Sunday*

A. L. Kennedy

DAY

A. L. Kennedy lives in Glasgow. Her previous books include three collections of short stories, five novels, and two works of nonfiction. She has received many prizes for her work, including the Lannan Literary Award.

www.a-l-kennedy.co.uk

ALSO BY A. L. KENNEDY

FICTION
Night Geometry and the Garscadden Trains
Looking for the Possible Dance
Now That You're Back
Original Bliss
So I Am Glad
Everything You Need
Indelible Acts
Paradise

NONFICTION
The Life and Death of Colonel Blimp
On Bullfighting

DAY

DAY

A Novel

A. L. Kennedy

Vintage Contemporaries
Vintage Books
A Division of Random House, Inc.
New York

FIRST VINTAGE CONTEMPORARIES EDITION, MARCH 2009

The Library of Congress has cataloged the Knopf edition as follows:
Kennedy, A. L.
Day / by A. L. Kennedy.—1st ed.
p. cm.
1. World War, 1939–1945—Veterans—Great Britain—Fiction. 2. World War, 1939–1945—Prisoners and prisons—Fiction. 3. Recollection (Psychology)—Fiction. 4. Psychological fiction. I. Title.
PR6061.E5952D39 2008
823'.914—dc22 2007017195

Vintage ISBN: 978-0-307-38631-1

Book design by Soonyoung Kwon

www.vintagebooks.com

Printed in the United States of America
10 9 8 7 6 5 4 3 2 1

Tha móran an so.

DAY

Alfred was growing a moustache.

An untrained observer might think he was idling, at a loose end in the countryside, but this wasn't the case. In fact, he was concentrating, thinking his way through every bristle, making sure they would align and be all right.

His progress so far was quite impressive: a respectable growth which already suggested reliability and calm. There were disadvantages to him, certain defects: the shortness, inelegant hands, possible thinning at his crown, habit of swallowing words before they could leave him, habit of looking mainly at the ground—and those few extra pounds at his waist, a lack of condition—but he wasn't so terribly ugly, not such a bad lot.

Mainly his problem was tiredness—or more an irritation with his tiredness—or more a tiredness that was caused by his irritation—or possibly both. He could no longer tell.

It wasn't that he was awkward, or peculiar, quite the reverse: he was biddable and sensible and ordinary, nothing more: but even an ordinary person could sometimes have enough and get browned off and, for example, want to be offered, every now and then, a choice.

That was only reasonable, wasn't it? A man had to imagine he'd got a chance at freedom, a bit of space. The interval between alternatives, that gave you space. But sometimes you would consider yourself and all you could see were obstructions and you'd be amazed that you ever were able to leave your house—your bed, never mind your house. You'd look in the mirror some mornings and wonder why it didn't show; the way most of you was always yelling to get out.

Moustache or no moustache, that wouldn't change.

The trouble was, you had too much to do: breathing, sleeping, waking, eating: you couldn't avoid them, were built to need them, and so they just went on and on. Where were the other possibilities, the changes you might want to make—like walking off beneath the ocean—not being a fish, he bloody hated fish, but being a man tucked away in the ocean, why couldn't he try that? Why couldn't he try out whatever he thought?

And thinking itself, that wasn't helpful and yet you had to do it all the time. It was there when you dreamed, when you spoke, when you carried out your very many other compulsory tasks. If you couldn't keep control and stay wary, you might think anything, which was exactly the one freedom you'd avoid. You could dodge certain thoughts, corkscrew off and get yourself out of their way, but they'd still hunt you.

You have to watch.

This morning he could feel them, inside and out, bad thoughts getting clever with him, sly. They lapped like dirtied water behind his face and outside him they thickened the breeze until the surface touching him, pressing his lips, was far more quick and complex than only air. Today it had the smell of blue, warm Air-Force blue: the stink of drizzle rising up from wool and everywhere the smell of living blue: polish and hair oil and that sodding awful pinky-orange soap and Woodbines and Sweet Caporal and those other cheap ones, the ones they gave away after ops: Thames cigarettes, to flatten out the nerves.

"Hello, looks like London Fog again."

Pluckrose had started them calling it London Fog: the Thames smoke haze in the briefing room—him first and then everybody. One of the things they had between them as a crew: "London Fog again."

But he wouldn't remember Pluckrose, wasn't going to ask him in.

Chop it. All right?

And this time I mean it. All right?

So the noise throttled back, obedient, let him be where he was.

Not that he was any too clear about that—his precise location—beyond the fact that he was sitting, sitting behind a young moustache.

They'd left the path an age ago, Alfred hadn't noticed when, and there was no doubt they were lost now, if they ever had known where to go. And that had been something of a pain, an irritation: arriving in nowhere, having to stumble and tramp along on a track that divided and twisted and then abandoned them completely: sent him sweating through ragged scrub behind a man who was a stranger—Vasyl—someone you heard about: rumours of bad history and a knife.

But this is fine. I am still enjoying my situation. It doesn't worry me a bit. Because I am choosing to be happy. It's all so big and flat out here that I can have room for that.

And it's a fine day and good to get a rest, clear off out of it into the open. So I won't be downhearted: there's no need.

Plus, at least this is peaceful and I always did appreciate a little peace. You can have enough of crowds. They pester your head.

One at a time, you could deal with people, but not crowds, and these last weeks had been very much less than deserted—being transported, lectured, ordered about—just like the old days—too much like the old days—you and the other volunteers. First rule of civilised life—never volunteer. So it's sensible today, when you're not required, that you should go and catch your breath, get settled down, and nobody can do that with an audience: it's neither possible nor dignified.

Vasyl, of course, is not an audience and therefore doesn't count. Men you hear stories about take no interest in what you do. They let you carry on as you want to and pretend they haven't seen. They act the way they hope you will for them.

It must have been a while since they'd packed in the walking, settled themselves on a patch of turf scattered with small yellow flowers he couldn't name. His view of the moorland was gently shuddering with heat and he realised he'd kicked pale dust all over his boots, his trouser cuffs. Everything he wore was loaned to him, not truly his responsibility, but still in some part of himself it was kit he was used to maintaining. Why else keep wearing it? He didn't have duties today, it wasn't necessary.

Look at you—filthy—all over the place—you'd have been torn off one for this, Day. You'd have put up a black for this. A proper disgrace to everyone concerned.

Sod it now, though, eh? No more playing silly buggers over that.

Not to mention that King's Regulations no longer apply.

And the dust, you might say, was so distant there at the far end of his body and nothing to do with up here and the neat, clean secrecy of private thought, invited thought.

A good roast of sun, it slows you, lets you relax—and out here if there's anything wrong, you can see it coming with bags of time to do what's next. This is the place and the weather for peace, for the cultivation of a friendly mind.

He wriggled his fingers and focused on enjoying the well-trained, emptied murmur that mildly ran his brain inside his skull, circulated the blood, kept him smooth and defended and working, imagining a thrum against his hands where they cuddled the back of his head and kept him from the lumps and buttons in his folded jacket. Battledress made a lousy pillow. You might almost think it had been invented with some other purpose in mind.

The wiry grass was pricking through his shirt, but that was quite calming for some reason, as was the din of insects, singing out around him for mile upon tussocky mile. Lying down like this: it was very good— a long time since he'd known it be so satisfactory and really improved by having this stranger with him, this Vasyl, this silly basket who was sitting and rocking and shifting and messing about, flicking an American lighter constantly, sucking on stolen American cigarettes. Very possibly he stole the lighter, too.

"D'you have to smoke that loudly?"

"I do, yes. I do." Funny accent, as if his tongue had been damaged, or was numb. "These are good. Highest quality. You want one?" And a dry voice, dulled—it made you feel some part of him had died, although you ignored that—nothing to do with you.

"I don't smoke."

"Everybody smokes, Mr. Alfred."

"Then I must be nobody, *Basil.*" Enjoying the thought of annoying a man it might be awkward to upset.

"*Vasyl. Vasyl.* Not a difficult name. A nice Ukrainian name. Also I can be called Slavko. This is another name I have. Better name."

"You mean like a middle name? Like Basil Slavko."

"I mean my other name. Other name for other things. *Vasyl.*" That sounded as nettled as a dead voice could, but still was not satisfactorily upset.

"Where did you get the lighter?" And adding, "*Vasyl,*" making sure to say it wearily and too loud, because nobody had to bother about people's names, not any more—insisting on details was absurd—and because maybe he wanted to pick a fight. Alfred wondered if this, in fact, was why he'd come—make a jaunt across the heath for exercise and education, have someone punch your lights out, then beetle off back. It would make a change.

But now Vasyl only giggled in a monotone that made Alfred feel slightly sickened and also ridiculous and, "You take one." The pack offered with a sharp little prod at his shoulder. "Have one. You would like." Vasyl leaning on his arm, breathing, sweating. "Real Chesterfields." His uniform possibly hotter than Alfred's.

Alfred waiting until the bleeder had retreated. "You have one for me. I'm nobody, remember? No other name. No other things."

"OK."

Alfred flicked a look across, caught Vasyl lighting a second cigarette, holding one in each hand at this point and grinning—deepish eyes staying worried, or certainly busy with some type of calculation, an urgency—but the mouth apparently friendly and content. Funny skin he had, pitted—made Alfred think of shrapnel, explosions. Which didn't suit his mood.

"And what you look like, I can't say." Alfred subsided, realigned his head against his palms and stretched.

"I look like a man with a great many of cigarettes." An emphasis in this, sharp, and next a hacking laugh that funnelled quickly into coughing, silence, then a regular drag to the left, drag to the right.

I never did smoke, no matter what. They said that I would in the end, but I didn't. Ma told me not to—wouldn't see me spending all my money and then she'd go mithering herself about accidents I could have—petrol and engines and fires. I told her she needn't worry. But you do what your ma says anyway, don't you, cocker? Have to try and keep to that.

And I sent her a bit of my money. Not enough.

Not that she asked.

She would never have asked.

I tried.

That's the thing. That I tried.

Oh, ar. I was a good boy. I've murdered and I stole and used big words, but I never smoked and I was a good boy. A grand lad, me.

The sky was staring down at Alfred, taking quite an interest suddenly, and he squinted up at it, felt a balance agreed between them, unwinding him, washing his limbs. "Must have been a storm somewhere." He was slow enough to stall completely, tip into a sweet, smooth drop.

"Ha?"

High gauzes and drags of cloud, in where the blue was strongest: he'd learned what that meant. "Cirrostratus . . . moisture . . . It freezes up there. Everything freezes up there." Catching the idea before it pushed in any further and turned nasty. "There'll have been a storm somewhere. Earlier." And he was glad that he hadn't heard it, that no one had, because he was very much soothed at the minute, but you never knew what might become a strain, what might become a trouble for somebody. People were unpredictable—eventually, being with them always showed you the same thing: there was nothing on which to rely. Anyone could splinter in your face.

Bit bloody miserable that, though: isn't it, our kid?

Which isn't like us. We're as happy as the bloody day is long.

Yes, but this bloody Day isn't bloody long. Five foot bloody four in my bloody socks, I thank you. That is short.

That is usefully short.

How Pluckrose always put it—"This is my friend and colleague,

Sergeant Day, Alfred F. And, before you mention, he is not a stunted little bastard, he is *usefully short*. Couldn't fit him in the turret otherwise, could we?"

Pluckrose who was also a sergeant, although it didn't suit him—not that a commission would have suited any better—his face was simply incompatible with Air Council Instructions: it had the wrong atmosphere and superiors took it amiss. Added to which, he never could shut up. "Well, I didn't ask to come." Peering over Alfred's head on the first day, beaming about at the hangar full of blue: men standing as if they could think to do nothing else: others searching as if they were late, as if they'd lost something, or had been forgotten: others not alone, beginning to be not alone. "Matter of fact, the King *asked me*. I got a written invitation—through intermediaries, that's just what you'd expect, but it should make a difference, you would think. Of course, I volunteered for *this* part. And not a soul's been civil to me since—except you." He beamed down and Alfred could see no doubt in him, no unease, only this sense that he was being entertained. "Wouldn't have turned up, if I'd known. I mean, it's hardly been efficiently organised, thus far. More like a total fucking shambles." And the amiability in his voice had made his swearing not a personal thing, or angry, more of a musical addition. "Truly. I mean, a man could catch his fucking death of cold here, for a start. And I suspect worse."

Alfred, his words in a lump under his tongue, ashamed of themselves, but getting out a decent-sounding, "Yes." He was keeping things short, sticking to the phrases he was safe with, the ones he'd cut away from Staffordshire, that could sound fully RAF.

He still practised in his head.

Yo bin and yo bay. Yo doe and yo day.

You are, or you have been and you aren't, or you haven't been. You do and you don't, or you didn't.

Everything getting longer when you started to say it that way—and harsh, too, the *h*'s everywhere to trip you, having to hack out each one.

I bin.

I am. I was.

The way I was. The soft way I was.

His dad had always said, "Doe talk soft." But he'd meant don't talk as if you're stupid, he'd meant Alfred was stupid. Now Alfred was talking hard.

Still, he didn't sound like Pluckrose, wouldn't want to—Pluckrose had come from another England. Pluckrose could have been on the wireless: a police inspector, maybe, a friend of Paul Temple, or a gentleman with missing papers who seeks the help of Sexton Blake. A gentleman with lots to say and currently engaged in listing his complaints.

"Some of those big tins of jam, you know—they're from the Great War. Plum and apple jam, rejected from the trenches. That can't bode well."

Alfred wasn't *going* to sound like Pluckrose, only like his altered self, his best guess at how a Sergeant Day would be.

For Alfred's other alterations there'd been drill, there was assistance, and he'd had taken to it all with a sort of delight: fitting his hands, winged into each other for standing at ease, getting the loop of the cocking toggle over the stud in one, checking the travel in the breech block, learning his movements, his new form—the man at the turret's centre, the heart of a gun.

And it had felt like choosing, like being free. Some mornings it lit in his breath: a permission to keep this fresh skin, to love the patterns and the habits of his airman's life. Now, though, it might be different, this was somewhere operational and serious, too busy for you to get help. Parts of him, like his speaking, they weren't quite right, they didn't work well and perhaps this was an indication of other more serious faults he hadn't found yet. He could see himself failing, washing out, disappeared up North to somewhere cold and pointless, erking away at potato peelings and latrines. And wouldn't that be a sort of cowardice: a fear you don't have to admit, because you just sneak yourself out of danger by making too many mistakes? And maybe you've hurt other people before that, because you were scared. That's what they always told you—panic and you'll damage valuable equipment, you'll waste us trained men.

Pluckrose was still talking, while glancing at the doorway, the ceiling, at Alfred and Alfred's forehead—which was frowning—and at the single wing above Alfred's breast pocket—AG embroidered at its root, the gunner's brevet, the sign of his qualification. The first test that Alfred ever passed. The first he'd ever taken.

Pluckrose winked. "Not out hunting for yourself, though? Under instructions? Go thou forth and gather up a crew?"

"I found you for the skipper." This a mumbled chain of Black Country noises—*I fownd yo fur the skippah*—but never mind, because here was the first time that he'd said it—*skipper*—and felt the sparking kick inside his chest, beneath the weight of that single wing. Alfred had a skipper, he was under instructions, he was all right. He was solid while the whole place was uneasy with confusions he couldn't fathom: restless men and the rattle of wind against loose metal somewhere and the lot of them left here after the pep talks to sort themselves out and knowing they'd have to manage, get this done right, because you couldn't end up with the spare bods and the runts, couldn't be forced into a crew with nothing but wazzock-looking baskets, the types who'd kill you.

He'd thought it very quickly, but very clear—*the types who'd kill you*—he'd allowed that, but it made no impact, perhaps because he'd hoped he was already a little lucky, being fixed up, crewed up, safe.

Lucky and almost showing a grin. He had his skipper.

He'd been able to tell Pluckrose, "So come on then. Skipper's waiting."

But the skipper needs to be first. If you've got to go dragging it up again, then you have to start with him.

The skipper is the one who stood behind you and a touch to starboard, stood and waited for you to know it in all that crowd, to see if you had a sense of him, had instincts. When you turned he was solemn, arms folded, staring at you, the peak of his cap leaned forward so you caught no more than a glimmer from his inspection: he was keeping mum about it, but already seeming close to satisfied. "You married?" Not making fun of you with this, not intending disrespect, letting it seem that you were pals in a way and you'd had other times together and this was the end of an old conversation, the last thing to check.

He angled his head for an instant and then you could see his eyes, what you were certain must be proper pilot's eyes—you hadn't a clue about anything, but they really ought to be like this: their interest too far forward and an odd temperature at their back. Later, you'd see the same in other men and you would think of the skipper, whether you wanted to or not.

You realised he was waiting for an answer and you choked out, "No, sir. I'm not," as if you were a boy, had never touched a woman.

And, then again, you weren't married and you had touched only yourself and then fretted about it and you were almost infinitely younger than you thought.

Infinitely: a word you'd learn soon—once infinity started to drive up and breathe against you. Infinity is fond of wars, they give it a way to come in.

"No, sir. I'm not."

"Decided I'd ask. Better to have all bachelors. Simpler. That's my plan." And he takes off his cap and he reaches forward and, before you can intend this, you are bare-headed also and shaking his hand. There's the grumble and shout of so many others round you, nudges as men pass, and you drop the grip, but are together now. He examines your face and stops you moving and you watch something hard turn in the light, light grey of his look and you feel that he'll do what he has to, whatever that might be, and it seems he's caught this in you, too, and is content. You will both do everything required.

"Position?" He's almost grinning.

"I can take mid-upper, if I have to."

"But you'd rather not? Rather be out in the tail turret on your own."

"You get a nicer view." And they kill you. You're the one they're most likely to kill—that's why it's been what you've wanted, from the very first time you heard. "I like a nice view." From the very first time you heard.

"Thought so." Said in a way that had warmth about it, when that was nothing you required—you only needed to get what you wanted, were asking to get what you wanted. And he gave it. "I thought I had the right man." And now he did grin. "I'm Peter Gibbs." He rubbed at his hair, letting you see that its colour annoyed him when he thought of it. "Or Sandy. For obvious reasons."

You had to raise your voice above a swell of noise and this had been known to make it unreliable, although at that moment you didn't care. "Day, Alfred." Surprising yourself by saluting properly, absolutely the way they wanted, the way a well-disciplined dog might if it could. You stretched up into it, you added lustre to the service, you believed in the rank and believed in the man and believed in yourself, even yourself.

After which you were embarrassed, naturally. Saluting with your cap off—how big a bloody fool could you be.

But the skipper was easy about it as you covered your head, felt a sweat—and he was grinning again: for you, not at you. An officer's accent, only not like an officer. "I do want a tight ship, Sergeant." This something he's considered which he tells you to make it true. "But I don't think we'll have much time for ceremony." His voice with a kindness in it that will take you and lead you to trust. "Picked you first, because you have to watch my back. You sing out and I'll fly us right up our own fundament if I have to. Make the attempt, anyway. Evasion will take place." And then, in case you think he's a line-shooter, "But I'm a rotten pilot, actually. So this is your last chance to get away . . ."

You grin to him for an answer, then press on, "Well, if all else fails, like, you can just take us round in circles anti-clockwise and screw the bulbs out of their searchlights . . ." Which is a very old gag, but you need it to cover the pause, because neither of you can guess how this will be, but it's impossible to admit that, no future in it, and so you let one plan seem as likely as another, because all of them have to be at least half mad and both of you have to sound certain when you are not and you suspect that you may start laughing, shadow-boxing, singing "Jerusalem": you can't predict: anything to lead your mind astray, because you are actually here and beginning to be aircrew and in a war—yourself in the whole of a war—and because you are so alive, so infinitely, infinitely alive.

The skipper coughs, not complaining, but he would like to be in charge, thanks, and you enjoy quieting down for him, having him make you focus. You can focus—a good gunner concentrates.

"Sergeant Day, I'm going to scout round for a bomb aimer. You get me a navigator, would you? Rendezvous by that fire bucket in ten minutes."

"Right you are, sir."

You're almost off when he touches your arm, bends in to be level with you. "Look, I should suppose a gunner wants to shoot things, yes? Well, I rather hope I never let you get the chance. Unless you can aim with your head banging off the turret roof. I want to get us through and bomb. It's our job to bomb. If you won't like that you should tell me now."

" 'Course. We have to bomb." But a disagreement in you, the taste of how they've trained you and liking to hit your target, understanding how to put yourself into a kill: one thousand, one hundred and fifty rounds per minute—you know the hot, dark trick of that.

"Sure? I mean arse-splitting turns will not be in it."

You let go, though, because you have to: he's your skipper. "If there's a fighter in my way and getting too friendly, I'll fire at it. But I'll be singing out all the while." You liked that *singing out*—the way he would put it. "Don't mind getting my head lamped when you dive—nothing valuable in there."

"When you say *go*, I go."

"When I say *go*, you go."

But he'll get his wish: the bombing will always be the thing, what you're for, what Chopper Harris says you're for, the Big Boss. He says you're to be the boys who bring the whirlwind.

And you don't only obey the skipper, you *want* to obey him and that makes a wonderful difference. Even if in the end it amounts to precisely the same thing. Saying more than you'd expected, "We'll bomb. We'll bomb the bastards." And you don't mither, don't flap, because you're comfortable with Pilot Officer Gibbs; you always will be. The skipper is safe and you know it. "Never mind me squirting tracer all over the shop—corkscrew us out of bother and we'll make it home."

"When you say *go*, Boss."

"When I say *go*."

Then a different smile from him, bigger, a bit half soaked. "That's the stuff, Boss. We're agreed."

No reason for him to call you Boss—maybe he wants to feel lighter, because you've just given him a command, or maybe because you're small and this makes it funny. You never can work it out, but from now on he does call you Boss and this makes the others do the same until, by the end of the week, it's your name. Silly one to pick when you've never been a boss of anything.

When you bring him Pluckrose, again there's a shake of the hand and you notice how the skipper moves: that he's gentle, precise, and you might mistake him for being not much of a man, but really there is just no waste about him. He puts himself exactly where he chooses and is still. If he hit you, he would do it very quickly and very well.

No bomb aimer, yet. "Sorry, Boss." Skip shrugs at you, enjoying that he's rueful. "Couldn't find anybody quite right. Who's this?"

Pluckrose in and explaining, before you can answer, which isn't a shock.

"Pluckrose. From a long line of Pluckroses: my father, and my grandfather and my so forth, all of them Pluckroses to a man and my mother, of course, picked it—plucked it—although possibly under the influence of drink—and so, having put up with it themselves, they were delighted they could pass it on to me." He doesn't appear to breathe. "Those of them still living. The others might well have been less enthusiastic, although who knows—once a Pluckrose, I'd suppose always a Pluckrose." And the skipper watches him, unreadable and still, and you wonder if you've made a terrible mistake in bringing him a Pluckrose. "You can imagine how much I look forward to meeting strangers—especially popsies—and, my, how I liked my schools—all eight of them. I have really no education to speak of, can barely add up, so I wouldn't rely on my calculations at any point—geometry is a foreign land to me—and foreign lands, of course: they're a foreign land to me, too. Struan Macallum Pluckrose, that's the complete set of luggage—the very tiniest touch of Scotland there on my mother's side." Pluckrose blinks down at the skipper, allows a moment of remarkable silence. "Would you like to see my logbook?"

Offering this before he's asked, his face fighting between resignation and a peculiar kind of glee, and the skipper studying each page very calmly, closing it, softly handing it back. "Well, nobody's said you're dangerous."

"I can be very plausible, if I have to."

"Which might come in handy."

Pluckrose exhaling, seeming to lower by half an inch and no longer close to bellowing. "I'd hoped it might."

"Peter Gibbs. Sandy." The skipper rubs his neck, glances at his navigator—which is Pluckrose—and then at his tail gunner—which is you—and then the hangar where more knots are forming, pairs and teams of men gaining definition. "This is only a guess, you know . . ." he murmurs just loud enough for the pair of you, his crew, "but I think we might take a bit of getting used to. So perhaps from now on, we should travel en masse, formate in a nice little vic and introduce ourselves together. Then they can take us or leave us in one go."

Vasyl had declared lunch on the grass, unpacking half a decent loaf, cheese in a greaseproof wrapper, three boiled eggs. Awkward that—you can't share three between two people.

"Is fine. I have my knife." Vasyl seeming a touch shy, smoothing his hand into his trouser pocket and bringing out a clasp knife, a small thing. It could still do you harm, but was nothing to fuss about. "My famous knife, yes?" Letting it lie on his palm for a moment until it became all innocence, cutlery, an object with no sense of purpose. Then he cut the egg lengthwise through its shell, very earnest, and making a good job of it, the blade plainly very sharp. "There, you see? Fair is fair." Holding out Alfred's half in a wide, reddish hand.

So they had one thing in common: understanding food.

Bash, we called it in the camp. Bash. Maybe that made it easier to cope with. You expected things of food, you had high hopes; never quite knew where you were with bash. And you had to be careful with it, keep things equal and correct.

Not that they didn't have more than enough at the minute. A comfortable ration for this afternoon and a bottle of cold tea apiece—real tea, none of that ersatz stuff made out of daisies, or God knew what—and meals laid on for the rest of the time, generous portions.

But you could still worry.

The thought of food had followed Alfred for six years now, long after the end of the war: that and the preventative hunger, the drive to take what he saw, whenever he saw it, in case there was nothing else after. He'd kept chocolate with him every day; and a new slice of bread each morning, to help him be at ease. This was how you discovered that you were an animal—you caught yourself hoarding, savage, feeding: mind shut.

You'd think all those books would make a difference, wouldn't you, our kid? That's what everyone said would happen. You end up around reading people, ones who like their words and are comfortable with them, and you show an interest, a curiosity, and that's your affair and no one else's business and you find yourself growing—a little chap, but big inside, quite roomy. Only then they pile in, the reading people, gang up on you and interfere and they want you to be like them, their boy, their babby, and they give you more refined concerns—according to them, you've never been bothered by anything worthwhile—so now you have rarefied worries and delicate problems, like your head's been turned into a parlour and there's nothing there can stand your touch—and they give you words that you can't quite operate to put in your new voice and this is supposed to make you finer and a finished man. A great opportunity for self-improvement, war.

Unless you're hungry.

Then you end up just like any other dog.

Still, they'd had a point. Being an autodidact—horrible word, autodidact, but one of the first you teach yourself: all by yourself, without the reading people, without anyone—being an autodidact had made a difference. Without the books, you might not have been so thoroughly ashamed. Or disappointed. Your shame might have been unavoidable, very probably it was, but not your disappointment.

Oh, give it a rest, though, can't you? All of that was years ago and you could have had it worse.

And you were warned—by someone who was taught in schools—Ivor Sands told you and his whole life is books—go scraping about in your past and you'll get hurt, you'll remember and hurt. But you wouldn't be told.

Alfred rubbed his fingers through his scalp.

Won't need a punch in the head at this rate—doing it very effectively from within.

He lowered his eyelids, turned his face to the heat and stared at the muffled light, the blood sun.

Time to get yourself in order, Day. No more self-indulgence. Think of your egg—your nice half chooky egg. That shouldn't be neglected.

He looked down at it, peeled away the shell, his mouth suddenly overinterested, wet.

My, but wasn't it all just a big, free university—the university of war—with HE and armour piercing and incendiaries, just for a lark. And so much to find out: the far edges of people and the bloody big doors into nowhere that you don't want to know about.

Enough of that, though. If you keep yourself in charge of your thinking then things stay friendly and polite.

So keep in charge.

And then what?

Let us consider the things for which we should be grateful.

For instance?

For instance, you wouldn't deny that it left you with a grand apprecia-tion of your grub. When there is food, you don't take it for granted. No indeed. It's just as if you can't help saying grace.

Amen, straw women, rubber babbies all a-swimming.

But those regulations no longer apply.

No more playing silly buggers over God now, either.

He focused himself on his egg and biting, hid inside that—the nice cling of the yolk, a dab of it slightly creamier where it was undercooked. "Nice enough, I suppose. No salt, though." When he licked his lips he could feel the tickle of hairs—eating was going to be different now, very slightly. He liked that.

"Apologies. I forget my head."

Vasyl threw across a twist of paper that did indeed conceal a hollow full of salt. Must have been a Boy Scout. If the Ukraine had Boy Scouts. Alfred suspected that Uncle Joe would not be all that keen and wasn't there some other outfit they had in Russia, some socialist arrangement?

"An egg with salt, now that's more like it." Bread made it better yet. Sip of tea. A modest slice of cheese. You couldn't complain.

"Want some of this?"

"Bloody hell." .

Vasyl brought out a tin of Klim and, quick as you like, had it open, something about this seeming a kind of threat. It had been four years since Alfred had seen a tin of Klim and the tiny shock of the banded label, the fat, square lettering, hurt him slightly, made him swallow. "Bloody, bloody hell." Klim had been behind the wire. It didn't belong in 1949.

"You don't like? Milk—is good for you." Vasyl watchful, more inter-ested than he should be. "Make you grow long bones."

"Bones are long enough, thanks." Being sure to sound sharp. "Wouldn't want to grow out of my clothes. At home we all have to economise, you know. Save pounds, get dollars, that kind of thing." Because you couldn't let him start assuming you would put up with any-thing. Unwise to stand out, or throw your weight around, but you couldn't let somebody mark you as a target, either. Show them you're not afraid and then you're halfway to winning the fight. "Just a surprise to see it. Klim. For some reason I'd have thought they'd blow every Klim production plant sky high and then bury every tin of it at sea. Bloody *Klim*, from bloody herds of *swoc*, eating bloody fields of bloody *ssarg*. I took it as a sign that somebody out in the world had a sense of humour. Very necessary, a sense of humour." This was too long, too big, giving Vasyl leverage he could use. Which was what he'd wanted, no doubt. Better not to get angry, though, because that could lead to weakness and other sorts of grief. "But maybe I'm taking things too much to heart, just because I still dream of the stuff. Often." Wrong—Alfred watched in Vasyl's eyes how this invited an intrusion, showed a fast way in. "And everyone's been so busy in the peace: keeping the rationing going, taking whatever they like, making sure that we stay cheerful and all get what we deserve. We've every one of us got what we fought for, hadn't you heard?" Alfred aware that he now sounded as bitter as Ivor Sands, when he wasn't like Ivor, was sure that he wasn't as damaged as that. Still, despite his complaining, Alfred reached and took the can, shook out a palmful of that old, dry sweetness. "Christ."

"Taste pleasing? The way you know?"

"Tastes like hell. And I like my tea black. You can keep the rest." A flutter in his stomach, so he lay back, breathed for a while.

But Vasyl was in the mood to take advantage, couldn't wait to dig. "Tell me a thing, Mr. Alfred."

Tongue at your top lip, cleaning away the memory. "No." That was the trouble with a moustache—it made things linger.

"You sleep?"

"Everybody sleeps."

"You sleep the way you like to? You enjoy your sleep? Is enough for you, your sleep?" The man in a rush for something, after blood. Like the doctor at Cosford, the trick cyclist. Same style. Wanting to steal what was left of you and pretending you shouldn't object.

"My sleep is more than enough for me, thank you. I sometimes have to wake up early, just to keep it from wearing me out."

"And now you are here in Germany again, pretending to be in a camp—now with this, you sleep?" The fucker guessing, correctly guessing, that insomnia—a charming word, that, full of Latin—insomnia had been a problem but, since coming here, had abandoned him completely.

Such conditions could go either way, Alfred supposed, but it turned out the hut noise had soothed him: the breathing, creaks, the shift of bodies, the chafing night din of a barracks, none of it annoyed him any more. Instead he'd gained a sleep like drowning, like being swallowed, a crush of grey taking him off as soon as he lay down and folding over him, thick and seamless, until they had to shake him at reveille, haul him back up to the light.

No need to mention that yesterday morning you'd gone round to have a swill, get yourself presentable, and had to pause, sit down on the clean, fake steps of some other clean, fake hut and realise you were tearful, ached, because the pretend camp, pretend fences, pretend guards— they had been what you wanted. The bastard thing had made you miss it. The fucking thing had put itself inside you so deep that you felt this happiness to see it built again and straggling with men: pretend Kriegies— *Kriegsgefangene*: all German, that word—pretend POWs, like yourself and more than only you coming back for their second time, volunteering for their prison, more than only you—and you were fucked off with yourself and fucked off with them and fucked off with the thing and its taste and its fear and its living in you and fucked off that it wouldn't be long before filming was over and they'd send you home.

And I'm looking for the faces, too. From when it was real. From when we were Kriegies.

Because some of it here can seem so much the same and that leads you to expect them, even when you're certain they're not coming: the boys you need to see.

Alfred rolled on to his side, saw Vasyl tip his head back and eat the Klim out of the can—just pouring it down too fast to taste. It made the bugger cough for a moment before he paused, spoke again, the words thick with milk. "I said, do you sleep, Mr. Alfred? In my camp—in my real camp. I sleep."

"Then why come and do this? If your camp is so bloody lovely, why don't you stay in it? Want to be a film star, do you?" Alfred felt his tiredness coming, inviting a pain in the head. "Or didn't you get enough of the fucking war?"

"Displaced Persons, we have no choice until they decide what to do with us, we must stay where they keep us. Work is a way to leave." Vasyl sighed as if he were a man of distinction and excellent schooling, someone cultured who loved porcelain and perhaps symphonies and it was a very great shame that a person of so many qualities should be suffering so badly and speaking to a so much lower type who was too stupid even to notice. He made a point of emptying the rest of the Klim out on the grass, wasting it, watching Alfred for any reaction

Alfred just made a smile and didn't shout and looked as if he might be stupid, because he was good at that—self-taught. Self-defence.

"We have to be very patient and wait very nice with each other and not speak a great deal, or ask questions. It is very dull." Vasyl lit yet another cigarette. "This making a film is a thing to do which is not concert party, or recital with poetry, or digging a field, or debate concerning democracy and the future—*in preparing tomorrow's peace, English influence will never be devoted to a policy of enslavement.* I have heard this enough times to remember. Always lectures. Always the same."

"Funny, I've never heard it at all."

"Swiss people, they say it in the war. What the Swiss understand is nothing. Very small people in their minds and thieves and trying to say what everybody should resemble." He licked his forefinger, dipped it in the little pile of Klim on the grass, licked again. "And we get paid. For what work we do with this film, they pay us six marks any day." As if anyone might believe he had need of the money. "Currency is useful and my intention is to improve my speaking English."

"You're supposed to be playing a German."

"German I know already."

"Me too, our kid. Me too."

Beyond which they ate for a while in silence and Alfred must have drifted, dozed, because when he woke the thought of the boys was with him again, the whole pack of them, staring into his head. Dickie Molloy there in a temper, kicking at a wall and then running off limping up the lane, yelling like stinko as he went, and Bill's mints, Bill Torrington's peppermints—inexhaustible supply he had from some cousin who worked in a factory that made them—never got anything useful, like sugar, only peppermints—and Edgar Miles who quietly looted them three seats for the mess from a bombed-out cinema—made everywhere smell of burning—and Hanson who was a bastard.

"Give us a look at your thumbs." Hanson with his frayed cuffs, his uniform that looked as if he'd been buried wearing it. "Come on. Thumbs." By this time Alfred and the skipper had gathered up Pluckrose, Torrington, Molloy and they were looking for a W/Op. Pressing on regardless, this scruffy article was following them, making straight for Alfred, "If you're a gunner . . ." when they didn't want him, when nobody wanted him. "Show us your thumbs." A round head and flat little eyes, needling.

"I am a gunner." What else could Alfred say?

The skipper and the rest had stopped, had turned to wait at Alfred's back and so he had to get this right and be the man they took him for, one who stood his ground. "I am a gunner."

"You *say* you're a gunner."

"That's because I *am* a gunner." This heating him in his legs, his neck and the weight of the crew behind him making him reckless, letting him prop his fists on to his hips and stand. "What are *you*?" And someone, he'd guess Pluckrose, making this low chuckle in his throat at that, appreciating the show.

Hanson wove his fingers together, stretched them, popped his joints. Filthy nails he had and the smell you would get if you slept with your guns. He glowered at Alfred from under dank blond hair, making a meal of things and raising up both of his thumbs. "Gunner's thumbs."

And, after a moment, the others had punched out a single, solid laugh between them and Torrington and Molloy had patted Alfred's shoulders, but he hadn't shifted, because Hanson had to be the one to move, to flinch, and Alfred's heart had seemed high in his chest and eager.

"Lord, it's like a mongoose with a snake." Pluckrose at his back, gentle. "To paraphrase Wellington—I don't know if they're going to scare Goering, but they put the fucking wind up me."

Hanson breaking off then, giving a grin. "Straight AG." And waiting for the word.

"What do you say?" The skipper at Alfred's side now. "Do we want him?"

He liked being given the power to pick. "Not sure."

"Do we need him, Boss?"

"Probably." Alfred surprised to hear himself. "Probably we do." He'd not looked at Hanson after that, had avoided the sight of him for the rest of the day.

Edgar Miles had wandered along to them soon after, yawned a bit, stood at his usual shambolic angle—looked so slack that you could pour him, carry him off in a bucket—and he said he would like to be part of a crew that laughed, which had set them off laughing again, nearly howling, this time Alfred and Hanson joining in, because this made the seven of them fit and seemed like the start of how they'd be and meant they were complete, crewed up.

Not that they weren't a lifetime away from knowing anything: they'd only had a round or two of training from madmen being rested between tours. Still, no need to worry, a lifetime wasn't all that long.

And they had so many ways to pass the time.

"Why don't you do her, so? Why don't you do the deed?" Molloy, a little drunk one evening, maybe two weeks since they'd met, and punching Alfred's arm, "If you have a lady friend."

There are things that you never imagine.

"You do have a lady friend." Molloy flushing a touch with the lateness of the hour and drink taken, but still mainly pale.

"I didn't say I did."

There are things you should never remember.

"Ah, but you have to. No choice. Special circumstances with a war on and such." Face and hands white as paper and the eyebrows, eyes, mouth—the features all dark, as if they were drawn on, added in black ink.

"I didn't say I had a lady friend."

"Ah, you do, though. I heard. Straight gen. You've one and another one for Sundays, surely."

Pluckrose nudging in, "You mentioned there was a war on? You know that would explain all the fucking noise." This in the low, square saloon of the Duke's Head, their earliest local. The Duck's Head—what else would they call it?

"You've a foul mouth on you." Molloy smiling and making his eyes round: a touch cracked-looking.

"Thank you kindly, I do my best." Nodding in a way that made you think of other Pluckroses, "And tell me, Dickie . . ." of admirals and judges and tall-headed men on horseback and hunting things, their long Pluckrose shins hanging down and their great, thin Pluckrose feet dragging on to the ground. "Tell me, dear Mr. Molloy—with whom exactly are we at war?"

"The Eskimos, you heathen bastard."

"Really and why's that?"

"Because we've stolen their fucking penguins and now haven't they gone and decided they want them back."

There are things that you never remember, because you are sensible and have studied unarmed combat. You defend yourself.

"But never mind that, so. You, Little Boss—will you do her or not?"

You defend yourself.

Wish her well if you have to and then get on. Not another thought.

You will not hold a thought of her.

You will defend yourself.

Alfred sat up, dry and vaguely breathless. His pack was leaning against Vasyl's on the turf, but there was no sign of Vasyl himself beyond a white mound of milk, ants working at it.

Oh, well.

He took a moment to imagine cleaning off his mind, washing it down with petrol, removing the stains. Sometimes this worked after dreams. The thing was to concentrate on something else and let them fade.

I suppose I could manage the journey back alone—the camp's about due west. I'd recognise the route, more or less. So flat around here, I'd be able to see it from a good way off. But if I went wrong, there are places out here you wouldn't want to come across. Things left behind.

No hurry, in any case. He enjoyed a long swig from the bottle of tea then stood, brushed at his trousers, thought how green the air was: a day's sun raising the scent of live earth, animal heat.

I don't get out in the country enough. I don't exercise any more. Still, I can change that. If I'd like.

He'd no time to consider how, because a clatter in the low trees and the slash of a stick being swiped into leaves announced that Vasyl was heading back. He liked to proceed by breaking whatever he could.

"Good evening, good evening. You are awake. This is splendid. We have just the time to walk and be there."

"You've seen it?"

"Yes, yes. I don't bring you all this way for no reward." He bent to his pack, couldn't help hefting it slightly, checking it, to see if Alfred had taken anything, disturbed it. "Your belongings, you carry them. We may not pass this way again."

Alfred checking his own pack on principle, slow. "We never pass this way again. That's the law." Happy he'd puzzled Vasyl with that, "All right, then. Lead on, Macduff."

"This is from William Shakespeare, correct?"

"This is from William Shakespeare, correct."

But I still have the advantage, because I found Shakespeare myself. Nobody just gave him to me in a school: I earned him.

There was a sort of rabbit track and Vasyl set off along this, through young trees and over uneven ground.

Alfred followed. "How do you know this is the way?"

"A British captain told me. They said the way and the place. He was there. He was with Montgomery also—saw him take the signatures for that first little surrender. He tells me one of the German officers has a briefcase with him: a very full briefcase, as if he would need it. As if they would let him keep it. That was a blooming good day, yes?" Vasyl monitoring Alfred's face as he said this, getting too loud.

Alfred ignored him and they started off, pushed to a broad rise of tawny grass, junipers rearing up from it in dark plumes, banks of heather showing the first bluish haze of flower. Vasyl's stamping about drove up a rush of small birds and Alfred hoped they were larks because he liked the thought of larks.

Once they'd walked to their little horizon another had stretched beyond a break of trees and laid itself down in a shimmer of sun. There were sheep standing in the distance, or else pale rocks, and a cluster of buildings that could have been barracks at sometime: perhaps still were, but for an unintended army. There was a thin road, a shine that could have been from the windscreen of a truck.

Alfred inhaled, the breeze sweet, tranquil, healthy.

"OK." Vasyl planted himself and folded his arms, staring firmly at a patch of grass. It seemed entirely like any other.

"What's OK?"

Vasyl frowned. "We are there."

"I don't see anything."

"What would there be to see? This is their whole aim, they don't make a memorial. He kills himself—in Uelzener Strasse, over in Lüneburg, you can go and discover—and they bury him where nobody will know except who did it. No bastards coming to put flowers." Vasyl turned his back slightly unsteadily, fumbled and began, Alfred realised, to piss. "You tell anyone I come here and I put what I like, which is best."

And what *should* you do if you're standing where they buried Himmler? Dance, maybe, if that didn't seem too frivolous, or wish him in hell if that didn't seem too late, or—why not?—piss on him. There wasn't a drill set down for the occasion. Plus, Alfred hadn't planned this far, not having believed they would find the place and not exactly sure they really had. The ground here looked just the same as all the rest, the air still tasting very fine.

Vasyl was dogged: emptying himself, you would have thought—an impressive volume. "You say to anyone who asks."

Say what, mate? That you can hold about a bloody quart? That you're like Mr. Woo in the air-raid warden song—could put out a fire?

Alfred rubs the skin above his eyes, concentrates. "How can you tell this is it?"

Because Alfred sounded annoyed and Vasyl maybe didn't expect this and so he snaps, "I can tell."

"But didn't they . . ." Perhaps pushing his luck here, "I'd heard they . . ."

Vasyl finished at last and faced him, fly rebuttoned, suddenly belligerent.

Alfred continued all the same. "I heard they came back and dug him up, cremated him." The little, harmless knife still sleeping in Vasyl's pocket, he was sure. "Is that wrong? I did think that they'd dug him up."

Vasyl stamped his foot, the dried earth under it sounding hollow. "I heard this. I know it. I don't care." The crickets had stopped. Everything had stopped. "He was here for months before that. You know a body buried for months?" He flickered a slow glare at Alfred. "I know bodies buried for months. They don't get him all out. Some of him is left here. Enough for me." He spat.

"Well." Alfred pulled his side cap out of his pack, set it in the proper place: badge in centre of forehead, edge angled to one inch above right eyebrow. "I suppose I should make my contribution on behalf—"

But he can't finish, can't begin, because there is a shout among the trees to their left, the sense is unclear, but there is running, drawing nearer.

A chase.

Alfred spinning, a stupid, huge fear jumping in him and nowhere to hide, but then here comes a young girl—ten, or so—laughing and running, enjoying the end of her day and brought up sharp when she breaks through the cover, sees men.

"It's all right. Don't worry." Alfred's voice sounded violent to him, like a threat, and the girl's mouth opened, but then only closed again. She was keeping a cloth full of something tight to her chest—perhaps valuables, perhaps food, something she's gathered on the heath. Her dress is close on her body, pretty, unprotective.

"Allusgoot. Allusgoot. OK?" You've seen it before—the way she won't move and can't understand you because she is terrified and no languages can reach her. You want Vasyl to help with this, but you can't take your eyes from hers, because that may make her worse and it seems that she also wants to look at Vasyl, be sure of him, but she cannot and now the other runner appears: a woman of about forty and quite plump, happy to be a little cross with herself and surprised with the way she is out of breath and having this fun, this time away from anyone's disapproval but her own. The joy falls from her in a step. She sees you. She halts and you know she would like to be closer to what is clearly her daughter, but isn't sure if this will help—maybe she must be the distraction that lets the girl try to get away, maybe showing no love for her will be safer, maybe open affection will make you be unkind. She looks past you to Vasyl and something complicated happens in her face.

"It's all right. Allusgoot. Goot." Easing forward and this scares them even more, which annoys you, although you know that isn't right—is not the way you should be. "English. Goot. Vassmackenzeeheer." The mother's hands are panicking round this square parcel she's got and her lips are moving, trying to find what would work.

And you can't let someone's mother be like that, not while the child has to watch, that's the worst thing, and you say to the woman evenly and slowly, "Come on now, there's a good wench—we'm pals, see? *Kine angst.*"

But there is a quality in her attention that finally makes you glance over to Vasyl and feel the air kick round your head, because he is holding a Luger: dressed in his costume, his *Feldwebel's* uniform, and levelling the gun at them, enjoying the way it is starting to make them look already dead.

"You fucking bastard. What the fuck are you doing? Vasyl! What the fuck are you doing?"

And the mother runs. She takes her chance, pulls at the child and makes this kind of high, whining scream and runs for the trees and Vasyl is going to chase her. He stares at you as if you are insane and then starts forward—this picture from another time—and he is giggling on one low, solid note, delighted with the way that he must look, the way that she must see him, her fear. And you are extremely, extremely—you are upset until you find that you are on the grass and cannot quite breathe and you have stopped him.

You are numb in places and twisting the weight of your hips and your arms operate without you, very smooth and calm, while you wrestle this man who has a gun and you are sure you are going to die and do not want to.

But you've forgotten about what you learned, all that while ago, what your body knows, and here is your foot on his wrist and also your opposite knee is pressing at his throat. Your position is unstable—you do need to make yourself secure—but you have smothered his struggling and he seems almost docile now. And underneath you both there may be some small part of Himmler, but more likely just a depth of earth in a heath where he'd once decreed there should be excavations to uncover an Aryan past, where he'd tried to prove his future—and this what you're mostly aware of, these strange and calming facts—before Vasyl jerks, unseats you, and the pistol is lifting towards you, but you have already caught him, because your arms are free and clever and you hold his wrist and you press your shin across his neck as hard as you can and watch him choke, feel his grip falter until you can take the Luger away and slap him.

You slap him again.

You decide not to mind how many times you slap him. Don't hit him, slap him, let him feel small.

This makes you smile.

You softly wonder if you only want to hit him and why not shoot him. Where would be the harm?

No one might come across a body here for weeks, buried or not.

One of Vasyl's cheeks is ticking, he is slippery with sweat, but he tries to keep his eyes open and to show you he is pathetic, wounded. He intends you to be more sorry for him than you might be for the woman or the girl and this annoys you.

But mainly you notice how carefree you feel, how glossy.

"If I let you loose, you'd better not try that again. You know I can beat you." This is probably not true. But you do have his gun now and so you sigh, lean back, and sit on Vasyl's chest, but otherwise let him be. He is heaving in air, wheezing, and your pressure doesn't help him.

You watch a breeze going over the far grass, wave scrolling after wave and dropping to stillness. You wriggle your shoulders, exhale. You angle your face to the sun, to the joy of it. You stroke your new moustache.

"You can't tell I won't shoot you?" Vasyl hoarse. "I just frighten some Deutsch cunts. It's a joke. You can't tell I'm a good person who loves England? I am a good person." He might almost be about to cry. "You make me afraid." He is perfectly convincing. "Please."

The labouring of Vasyl's ribcage very noticeable underneath you as you sit and understand that you would like it if he were really afraid and if that was to do with you.

"Please. You must let me breathe."

But your hating him fades quickly—you haven't the space for it. You are shut in a kind of private uproar which prevents you from thinking anything except that you are so surprised, because it's back: whatever it is that stops you dying has come back. You hadn't wanted to be killed.

You didn't know you'd feel that way again.

The following morning he fainted which was daft—if you have someone pointing a gun at your face, you'd expect to go down there and then, or maybe when the danger's over and you think you can relax—anything earlier being, on the whole, unsafe and not recommended. But passing out a whole day later, that was something you shouldn't do. What was more, you might want to avoid passing out altogether as injurious to your health and dignity. And you never could tell what you'd miss while you lay unconscious—the world, as you know, being full of such lovely surprises.

Although Alfred had to admit that fainting was not in itself any type of surprise. There'd been a time—mainly '46—when he'd dropped off the twig with great regularity. He'd grown quite used to the seconds of grey sinking that would signal an episode and, glad of the warning, he'd then avoid sharp edges, dogs or kiddies and hope to aim himself away from roads. He'd taken it quite calmly, he thought, been philosophical, and the trouble had cleared eventually, almost stopped. More than a year must have passed since he'd last found himself unwittingly horizontal.

But at 10:56, down he'd gone. He'd been standing to attention in a mocked-up *Appell*: everyone out on parade for the fake Nazis and a camera grinding by on rails, peering at the ranks in one direction and then sneaking back like an untrusting sergeant, inspecting them again. Meanwhile, the actors had this or that to say and this or that to do—he was too far away to catch the details. Then along came 10:56 and the colour dropped out of his morning, while his head pulled him down and forward through the usual, opening hole and he tried to slacken out his limbs, to roll into the impact he wouldn't feel.

Should have been a parachutist.

Too late now.

Two chaps had broken ranks, lifted and carried him into the shade of an empty hut. The director had liked the look of the whole palaver, and wanted to work it in, so some poor bastard (formerly of the Pay Corps and perhaps with an eye to future acting work) then spent the next two hours being required to crumple up and hit the deck: with arms flung out, with arms tucked in, with head back, head dropped, head lolled sideways, left and right, with every variation you might think of and more besides and then just one last time for luck, please, thank you. It was a fine game, filming.

Alfred sat on the ground and watched, staying in the cool, leaning against a wooden wall that still reeked of sap. He sipped the water he'd been given, didn't think where his mind had gone while he was out. Vasyl and another Ukrainian were off near the perimeter in regulation get-up, pretending to be Hans and Helmut on patrol. They were highly convincing, reproduced that odd wary/lazy trudge you would find in guards—so much so that Alfred was almost nervous to see them, felt vaguely confined.

Naturally Vasyl had spotted him hitting the deck. First thing Alfred had been aware of when he'd come to: the Ukrainian watching, then smoothing down his expression, nodding for some reason.

Alfred, for no reason, had nodded back.

Funny old life, ay it, cocker?

He looked up again now, but the pair had scoured on, were disappearing behind the mess hall and someone new was in the way.

"How are you feeling?" One of the men who'd helped him—lanky type of customer, overbearing. "Hm?" You had the idea there was something wrong about him, that he'd stick if you touched him, that he'd cling.

Alfred wasn't in the mood for company. "Not so bad. How's yourself?" but he did make the effort and was polite. "Thanks for . . . hauling me out of the way." You never should make the effort—or be polite.

"Couldn't have left you lying. Untidy." The man squatted down beside him on the soft earth, this suggesting the start of a conversation. "You're not the first." He seemed smug about this.

While Alfred thought he really didn't care. "Good. I suppose. Or bad." He fancied a nap, as it happened, but that might involve him in dreaming, so he supposed he'd better leave it be for now.

"Came a cropper myself on Monday. When they had us doing all of that running about and shouting." The man's tone implied that running about and shouting both might kill you.

"You don't say." Alfred intending this as an instruction and studying the pine trees past the wire—a long while since he'd done this: tried to think himself fifty yards away. Not so very far, but fifty yards that mattered all the same. He brushed the knees of his trousers—getting filthier each day—and prepared to stand. The medic had recommended he should go on sick parade, said at least to call in at the medical tent if he started to feel a bit badly. Alfred pondered this and also the lanky man, the idea of another ten minutes with the bastard whining at him, fishing for misery. Alfred soon convinced himself he was growing dire new symptoms— could be he should cut along sharpish, his being a desperate case. It was either that or go and fetch the Luger, show the director something he couldn't repeat. Not that you can't repeat killing—you just always kill someone new.

"I do know." The man intending this to halt Alfred's departure.

Ar, but do you know that if I think you gone, then you might as well be, do you know that I can do that—had years of practice? Do you know that's your safest bet?

But on he comes, persistent fucker, keeps picking at his scabs. "You know? I do know." A reproachful dip in that last sentence, as if he shouldn't have to add that everyone from the services is a comrade and a friend in need. Suffering, he'd like to tell you, has forged eternal bonds. As if they weren't the last things you would want.

Worst of it is, there *are* bonds and it would be bloody typical if they *were* eternal: it would be very much your kind of luck.

Your friend in need attempts a humble-but-heroic delivery—like a cheap Leslie Howard—it doesn't suit him. "Still, they didn't kill us."

Yes, but pretty much everyone else did get the chop. One way or another. And what sort of shape did it leave you in, mate? And, as if it mattered, exactly how buggered am I?

You see him take some of the dusty soil and then let it creep out through his fingers. He does this again. And again. Your own hands are still shaking from your fall, will keep on until this evening at least, and you don't want him to notice and say he understands the way you feel. You've never seen the point of understanding, it can't change anything. You stuff your fists into your pockets like contraband while he talks.

"I ended up in Fallingbostel. Over that way: across the heath? Came out three stone lighter."

You ignore him, watch the parade ground where a tumbling faint is practised, then performed—it looks rather splendid—before two men run in and stoop to cart the body off. The pair seem alert and athletic, but also tender—and the director has picked them to match, they might be brothers and are both most presentable, much neater than the fellows who lifted you. You also find them more convincing—the one who's fainting, too. He is undoubtedly better than you are at being you.

"I can't seem to keep the weight on now."

You have a pressure in your neck. Which is as close as you should get to being sad. Or maybe angry—you might also be that.

"The wife gives me potatoes and potatoes, piles 'em on, but it makes no odds."

You haven't got a wife. You've got two cardboard suitcases you've had to leave in Ivor Sands' back room and some books he'll have sold, although he promised not to. You can't trust him when he says that he won't do something you've not even mentioned—always means that he's actually bearing it in mind. Dickie Molloy was just the same.

You hear your voice say, "I ended up in a field beside a corpse. I stole his coat."

And you want to tell this Fallingbostel man about the corpse — that it had been a particular pal of yours. It broke your heart to take that coat, only you didn't especially feel it at the time.

Because you were being happy that your pal was much bigger than you, so glad he was taller, and eager to fit his shape down around yours, wrapping yourself up inside him and going to sleep beside a shattered hedge.

Your broken heart, it's still not right. You don't forget, because of the days when you turn too quickly, or you roll over in your bed and the pieces of heart are jolted in together, still sharp. Makes you cough.

And the thing is, as you watch the filming: the phoney German officers — real Germans: Good Germans, but still real — and the phoney guards and phoney ranks of blue and grey and khaki and the whispers, the taste of plans evolving and the phoney CO with the gleaming rented boots — as you watch it all you ask yourself why you came and you can't answer.

Ivor asked you first, ages ago — pounced on you in the bookshop while you were sorting out new stock — and you couldn't make your story straight enough to tell him. Always a stickler for explanations, Ivor.

"Why, dear boy?"

"Why not, Ivor?"

"Inadequate response." Ivor's face not too good that day — the burn on his cheek seeming vicious, keeping a tight, pale grip on the flush of his skin. "Come on. You know it'll send you round the bend."

"I am round the bend." Alfred opening *The Mesolithic Settlement of Northern Europe* and finding the pages smelled of damp and lilacs and maybe lamb, he thought lamb. Books remembered their old houses, their old owners. "D'you think anybody would buy this?"

"Students, yes. And it's in good condition. Don't change the subject. Why go back? And why to a camp? And what do I do for assistance while you're gone?" He glared at *The Allegory of Love*, but set it on the pile for shelving. "You've only just managed to make yourself irreplaceable."

"Don't talk balls." The shop empty, or Alfred wouldn't say this — no call to shock the book-buying types — Alfred had a soft spot for their customers: they were mainly the comfortable kind of strangers, reflective and sparse. Even the demanding ones didn't scare him, only wanted books.

"I'll talk balls if I want to—cock and balls if I want to. You shouldn't go."

"Why not?"

"Because you won't come back."

And Alfred had realised this might be true and wondered why he hadn't thought of it before and Ivor had slammed down *Tropic of Capricorn* and battered out of the back room, out of the shop, leaving its comfortable quiet behind him and Alfred had stopped the sorting and made a cup of tea and sat still with it in his hands, not drinking.

It had seemed very light, to imagine leaving, not having to carry on. Calling it a day—Pluckrose made a joke of that all the time, pointing at Alfred, across counters and dance halls and the briefing room: "Let us call it A. Day"—that afternoon, though, it had meant a new thing—soothing and final and mild.

But the film camp hadn't been as he'd expected. At first it was only gentle and he'd thought he was fine about it, more contented than he had been in years. It had seemed not unlikely that he could work out his own little pantomime inside the professional pretence and tunnel right through to the place where he'd lost himself, or rather the dark, the numb gap he could tell was asleep inside him. Something else had been there once, but he couldn't think what. He was almost sure it had come adrift in Germany, in the real prison, in '43, or thereabouts. So it could possibly make sense that he'd turn up here and at least work out what was missing, maybe even put it back.

When the film people had driven them up to the gates in their rented Bedfords he'd felt—there was no other word—victorious. Perhaps a good few of them had, because they'd paraded in. There'd been a sense that the marching started as a joke, but then it fixed them, firmed, and their arms swung and their rhythm snapped and some Geordie-sounding bugger at the back shouted them round, halted them, stood them at ease, then allowed them to be dismissed.

Alfred had noticed some of the technicians pausing and a couple of them making what he knew must be smart remarks, but they were worried, too: they were thinking they weren't certain what they had here and that now it was caught inside the fence with them.

The fence itself was quite accurate. The guard towers, too, and the blue-and-white-checked coverlets and the bare board floors and creaking bunks, they were as true to life as they could be and, in a few days, they'd bred what they were meant to: boredom and queues and a kind of anxiety that silted down and stayed.

Which would really be why Alfred fainted, he supposed. Because the camp was winning, beating him again, and the edges of his dreams had dogs in them and they were running closer.

Jesus Christ, it isn't much to ask — the chance to recuperate undisturbed.

The Fallingbostel man still wasn't taking the hint: sitting with his eyes shut at this point, pretending to be contented because he was in the company of another bloody Kriegie and because bloody misery loves bloody company.

Alfred did what he could under the circumstances, wishing himself out towards the pine trees and filling his skull with the deadened drum of footsteps over layered needles, the clean scent of resin, branches springing against his arms. The scraped earth he was staring at didn't disappear, it only stopped meaning anything, while he made a ghost in the woods.

Wishing will make it so.

Not that it ever did. God, but he remembered the song — the Bastard loved every note of it. And he'd a sweet voice. Alfred found it eerie, watching the Bastard's thin, little lips move in his usually unwashed face and this nearly girlish, choirboy sound emerging.

"Wishing will make it so, just keep on wishing and care will go."

The crew generally ignored him, that being the only way, but one night Molloy had broken out. They'd been walking home, missed the bus, and Hanson warbling on as if he was somebody, running the chorus round and round beneath a low, waning moon. She'd seemed so big that night — the scar of shadow on her, but her shape still clear, the curve into her bright half, and the cold look she gave back to you whenever you caught her eye. No wonder you shouldn't fly when she was full — and not only because she'd light you up just as clearly as the target. You could tell you'd more to fear from her than that.

"Dreamers tell us dreams come true, it's no mistake."

Then Molloy tearing past everybody and kicking at the wall. "Shut up with that fucking nonsense, will ya?" Kicking and then turning to the Bastard and plainly wanting to kick him, in a sweat for it, but going back for another lump of wall instead. "It never made anything so."

"Very clever, I'm shewer. Fuck you."

"You can fucking wish yourself . . . you can wish yourself . . ." and then Molloy was running off up the shine of the lane and over the rise and away from them.

"And wishes are the dreams we dream when we're awake."

Alfred had almost started after him, but the skipper had told him not.

"Hanson, that isn't a song that we like. And don't try another, please, old man. Let's get some peace."

The crew sticking to that after, silent, the Bastard behaving himself and their feet echoing somehow, the way they might if they'd wandered into some high, empty room.

Funny: the music had been hopeless since Alfred had come back to Germany. There were gramophones and some wirelesses, all right, but they never played anything he could like. Perhaps it was just as well, though—bring back the songs he'd been used to and he couldn't think what would be next.

You always were a soft git when it came to tunes.

He blames his ma and Wesley: Methodism—less of the preaching, give us a song. You couldn't take the sermons seriously, anyway, not when they were coming up out of some lay preacher you knew, someone who was only a person. Even the vicar seemed watery when you saw him. But the hymns, they'd roar clear through you, then pack you with faith.

"My chains fell off, my heart was free,
I rose, went forth, and followed Thee."

Just another way of saying that your wishing will make it so.

But it's still got a punch to it—imagine a touch of the melody and it drops you back. Young Alfred with his Sankey hymn book and the Sunday dust that smelled of aunts and tight, clean collars and happy ignorance.

Ma, she always kept faithful, no matter what. She loved it. I think she even loved that it was pointless, unrewarded. Singing in the chapel, she'd seem a girl, she would be lit. Except no one wants to be lit—it just draws attention.

The Fallingbostel fucker has tucked himself close beside Alfred and is breathing too loudly, managing to make his presence push in and nag, so Alfred faces him and, "The smell. That was the worst. Not the latrines, or the damp, things getting reasty, rotting—I mean the way we stank— human beings—us. When I got back, repatriated, they DDT'd me and then I don't know how many baths I took until the water stayed clean— they let you do that, were used to people needing it—but I didn't get rid of the stink for days. And sometimes it's here now, in my skin. Human beings, we're the worst stink in the world, like a disease. It's in us. Like a disease." And this causes offence, which is what Alfred wanted.

The man stands up and you could almost be ashamed for him, because he is too clearly lonely and not mithered about who sees. Alfred keeps more orderly that, "I won't talk to you again." Watching the back of him, how it's round-shouldered. "I don't know you. You don't know me." Although this was too much, being purposely cruel, when Alfred hated cruelty.

Sod him, though. He should have expected it.

Because you can only meet so many people in one life and then you're not able, your welcome's worn out. Gunnery training at Jurby, the Initial Training Wing, the Operational Training Unit, all the training and training and people and people before you reach the station, your station. You get tired of new bods. For instance, maybe seven men are walking out at the end of a movie in Boston and they're a crew the way that you are and they've managed half a dozen ops and they have a bomb aimer who can sound like Tommy Hanley, or Lord Woolton giving Home Front tips—saying how *naice* his recipe for pie is—and then by the end of the week you don't have to meet them again and don't need to remember their names. After a while, you can't see the use of other people. You have enough with the skipper and Pluckrose, Miles and Molloy and Torrington and the Bastard. There's no need for anyone else.

Although you're not an idiot: you do realise that some night your crew will most probably get the chop. You don't brood, but the odds suggest strongly that they're done for. And this might depress you, what with all of the efforts you've made to know them well—it might seem that when you're together you're wasting your time. But naturally the mercy is that when they go you'll be there with them: dying, too. You'll be together. Or, even better, the chances are that you'll go first. So it's OK, you can be fond of them, or have any other feelings you decide.

By that afternoon Alfred had firm orders to take things easy—they were having a rest from the crowd scenes, anyway—so he sat on a borrowed chair beside a few vegetable patches and started on his Sherlock Holmes stories, *His Last Bow*. This was a book (not paid for) that he'd brought with him from the shop, but he'd first read a copy in Germany, inside the wire.

At some point in '44 some WRVS women, perhaps from Epsom, had sent out a crate of reading matter, mainly crime fiction and adventures, which they must have supposed would please your average captured combatant—combining as they did both gunplay and imprisonment.

We couldn't fault their logic: derring-do and shooting, a pinch of death, and adventures mostly ended by a long spell in the bag. Why wouldn't we all adore that? So we thanked them for their kindness and their letters and did not in any way explain that holiday camps and prison camps were sometimes not quite alike—less, hiking, for example, and no tennis courts for us.

And ta very much, though I never said so, for the taste, when I opened your books, of thin gravy and old pruning shears and long, dry maidenly evenings, tucked up tight.

But the Kriegies had been genuinely grateful for the books. Even though the Epsom matrons had managed to omit anything racy: they wouldn't want to shock the boys, or lead them astray. So no *I'll Say She Does* and no *Miss Callaghan Comes to Grief*. The boys had looked very thoroughly to make sure, searched high and low, in fact. Still, Alfred— good lad and, by then, a keen reader—had worked his way through every book, enjoying the Conan Doyle most, because it was so long ago. He would try to have dreams of the Baker Street fireside: bustle down in the horse road beyond the windows, Holmes and Watson off defeating evil and nothing for him to do but be warm and slow and read papers chock-full of completely irrelevant news. Then Mrs. Hudson might come up and lay out their tea: kedgeree, chops, bread and butter, a roast of beef. Some days the tea was all he'd picture—other times he couldn't stand it.

And trying not to see her, not to act another chase out through your sleep, searching houses you don't know, bomb sites, running round a strange, deserted aerodrome, knowing that Joyce is there and hiding, that she doesn't want you.

Dreams: ninety-nine times out of the hundred, you could shove them up your arse. Bloody hopeless.

He started the first story and made himself highly interested in the urgent telegram of Mr. John Scott Eccles, but the paragraphs still slipped and fell, not letting him in. He drifted into staring at a Ukrainian in ferret's overalls who was hoeing the earth between rows of young leaves, occasionally smiling in Alfred's direction, but mainly just smiling.

Of course, in the beginning the film people made the gardens. They'd bought up a load of cabbages and such, raked out squares of ground and then sat the vegetables on them to dry up and die in the heat. Which was bloody ridiculous. And anyone could have told them what would happen next.

Within days, everything had been stolen, sold, bartered, cooked and eaten in the DP camp, or elsewhere. How could it not be? Food left and going to waste like that: it *had* to be stolen—stealing was the only possible, moral response.

This made the film people unhappy, because they needed scenes showing prisoners working at cultivation and, in the process, concealing the soil they had sneaked up from their tunnels. These sections would suggest a sense of humour among Kriegies and bravery, too—but nothing that might be unpleasant, or disturb an audience. Without the dying cabbages and so forth, they'd be left with just a scruffy mob of lads prodding round in sterile squares of dust. The film people complained, called a parade and uttered threats, forgetting that senses of humour and bravery (even in tiny amounts) might make such efforts quite counterproductive. The atmosphere turned a trifle sour, until it became slowly, quietly clear that the miniature gardens were filling again, as mysteriously as they'd emptied. This time they held real seedlings, proper life.

The growing weather was good and everybody saved their washing water to pour on what they thought of now as their allotments. The film people said they were pleased and that everything was for the best, but they also started keeping to themselves, eating their meals in a team at one corner of the improvised canteen, not joining in with the cricket games, or the football.

Out in the rest of the camp the Ukrainians and their willing prisoners were rubbing along not too badly.

"Lend a hand on the land, eh?" Alfred assumed that the gardener would not understand him, but grinned as you should in such circumstances and got a laugh in answer.

"Winston." The Ukrainian's turn to grin.

It was as good a greeting as any. "Winston. Yes."

Next, with considerable concentration, "This is a splendid afternoon."

"This *is* a splendid afternoon."

"Monty." This said with finality, the Ukrainian shouldering his hoe and waving as he tiptoed out between the brightness of the seedlings.

"Monty." Alfred waved back.

He shifted his chair across into the shadow and dived down again to reach Holmes and Watson and John Scott Eccles of Popham House, Lee.

He's not the one with the severed thumb—he's got a disappeared governess and a murder, or the fictitious business in Birmingham, I'm not sure.

The cases had blended together, but that was fine, because being unsure of what ended up where meant the stories could stand a few readings, twisting into each other more closely each time, while you went to them increasingly for nothing but the chatter between Holmes and his best friend and the hours you could spend constructing how they lived when you weren't there to see. Maybe not the best use of your mental energy.

But stops you wondering if she ever constructed how you lived when she wasn't there to see.

Chop it.

The trouble was, after a while tucked up in the Luftwaffe bag, you had truly felt fictional and afterwards it didn't leave you. The idea there was somebody beyond you imagining, picturing, guessing—it could make you seem more solid, more likely to survive, and worrying—you were ashamed of this—but if they might worry about you, that could wish you almost human again. You were certain on some days that worries could be a great power.

How to calculate deflections, how to clear jams and keep firing, how to apply to the station commander for leave not exceeding seven days, how to think of her thinking of you, how to believe it—you'd ended up with all sorts of habits that didn't suit you once your war was gone.

While I was in the bag, though—there are things you can't help, you just need them.

That she would think of me.

That she would worry.

Should have stuck to studying. I had a chance at learning Greek: we did have a primer. And before that, the RAF would have taught me Persian, but I never asked. Probably they'd have preferred that I just kept shooting. But I could have asked.

I could have done all kinds of things.

"Little Boss, will you do her or not?"

Hoping you'll make the right choice when for you there won't be one. That's the way your world works, that's your regulations, the ones that will always apply—never mind any more that service dress should be worn in the sergeants' mess during working hours, no flying clothes, and never mind any more that your chaplain should be regarded by all ranks as their friend and adviser—only this is still the truth: Alfred Francis Day will be nothing but wrong.

You will always be wrong.

Alfred abandoned the Conan Doyle, shut it up and put it on the ground: carefully, because you should be kind to books.

He sighed. Then he sighed again. Because he could.

Lucky I've got a nice nature. Lucky I'm not easily annoyed.

He'd sat in a school where he wasn't intended to learn for eight sense-less years. He'd said prayers which served no purpose and must have taken days from him: weeks, if you added them together. He'd read about Physical Culture and the Great Sandow and Charles Atlas and the Mighty Young Apollon who kept an eye out for weak fellows who were discouraged and then gave them muscles and tendons of tempered steel. Alfred had saved and sent away for a chest expander, propelled himself through more days and weeks of repetitions with it and he maybe had gained a little weight, but then he'd been growing anyway, he'd been young. And he'd worked in his father's fish shop at cold, foul, stupid jobs.

Lucky altogether, really, aren't you? Can't think why you don't back horses and be done with it — lose the last of yourself: both your suitcases, get rid of all your excess weight. A regular Jonah, you are.

But only to yourself.

You never have to jinx anyone else, that's not allowed. Better to keep away if you thought you might.

Oh, and the waiting, you couldn't underestimate the practice he'd got in at waiting, he could win cups for doing that: waiting to get something, or leave something, or sign for something, or to grab hold of his ration of something, or waiting to go and do much the same, but somewhere else. Now, if anyone kept him hanging about for more than a minute or so, he'd find himself laughing out loud, howling sometimes, as if he was having the finest fun possible, because otherwise he knew he'd do some kind of damage: violence would be unavoidable. Safer to laugh and have them think you're cracked.

Twenty-five years old and laughing in queues. Twenty-five years old and already he'd done too much, or else too long, more than you should. Twenty-five years old and he'd never decided anything for himself.

No. That wasn't true: he'd made, he thought, four decisions. Four in a lifetime; and you could wonder about them, you could raise doubts with regard to their merits. At least they were his, though, all his own — the four moments when he'd acted like a man of vitality, health and endurance, the sort of chap Physical Culture should produce.

Alfred had decided to join up before he was called up.

Alfred had decided to be a tail gunner and nothing else.

Alfred had decided to kill his father.

Alfred had decided he'd come back to Germany and the fake camp.

At least you couldn't call me half-hearted — not once I make up my mind.

He'd only prayed before the first one, being then at an age when he did still talk to God. And there were special circumstances that might have made anyone call down extra help, because he was only fifteen when the war broke out and it might have been over too soon, he might have missed it. There could have been another agreement like Munich, or it could have stayed phoney and fizzled out, he hadn't been able to tell at the beginning. So he'd prayed for the war to be serious: good and long.

And don't think I haven't thanked myself since. And God.

That Sunday morning in September, the weather so good, looking set for an Indian summer, and the church bells sounding and a conscious stillness up beyond them, a sweet ache of a day—he wouldn't forget any part of it. He'd sat with his ma in the kitchen—she couldn't go to chapel because of the pain in her leg and that wasn't good, it made a familiar rawness in at the back of his thoughts, still Alfred and his ma, they kept things cheery. They were fine. They were being comfy together and they'd eaten their sausage, eggs and bacon, not talking much because they never had to, and everything today could be late and slow—they'd get away with that—and they were having extra toast—he didn't know then she made the best bread he'd ever taste—and the house would be at rest for another two hours, at least. The back door was open and the smell of their last roses coming in and a wedge of sunshine fallen down into the hall with the cat lying in it and purring, you could tell by the set of his head before you even heard a sound. Then Chamberlain comes on the wireless and Alfred had never liked him, never taken to the tone of him—the way he seemed like some thin, grey relative you wouldn't want to sit with, all his sentences fading away and breaking if his voice went low and everything being so sad and hard for him, even though there were other people in the world who weren't enjoying themselves that much. Like the Czechs. Or the Poles. You could bet they weren't happy. But here was Chamberlain in the Cabinet room—which Alfred imagined to be like a kind of parlour: Mansion Polish and china dogs—and he was saying in his pretty accent that he'd had a bitter blow and there was nothing else for it now but to be at war. He'd needed to hear from the Germans by eleven o'clock and eleven o'clock was gone. Which suited Alfred nicely, thanks ever so much.

They'd brought in national service the day before, which had put Alfred's father in a mood. Not for himself: he was too old for anyone to want him: but he'd worked out they'd be after Alfred soon.

Alfred had been put in a mood, also, because of being fifteen and just those few months, only six, which meant he'd have too long to wait. But as soon as he could he'd volunteer. He'd decided. So he wouldn't have to walk about in fish guts till he died, wouldn't have to listen while his father made that same sodding joke every day: a blind man walks past the fish shop—"Morning, ladies." Alfred would go and he'd pick his service, that was how it worked, he hoped. Up in the clean air, up free with the blue, that's what he wanted. At least it would be, if they'd have him. So he'd exercise more to please them and strengthen himself and then he'd volunteer. Of course he'd fucking volunteer.

Ma, she'd heard the announcement and stopped eating. Alfred had been so busy in his head that he hadn't paid her proper attention and she must have sat perfectly still for a long while before he noticed and was jolted, damaged somewhere by the way she raised her eyes to him.

She was normally very sensible about crying and didn't do it. Today, though, she'd made a mistake and so they both started seeing what they were together—truly seeing, because they couldn't help themselves, and so they had to know what they meant for each other and how it would be when he'd go. They were harmed by it, by too much feeling. He might as well have been leaving that afternoon.

And he hated that they were trapped inside this, had to rush through the way they would be months in their future, for fear of his father, the thing still asleep above their heads. Later his mother might not find the chance, might not be allowed, so she had to weep in the kitchen when nothing was different yet. Without ever intending, they were making their one goodbye.

His mother lost herself for a while in little cries that seemed to leave her frightened, woman's sounds, and her hands fluttered and tried to shield her head and he went around the table and held her, the twitch and flicker of pain in her, and he touched her hair.

Didn't pray for her, though, did you? Only for yourself. You asked if God could make you strong.

Because he'd heard what Chamberlain said about Mr. Hitler and the way he was *using force to gain his will.* Alfred understood about that. And before it was mentioned, he knew anybody who did that *can only be stopped by force*—it seemed daft that Chamberlain bothered to say so when it was just obvious. Unless he was trying to let people see he was like them and had problems they'd recognise, even if he owned a Cabinet room and no one else did—as if he was trying to say this Hitler was nothing special. That might be the kind of message a prime minister would pick: hoping you'd think him a pal and meaning you all to keep cheerful and ready for fighting the war.

Alfred hadn't cared. He'd smelled breakfast and roses and his mother's skin and his heart had stammered.

And the sirens—they set off the air-raid sirens, just for a practice—although we didn't know it wasn't real, not then—and the howl of that, I could feel it in her arms, I could feel the noise scare her.

She'd almost begun to stand: thinking of hiding maybe, of the shelter she'd never been to and didn't know: but he'd held her, rocked her, where she was to make her safe, to be her safety—he'd made her stay just where she was with him—and he'd closed his eyes and prayed again to be a strong, strong man.

Another waste of mental energy.

He stretched out his legs, leaned back and let the sounds, the rhythms of the camp, coddle in around him: a game of kick-about scuffling off beside the nearest huts, a curse as someone fell, distant sawing, the film people's bad piano limping out with a bounce of jazz, the player trying to be smarter than his fingers. Strolling feet approaching and a murmur of gossip to his left—odd how fast there was gossip when nothing here mattered and hardly any time would pass before all this was gone.

It came for him then, the true press of his mother's scent returning, speeding in at him and when he'd seen her fall and the little start of blood that time above her eye and being able to do nothing.

You see too much and have no words for what you see and see and see until it doesn't reach, is nonsense, there without you.

The woman in the forest when they were marching, when the Germans were pushing them west; she had a man with her and wanted his help, there on her knees and blood on her and shouting because he should help her and make this less terrible and let her be not alone and the man doing nothing, of course, being dead already and her screaming in German at a German soldier and him raising his gun to make her stop. And walking into the house with the blue window frames, neatly done, the place were the Russians had called and got drunk: Alfred hadn't known what to expect before he saw: broken things in the good front room, the foreign kind of parlour, and where they'd lit a fire on the rug and the hair, meat and hair, hidden under the kitchen table, or maybe just there by accident, maybe no hiding involved. Her breasts, she'd been cut on her breasts. The child cut, too. Beyond recognising.

Too much.

And having to keep all you love in your head, saving it all from the rest of the world and yourself: your nature, your training: and holding it, hiding it away—intentional hiding—crossing your arms now where you sit on a wooden chair which is not your own, in the dusty sun of a game you are playing with all of these other madmen, because as soon as you saw the advertisement, you knew you'd have to come here and it all just thins and fades until you can only feel her, where her head would rest at your right shoulder and her breathing, her life inside your arms, under your fingers, knowing what she thought by the give in her, or the little tensions, twitches, and how she never seemed possible—the touch of her standing against you something no one could deserve. Joyce. Her making you a man of silver, bathed with light.

Too much.

Caring for her more than your mother, more than the skipper—of course, more than yourself.

Too much.

Alfred discovered that he was bent forward, elbows on his knees, eyes fast shut. His head stung, drummed. And this was the clear result of a failure in his discipline.

The piano music had disappeared, he'd no idea when, and the air was beginning to redden, slow, the shadows tipping forward, one of them already thick across him which would explain why he was chilly. He stood, picked up his chair and his book and started walking. Dinner would be served up soon, he could smell it: some kind of soupy effort involving chicken, he thought, and afterwards vegetables and mutton: the moorland sheep disappearing and meat turning up in the pot. He wasn't that partial to mutton, but if it was there he would eat it, no question.

Before they started calling people in, he wanted to go back and be in his hut, check in his hut for the Luger. If there was no one about he would like to see it, have it in his hand.

.   .   .

The Bastard had been the first of them to kill.

Unexpected it was, in an easy January afternoon, their fresh, operational station drifting and darting out ahead beneath a heavy mist. It seemed purposeful, orderly—the end of their road, although Alfred had felt that most as an achievement, not a threat. This was a good day for the crew, swinging down from the truck, shagged after the journey, but ready as well and smart. They'd peeled away from the rest of the crowd, caught themselves trotting and had to ease off. No call to go looking too keen, too confident. Sometimes they were, but not today—they were only a little wary, nervous today.

"No need to rush now, lads." Molloy with his cigarette glued to his bottom lip. "They'll keep the war warm for us while we unpack."

And they had laughed, because they were a crew that laughed, louder than they needed to be, warming the space between them and the low white sky. Alfred had turned his head from side to side, searching.

"What's the matter, Boss?" Skipper checking him, keeping in touch.

Alfred might not have told anybody else. "Lancs. I can smell the Lancs. They're here."

The skipper cuffed by the side of his head. "Yes. I think that was rather the point." He made another few paces. "That they post us to where they keep them. Makes all our training that bit more relevant."

They studied each other for a moment and Alfred wondered if his face was different in the way the skipper's was, if the closeness of operations was so obvious in him, and that unsteady lift in his hands, under his boots, that fear of the next breath and its power to drag him forward, that fear it wouldn't drag him fast enough.

Formalities concluded, they'd set off for their new quarters. Pluckrose took the lead in the sergeant's party and drew Alfred up beside him, Edgar following on and the Bastard last, trailing, proving he could handle things fine without them. They'd hurried under the frost, rushed themselves inside, but then had to pause at their new room's door, because this would be their place now, a kind of home, but four of the eight empty beds were already owned: pictures on their lockers, a pack of cards, a collar, dress shoes, signs of life. They didn't like to be intruders and were unsettled.

All except the Bastard who brushed in past them to sit on a corner bed, bounce the cover slightly loose.

"Steady now, Johnnie — that one's taken." Pluckrose smiling, but not happy, making a point of setting his kitbag down gently on a free bed. "Doesn't much matter where you bunk, does it."

"So then it won't matter much to him. We'll talk about it. Have a darn good discuss." He lay full out, claiming the space. "Loverly. Sheets — don't get sheets in the army, but we do." Boots on, rubbing that filthy hair oil of his into the pillow. "And I got to have a wall at my back and at my head, can't sleep otherwise. You wouldn't want me not sleeping. Someone has to be alert, keep an eye out."

Very clear this was a dig at Alfred, at his gunnery and observation skills, and so he had to answer, his forearms getting tight, "We can't help it if you're used to living in a cell." Hanson ignored him so he had to go again, "You can't do this." Which sounded weak.

"Just did, *old boy.* Just did." This with his eyes shut, trying to show that he was the gen man and entitled. He'd managed two ops before he broke his leg in a way he wouldn't tell them and effectively had to remuster and start again. The two ops were supposed to make him someone. But he'd had to go back and get more training and conversion — the RAF hadn't bloody well thought he knew everything.

Miles sucked on his pipe and looked as troubled as he ever could and there was silence. So nothing was settled beyond Johnnie Bastard Hanson getting his way and putting up a black for all of them. He never was happy till everyone else was upset. There might have been a fight, Alfred could feel one was coming, but there wasn't time.

Because then the two officers from adjustment came in, very quiet, almost apologetic when they saw they had company. They glanced about them for a minute and seemed confused. They frowned at each other. They turned to the Bastard, the pair of them solemn, vaguely disgusted, and eventually he sensed it, opened his eyes. When he saw them he almost flinched, scrambled up, slid away to one side and fumbled his cap on. It was nice to watch, Alfred thought.

Then they made the adjustment, while everybody had to stand and let it happen and Alfred wanted to leave, only that might look yellow, or not be the proper thing. The framed snap shot by the bed was taken— pretty girl, but rather heavy-set—a drawer was emptied, the traces cleared and put into a box: letters, a magazine, little things which seemed too insubstantial for all that a man would leave—not a memorial, more like a mess.

The taller adjuster searched out the dead man's clothes, folded the shape of him flat. Probably, they'd emptied his locker already. Nobody spoke, but it seemed at last that everyone stopped moving and looked at the Bastard. He'd taken the man's bed and now the man didn't need it. That wasn't a lucky thing to do. That was like murder.

The shorter adjuster—pilot officer, slapped-looking face—when things were finished he drew to a kind of attention and Alfred knew they were all remembering that no one had saluted, that something in the room had stopped them.

"We'll sort through everything elsewhere. Has to be done. Wouldn't want to send a shock back home. Not an additional shock."

The other man, a flight lieutenant, started to walk out and then hesitated. "You're new bods." Nothing in his voice to soften what he'd just done, only a need to explain. "Well, this is what you get. If you're not careful and don't follow procedures and remember your drill this is what you get. He got the chop last night. Over Essen." He realised this sounded wrong, a type of insult. "He was a decent man. You should hope you're as good."

Alfred swallowed and wondered what he should be thinking, how to show respect, how he should be.

Didn't know him, so how can I be sad? If I was, it would only be for myself—in case I get the same. But I'm not sad. I could even be happy, because it wasn't me. It wasn't one of us.

The adjusters walked out, the flight lieutenant holding the box awkwardly, as if it should be treated like a coffin, but was too small, or maybe as if it just shouldn't be touched. He could have been unfamiliar with the duty. It could have been hard to get used to.

"Well, you all heard. It was last night. He bought it last night." The Bastard having to break the silence. "Nothing to do with me." He didn't sound convinced.

Nobody agreed. Nobody said anything.

"Suit yourselves, then." He didn't go back towards the bed. "But it wasn't my fault. The fucking Germans chopped him. Not me." And he stood for a minute, longer, although everyone knew that he would have to go back—make his bed and lie in it—because it was unlucky, now, like him. No one else would have it, or would let him leave it for another new bod, coming in.

So that was it. The Bastard making their first kill. Which was like him.

The station, though, Alfred got on with it, felt settled in as soon as he'd arrived and never mind the unlucky bed—he'd never touch it, but he didn't mind it. And for once he'd been posted and not caught a head cold straight after. He was always mithered about his ears, hoping they wouldn't get infected and object to the pressure changes, go US on him, but now he had a fair chance to stay healthy.

At least on the ground.

He enjoyed the sense of age about the place, more brick and less bloody corrugated iron—iron was so sodding noisy when you were trying to get a sleep—presentable hard standing, neat dispersal and low trees— he preferred them low for take-offs, out of the way—paths that might be green if he saw them in spring and a run with six hens that some ground- crew bods looked after. If they could keep chooks alive it boded well. And the near beer in the sergeants' mess tasted quite close to the genuine article.

Not that Alfred hadn't signed the Pledge—three times, when he was too young to care and he'd only known that beer was to do with his father. A red blur of sweat and yelling, the pub and crib and poker and lost money and the bad, bad nights—that was beer: everything to hate about his father, the gleam it would put in his voice.

Alfred could take it now, though, put it in himself where it was nobody's business but his and it made him smile. In the Duck's Head. Always in the Duck's Head. The crew—at least Pluckrose—had decided, whichever pub they chose to be their own would always be the Duck's Head.

"The Duck's Head, Boston—the Duck's Head, Piccadilly . . . this way, we'll always know just where we are."

"Yes." Molloy nodded as if this was maths, or philosophy. "We'll always know we're in the Duck's Head. Good man, yourself." He surveyed their fourth or fifth pub of that name with proprietorial admiration.

"Better than a bottle party—you never know where you are with them."

"Fast girls."

"Hotter than incendiaries. More harmful."

"Thank you for sparing me that trouble, my good ol' pal."

"The least I could do. And remember—a bird in the Strand—"

"Isn't worth two in Shepherd's Bush."

They gave each other the sign for victory with some inaccuracy.

As they did, Alfred stretched up to meet the idea of himself standing, which seemed a little slower than it had been at seven this evening. "I'll get . . . the same."

The faces crammed at the table nodded to him and he wound off through the muddle of civilians, a couple of brown jobs over by themselves and blue and blue and blue. Old blue—men who'd finished with the preparation, who'd fired at drogues, who'd done their fighter affiliation, their cross-country exercises, who'd flown out with other crews, old hands, to learn the ropes, maybe had that childish fluster at the thought of separation—men who were on ops now, already working at the job—they were doing it, weren't still waiting, weren't unsure. Alfred and his crew were almost there, but almost there was nowhere.

"Surprised meself."

"How d'you do that, then?"

A pair of sergeants leaning into each other at the bar, hands slapping down slowly on a thin puddle of beer across the counter, palm over palm, as they spoke, peering close at each other's faces.

"Oxygen mask fell out of the hatch at twenty thousand feet."

"So?"

"Was wearing it at the time."

They didn't laugh, only ground on, hands dipping and then rising off the bar top.

"Fall won't hurt you. Have my guarantee. Air's the softiest, bounciest stuff you'll meet. And it's very thin that high."

"S'right."

The brown-haired sergeant rubbing at the black-haired sergeant's neck, nodding and rubbing as if he couldn't stop. "Just don' land."

"S'right."

"Thass the only part that hurts. So don't you try it."

"S'right."

" 'Less you got a chute."

" 'Course, got a chute. 'Less it doesn't work."

"Take it back and complain."

"If it doesn't open."

"Take it back to the girlie and complain."

"S'right."

Alfred had never asked, never gone to someone who was aircrew and actually tried to find out what they knew, what they really knew, and here it seemed there might be an opportunity. "Excuse me." If they thought he was a twerp, then at least they'd not remember in the morning. "Excuse me . . . if you wouldn't mind." He'd sound soft, but that wouldn't matter.

They blinked at him, mouths pursed. "Wouldn't mind?"

"What wouldn't we mind?"

They were watching a movement he couldn't see, something beyond him. "Did we mind?" Hands still folding in across each other, wet with spilled beer.

Alfred cleared his throat. "What's it . . . If you wouldn't mind." Only one shape for the question. "What's it like?"

Their eyes were pink, as if they'd been crying, or were sick—as if when they looked at anything it would be sore. They both had the rash from their oxygen masks, that mark.

Alfred waited. "What's it like." A soft kid's question.

"And who are you?" The black-haired sergeant suddenly more sober. "Exactly."

"Day. Alfie Day."

"Says he's Alfie Day."

"Is he now. Is he."

"Wants to know what it's like, Dusty."

"What *is* it like, then, Mogg."

Mogg and Dusty leaned their foreheads right in to touch, skin against skin, and rolled the contact back and forth. "It's bloody awful."

"Wha' did he think?"

"Dunno, Dusty. Less find out."

They broke off and faced him again. Alfred answering before they could say any more, "I didn't know. I don't know. Why else would I ask?"

This makes them twitch before Mogg begins gently, "Know about the breakfast, do you? Operational breakfast: real fresh eggs and bacon, maybe sausage. Traditional."

"Traditional."

"Home you come."

"Home from the sea."

"From the sky, Dusty."

"My mistake."

"From the sky."

"And you get your eggs and bacon hot. Treat. Know why you get the eggs, do you?"

Alfred shook his head and so they gave him their catechism.

"Penguins. Which is to say, all of the flying creatures—"

"Which is airmen."

"Who do not, or cannot fly—"

"Which is penguins."

"They sit at home while we go out and pay calls on the Hun and they lay us the eggs to be ready for when we come back."

They give Alfred time to nod, although he barely does.

"Tell him about the bacon, Mogg."

"Ah, the bacon. Yes. Know why they feed us the bacon?"

And Alfred wants never to be like these men and never to wear their grey sweat, their weariness. But he knows that he will—if he's lucky, if he lives—and this makes him giddy and too loud when he tells them, "No."

"Shhh."

"Softly does it, sprog, or the Huns will hear. The snappers."

"Bacon, laddie. They feed us up on bacon, because bacon is our meat. Wait till you catch it, or some bugger lands with a burning boy on board, wait and you'll understand. We're all just pork."

"Cook us up and we all smell the same."

Alfred sat on his make-believe bed in his make-believe hut, a rolled shirt on his knees. He hadn't opened it yet, but he could hear the gun inside it, breathing.

They eat, they shit, they breathe—don't ever mistake a gun for something dead.

He wondered if there would be noise at dinner, which he wouldn't like. He wondered if there would be ice cream. He wondered when the first change in him had come and when he had gone beyond where people lived: lost the God-bothering, his clean self, his redemption.

I feel the life His wounds impart.

He wondered why he'd ever thought that he could touch her.

I feel the Saviour in my heart.

He wondered where he could go now when the day came and he had to leave the camp.

My chains fell off, my heart was free,

He wondered about the gun there in his hands.

I rose, went forth, and followed Thee.

The gun that was watching, asking.

All kinds of being free, our kid, all kinds of escaping.

But what difference would it make. My heart's not free.

By the end of his time as a prisoner Alfred had been different, a new thing and surprising to himself. He lived in a way he couldn't recognise: light and distant, as if his release had already come and unlocked somewhere underneath his skull, parted him from his dirt, his flesh. He didn't need to feel any more, he didn't need to eat.

Convenient really, because there was no food. '45 coming in cold enough to burn your lungs and all of the world crawling westward, driven, or folding up asleep in the snow, dropping out into one last drowse that seemed like drinking, or wading, or fighting if you happened to watch a man step off and catch it, if you were able to pay attention. Men who lay in the morning and never rose, men who forgot how to walk, men who slipped at the crack of a bullet, tumbled. Men who were things.

There were roads and woods and railway trucks and there were driven things moving beside you—ahead and behind—and they might look at you, which you didn't want, should be afraid of, their lost and dead and dangerous eyes—just like your own. And there was no food and no reason and no longer any pretending you'd find either.

Your chance to see the true world. Your chance to know you live where there is nothing for anyone.

Sometime in that spring, he'd noticed his fingernails and seen they were still growing: his beard, his hair, they were still turning out more of themselves when the rest of him was reconciled to leaving and would have been impatient if he'd had the energy—there was only this final tiredness to get through, then he could be done. It seemed he'd become an argument now, a silly row over when he would let himself be peaceful, stop.

Earlier, in the camp he'd still eaten, of course—and been hungry, of course.

Clemmed.

He'd grown up being *clemmed*, but *hungry* did just as well and then proved itself a more suitable word for the hard, deep, stalking thing that came to get them.

Behind the wire they'd given each other lectures about the faraway and generous English countryside and collective farms and the early Christians and Plato and hygiene and modern art and he'd sat three examinations by correspondence and he'd taken extra time in the *Straflager* cells to study with no interruptions and he'd read whatever he could find—and *Anna Karenina* and *Madame Bovary*, because he ought to and they were there—and he'd thoroughly improved his handwriting and had meanwhile learned, along with everyone, each of the ways you could be hungry.

Extra bash—always trying to wangle extra bash.

He'd found potato peelings once: spilled, possibly on purpose, when someone had taken the rubbish away from the back of the kitchens. Potato peelings. Wonderful. He'd rushed to tell Ringer—rushed in the sly, compressed way that you must if no one else is meant to see—and he and his best friend: quiet, tall Ringer, his best friend: they'd scuttled back and liberated them. Cooked everything in the hut, shared with the boys in the hut, filled themselves with slimy ounces of green potato peelings—sick as dogs the following day and wasted their rations—my, hadn't they laughed. And why wouldn't they laugh: their bodies turning comical, shrinking until their uniforms were absurd, asking them for dinner and then chucking it away.

He'd lie at night and try to fool his stomach into resting, letting him sleep. But it was clever and alert. He'd picture it under his skin like a little fist, twisting whenever he shifted, reminding him that it was changing and making him changed, too. It was eager to keep his panic, his fear—it just wasn't quite predictable with eating. And somehow it had swallowed his lack of Joyce, his certainty they'd never meet again, and at any quiet time it would let him understand her as a hollowness beside his spine. When he took his bread and tea, he would be careful, shy, not wanting to disturb her.

Then, of course, the war had come up to find them, had sung and howled and thumped beyond the trees and Alfred had assumed they would be shot soon, but was wrong. They were told to prepare for a journey and given Red Cross parcels—hadn't seen even a hint of one in months—and the tins were so heavy to take with you, but you couldn't leave them and maybe, anyway, the journey was a lie and you'd be dead this time tomorrow, earlier, and what was it best to do—you didn't know.

He'd sat with Ringer and they'd tenderly eaten tins of bully beef, fought it down—with doses of cocoa mashed into butter, the miracle in a tall can each of proper butter—and Ringer had stared at him with his too big eyes and seemed worried.

"It'll be all right, our kid."

But Ringer not answering and forcing in more meat with his head dropped—everywhere people eating, or vomiting and swearing, or trying to barter tins of cocoa with the guards in exchange for bread—pack the tin with brick dust and a layer of cocoa on top and hope they won't take offence about it later.

"Ringer. It'll be all right. After this, we'll sew our shirts up into packs and then we'll sort through what to take." He'd got her letters ready. They had to come in his pocket. Not that he should bother, because it was over. "Stick with each other in the morning and off we'll go. We'll manage if there's two of us. Get that fittle down yo now—a nice bit of bash—keep your strength up." But he was welcoming the tiny, sharp thought that he'd be found with them in the snow—her cards, her notes, the last of the photographs—and maybe somebody would tell her later, or maybe write to her address, or maybe he was deciding to die with something she'd touched, touching him.

That was the one good thing about it, the starvation—you were light-headed already when you realised you didn't need your pride, you could let it be. No more of that or anything like that. You weren't bothered. Now you only needed what you needed and wouldn't get. That made everything simple.

"You think the Russians'll catch us?" Ringer interrupting. "You think?"

"Good if they do, isn't it?" Alfred breathing in meat grease and thinking he can't get another mouthful down and past his clack, not another bit, but mostly he is far off and somebody could execute him now and that would be fine, or he could even talk to Joyce, explain every detail, and be very calm. "I want to see that dixie emptied."

"All right, Boss."

His name from a hundred years ago that Ringer had given him over again.

"I'm not your boss. Just somebody has to decide. And keep you right."

Only Ringer is sad now and holding his spoon as if he's ashamed of it, setting it back in the tin. "I'll go again later." He rubs at his hair and it ignores him, goes off at its own angles in the way it always does. But he smiles so that Alfred will smile. "Are we downhearted?" So quiet it might have been a thought they'd had and never spoken.

"No." Alfred's stomach cramping and his mouth sour. "No."

But that was before the full change.

On the march or in the sidings—it had happened there, he thought—being turned to a thing that crept and lost its voice and couldn't shiver. His lips grew this layer on them, since he didn't much need his mouth.

He would still remember holding Ringer's hand, or sleeping against his back to know he was breathing. But if he thought of Ringer, allowed that, then things would slip on to the day when it went wrong and Ringer was took bad and messed himself as he walked and couldn't be contented after that, stooped over more and wouldn't look at you. Alfred had brought him clean snow, no shit near it, no fucking dysentery near it, but he wouldn't take it. You don't last without water. They could have gone on without eating, but not without water.

And Alfred had been happy to die. Almost keen—why not be? Who was there to want him alive? Only other dead men.

Even back in Cosford where they built him up—those children in blue uniforms, faces as if they'd been packed in gamgee cotton for the duration, milky—they'd brought him all sorts to eat, nothing too complicated at the start, but then good stuff, and some of it he'd managed, acted grateful in the way they wanted and supped it up, but he'd never believed that it would work. He'd mainly lain and waited and hoped they'd forget about him so that he could, too.

And then everything had gone comical again: whatever he was made of changing its course and lifting him, stinging. One afternoon, there'd been this rushing inside his arms and his heart doubling, racketing about—there was no way to misunderstand the terrible life that roared back in. He'd been caught again and no escaping. It all would come for him and hurt him and he wouldn't die, he would only want to and not get his way. He would have to be there, be Alfie Day and feel.

Alfred had never quite believed in him, not at the start.

"Day! What are you doing, Day?" Sergeant Hartnell just looked too much like a sergeant. "What is it that you are trying to do?" He had a rectangular head. Four corners at the top, four corners at the bottom—he had a head with corners.

"Don't know, Sarnt."

"I know you don't know." He looked like an actor, or like the instructor they'd seen in their first training film, who might have been an actor. "Everybody here knows you don't know. The baby Jesus and all of his angels knows you don't know."

Except Sergeant Hartnell was real and sweating with the effort of shouting at Alfred. Shouting made him sweat more than exercise ever did. He seemed very sensitive that way. "I should expect your bloody mother sitting back home knows you don't know. She's had the whole of her bleedin' life to get used to you. But you came as a norrible bleedin' shock to me."

Your bloody mother.

Alfred found that offensive, which it was meant to be. He also found it too large to breathe round and this started a throb in his head which was not convenient and he wasn't far from losing his temper which was worse—then again, if he didn't, it put his personal Moral Fibre into doubt. A chap with Moral Fibre wasn't meant to tolerate offence. Then again, offence from a sergeant was something you had to enjoy, so maybe that left you right back where you'd started—standing still while the man called your mother a bad word.

My bloody sergeant.

But Sergeant Hartnell intended to see Alfred's Moral Fibre, needed its proof.

Because Sergeant Hartnell did not like him.

The trouble was, they'd got along at the start of basic training. Alfred had been relatively fit and keen to do better—he'd enjoyed the exercises: swinging and pressing and marching and squatting and jumping alongside lads who'd sat in offices all day, bods who were not determined, who had never heard of the Great Sandow, or anyone else. There was a proper gymnasium here—barbells and clubs and beams and ropes, the things you would need to improve yourself, already set in place without a word—no more mucking about with chairs and door frames and what you could rig up from drawings and instructions—it was all on hand. Alfred had taken to Sergeant Hartnell's training, had enjoyed himself in a way: so, although he'd tried not to, he'd stood out, which is never a thing you ought to do.

And, having caught his eye, Alfred had raised Sergeant Hartnell's expectations.

"Day, you are spreading alarm and despondency. You're supposed to save that for the bleedin' Nazis. Or am I wrong? Day? Have I been mistaken?"

"No, Sarnt."

Now Alfred was disappointing him.

"What is it you did in civilian life, Day?"

Not a question Alfred liked to answer—it could lead to so many nick-names you wouldn't want.

"Day? What is it they discovered you could do?"

Alfred could see in Sergeant Hartnell's face that he still thought there was promise hidden somewhere about Alfred's person and that he was guessing Alfred had been in a decent, respectable line of work: a police-man, or better still, a farrier, or even a mounted policeman—Sergeant Hartnell especially liked men who'd worked with horses, no one knew why. Although some wag did once suggest that his mother had won the Gold Cup by a furlong in '38.

"I was in a fish shop, Sarnt." Don't think about Hartnell's bloody mother, it will make you laugh. "Wet fish." Don't think about—*Why the long face?*

"A *fish shop?*" He makes this sound like a disease.

"Yes, Sarnt."

"*Wet fish?*" A gentian-violet-painted-on-your-short-arm-and-your-bollocks type of disease.

"Yes, Sarnt."

"Well, then pretend he's a bleedin' haddock, Day, and *kill 'im!*"

Hand-to-hand combat, all-in fighting—Alfred was no good at it. He wasn't so tall and that could be a disadvantage, but he was strong and he had balance and flexibility and he'd practised making punches for years: he understood punches, the theory of hitting people. You punch from your arse, from your hips, that's where it comes from. Too late once you've got to your arms: if you only use your arms, they won't give you enough, even if you get that snap and twist in at the end, you'll be no use.

Alfred's father didn't understand the theory and was not fit. He just hit people. He hurt them. Alfred found that offensive.

And it wouldn't be a thing to think of: not now, not to keep your temper.

Sergeant Hartnell had taught them how an RAF man ought to walk and ought to stand and ought to clean his kit and use it and then had taken them out to the football pitch and put them into pairs for combat training, let them square up to each other—grievous assaults for the use of—and learn how an RAF man ought to fight. He explained to them the softness of the throat, the invitation to damage beneath the jaw, the weakness of the neck, the knees, the ankles, the fear you can put in your enemy when you go for his eyes, for his balls. Sergeant Hartnell had a special fighting knife of which he was very fond. He said that it would always do the job.

"Worked with a knife, did you, Day?"

"Yes, Sarnt."

Worked with my hands frozen, gutting stinking little bodies with stinking little eyes, cutting my fingers and never feeling it. The pail full of heads and the meaningless fucking eyes. The pail full of staring.

I wore gloves to bed and still couldn't sleep for the stink of fish. In the end, you know you won't notice it any more and then you'll be done for—you'll be a fish man the whole of your life and not have to care—so you run for the RAF, just as soon as you can. Self-defence.

"What does a knife do, Day?"

"The job, Sarnt."

Alfred understood this was true, but also knew that if he was sitting behind four Browning .303s he would do the job on Sergeant Hartnell *and* his knife, would cut him in half.

"Come at Sims again, Day, overarm strike with the knife—even if you'd be a fool to use it—overarm strike to give him practice, Day. And this time, *mean it.*"

Alfred stepped back, tried meeting Sims's eyes and saw that Sims was close to laughing, which should have helped, made him annoyed—only it didn't, because he couldn't let it, couldn't tell what would happen if he did. His wrists got heavy and bumped against his thighs, his spine curled, lost faith.

You never would do this when he's waiting for it. You hit your man when he's sleeping, drunk. You stand on his bollocks when he's passed out drunk. You kick him when he's fallen, when he's lying in the passage and won't remember. There's nothing you can do like this.

Alfred lifted his arm and immediately felt he was inside the wrong shape. He pushed himself off from his left foot and landed flatly on his right. He was almost no further forward, which was odd. A small breeze shoved at him from across the running track, reminded him of his sweat.

"Day! You are upsetting me."

Alfred froze, wobbled.

"Do you want to upset me? Don't you love me as I love you, Day, Alfred F.?"

Alfred supposed he shouldn't answer this, stood, panted against the hot weight of being stared at by the rest of the men and found it made him more unsteady. Close to his ear, Sergeant Hartnell sighed.

"All right, Day. You defend and I will attack you. Defend yourself, Day—or you will be killed."

Which did it, cleaned the day back to its bones and made everything so white that Alfred couldn't see and it let him lift, fade, disappear up into a beautiful burning. All he could ever recall of what happened directly after was his own, huge smile.

And then looking down at Sergeant Hartnell while standing with one boot stamped in his superior's armpit and twisting and also holding, folding back his sergeant's wrist. The breath packed high in Alfred's chest leapt out as a type of bark and he thought that he seemed decidedly well in himself, all of a sudden cheery. He waited, because he didn't know the form for when you have attacked a sergeant and made him let go of his favourite knife.

"Not so bad, Day." Sergeant Hartnell eyeing him from the ground, perhaps choosing when to move so there would be no unseemly struggle, perhaps deciding how he might need to injure Alfred and set the balance back to where it should be. That was all right with Alfred, he'd not mind. He opened his hands and made them soft.

Freed, Sergeant Hartnell paused and then sprang up neatly to his feet, making Alfred blink.

"Not so bad at all. But I need that every time, mind. Every time. Harnessed aggression. Or you will be unable to save your life and I will not be there to save it for you."

"No, Sarnt."

"Because I do have other things to do."

"Yes, Sarnt."

"Spending all my bleedin' time running round looking after you great hopeless shower." Sergeant Hartnell grinding clockwise on his heel, surveying his charges. His squad studied the grass, shifted their boots, tried to look savage.

"Yes, Sarnt."

And then the exercises continued: the heaving and the quiet blas-phemies as they swung each other on to the grass, ran knowing they'd be tripped, struck knowing they'd be blocked, harmed each other enough, slightly more than enough.

At the end of their games, the other lads were always in good spirits, a brightness to them you didn't see when they'd been out square-bashing, or down on the firing range. Alfred, on the other hand, only lost his con-tentment, had to swallow more often, his mouth filling with the taste of coal and damp and his mother's kitchen and he had to spit and needed to wash himself, wanted to go off and stop fucking pretending, just run into a fight, disappear all of the way and be in proper pain and fucking kill somebody. The same every time: he'd want to fucking kill somebody, when there never was anyone spare that you could kill. Would have been frowned on, you could bet.

"Your bloody mother"—you never should say that to anyone.

He'd much preferred the range. He had good dreams when he'd been shooting.

But that was long before the skipper and the crew.

Before all kinds of things.

The crew which didn't like to think of itself parted, wandering loose across so many other places in the times before they'd met. None of them, Alfred was certain, really believed in the schools that Pluckrose went moaning and binding on about. They refused to imagine Miles get-ting through an assault course, or indeed breaking into a run at any time. They wouldn't accept the skipper had ever been without his wings. They were the crew and nothing other than the crew and that would be for ever and they'd have their picture taken to prove it, the family of them together; but not until the thirty ops were over, not until they were complete.

Because you didn't want to jinx yourself, but also because of tradition and wanting to be traditional squadron men—traditions being excellent things—and even more because of what it said about their time. The crew was extremely particular whenever it dealt with time—it woke and was live and moving in its moment and in that moment only. It would not be concerned with its past and had no business thinking of its future:

its cleverness was in drinking up its minutes, second by second, and making sure to drain each one. It looked at the bods outside it who did not grasp this, looked at the sleepy civilian types—the spivs and 4Fs—and saw how close they were to being dead: how the time streamed off other people like rain and ran away without them missing it. The crew didn't like that—they found it offensive.

"D'you know now, if you're quick, you can put your hand inside a second." Molloy there with Alfred, the two of them leaning over the fence at the bottom of the station and having a look at the neighbouring farm, the fields, birds moving among the furrows, brown and small as stones. There were partridges in the woods, very dapper Alfred thought them, a nice sight—but none today. People tended to shoot them. It was a shame.

Sometimes the farmer would turn up to chat, pass the time while Alfred didn't think of the bowsers refuelling behind them, the bomb trains receiving their loads, the tail assemblies being fitted, tested, pins and clips reinserted for safety. The farmer would tell them about his crops and what had grown where they were standing, over on the war's side of the fence. Mostly, he said the same things in that dreaming flat Lincolnshire way, slower even than Torrington, repeated himself word for word, but they enjoyed that, let it comfort them.

We made him one half of a bargain. If he would keep being there, then so must we. It doesn't do to miss appointments.

That afternoon, though, they'd been alone, balanced in the while before Alfred would go and check his guns again. They'd been fine on the test flight and he trusted the armourers, of course, and he trusted himself. But he would check his guns again before they flew. He would clean his Perspex, polish away scratches that weren't there and he would practice seeing, scanning, quartering the sky and he would breathe in the smell of his one chosen home: the tight, exciting reek of working oil and skin and his never-to-be-washed flying suit and the good metal and the brassy sting in his throat from ammunition, the choke from hot firing, his trade, himself.

"You can open your fingers and stretch it."

"Stretch what?"

"A second." Molloy would say these things as if they weren't strange.

"Put your hand in it the way you would into a woman." Talked about women as if they were a known, sad thing to him. "When the engines run up, the whole orchestra there—starboard inner, starboard outer, port inner, port outer, the swing of the torque and we're going, taxiing, we'll not be scrubbed now, we're going off—then I open my hands both together and I work inside them, those seconds, until I have them on me like another pair of gloves—the last free seconds there until we're back, you want to keep a hold of them."

"You're mad."

"Bomb-happy. Aren't we all, so?"

"You're madder than the rest of us."

"Maybe that's the sensible thing."

Alfred aware, as he taps the fencepost, that he can hear this wonderfully clearly, the meeting of his fingernail and the wood: that since he began flying, operational flying, he believes he has heard, seen, tasted more. He hopes this does not mean his life has been creased over on itself, thickened and made more of, in anticipation of its being short. He hopes that it means he is a gunner and gunners are watchful, hungry, awake.

"Would you say, Little Boss, that you knew why it is we do this?"

"Because it's such a lark."

Molloy looks at him, sharp, disappointed.

Alfred tries to do better. "Well, if you want the only reason I know, it's because we're told to."

"That's what I thought." Molloy tossing the end of his cigarette into the field as if it had upset him.

Alfred wanting to say something helpful. "It would be different for you, though."

"Why?" Still the sharpness.

"I don't know . . . because Ireland isn't at war. You don't have to be here."

At this, Molloy gives a laugh, lets it be single and sour, and some of the birds beyond them lift and circle away. "That's true. Yes, this would be me at war on my own behalf, my own decision, because why not. What would I be doing, otherwise? Leaning over another fence back in Ireland and out of my mind with looking at the same people for all of my life. Or pouring concrete for an airfield over here, I suppose. Could have done that. Stay at home and put yourself in pain, because you've nothing else, or come away and have other people put you in pain—that's a nice change for you there." He lights another cigarette and holds Alfred's arm for a moment, frowns at him. "Two of my sisters, they got away from it— they're in a hostel near Nottingham, I think—making our bombs for us. They got away." He swallowed down his smoke then growled it out again. "Yes, I have freely volunteered to wear the hated British King's uniform. Couldn't sink all the way to brown, but I could manage blue. And I do what I am told. And the boys over there," he jerked a finger towards the East, the opposite coast, "they'll be doing what they're told."

Alfred felt the slight, metallic resistance that always seemed to lean in against him when he turned and knew he was facing Europe, the edge of the night that rose up and waited for them, high as thinned air and ice. "Some Gestapo man would see to them if they didn't. Or they'll like the job and want to do it, I don't know. They seem . . . they do seem keen, Dick. Enthusiastic." This the first time he's aware of having used the word—*enthusiastic, from the Greek.*

"Aren't we all the obedient fuckers, Sergeant Day?"

"Saves time."

"Saves thinking."

"Well, I'd rather not think, our kid."

"Bollocks to that, young Alfred. Thinking all the time, you are, and reading your books. Studious bastard, you are, and why should you not be? You think. We all think. But we do as we're told, no matter what. Grand life, isn't it? I come here to be away from the fucking Brothers and the Fathers and Little Fucking Sisters of Eternal Pains in Your Hole and all I do now is what I'm told."

"Nothing wrong with that." A fear in Alfred, because this is part of his crew unhappy and shouldn't be. He is responsible for setting this right. "That last exercise when it was dirty as all buggery, when we couldn't see our own props and the pitot tube had frozen and the altimeter went US—we wouldn't have come home without you."

"What, were you thinking of dropping me out?"

"You know what I mean."

Being locked in the turret on their final training flight: a cross-country navigation exercise and the weather gone to hell: nothing beyond the Perspex but a din of sleet, moisture clawed away into the slipstream, a slicing dark. The crew voices blurred as ever, shaken and thinned in the wires before they ghosted back to him, but it had still been clear that they were lost: Pluckrose muted, the instruments failing, the storm kicking at them as if it knew, would split them out and have them now.

"I'm supposed to mend things. So I mended the altimeter."

Alfred had scanned for any landmark, any meaningful shape, until his mind was slipping mirages up to jolt him—very plain for a moment, something like a young girl's face, a staring, hating face.

"If you hadn't mended it, we'd have been spread out across a cloud with a solid centre. You know that. They'd have been scooping us up off a hillside with egg spoons."

"I cut it open at the back and let the air in. That's all. Just physics. You do have physics in the wicked English Empire?"

The skipper had talked them through the night, keeping them aloft, Alfred needing those brief shudders of sound, the way they noted failures calmly, asked for fixes, held everything. Alfred had rattled over nowhere, watching the night swarm down behind them: his back to the skipper, his back to the crew, four Merlins hauling them forward and him with his back to it all. He had made sure to believe they wouldn't die.

He'd almost prayed, but there hadn't quite been time, or else he'd resisted, and then he'd heard his skipper tell them the altimeter was back.

"That was down to you, Molloy."

"What was?"

"That we made it."

"It was down to the skipper."

"And you."

Molloy almost smiled, stretched instead. "Well, I'd be happy with a nice easy exercise like that tonight. At least there wasn't any flak. Except over Liverpool—they were very touchy, there. Almost as dangerous as the navy. Bet we won't be bombing Liverpool tonight. That, they wouldn't allow."

Which meant he'd put an end to their rest and now they would have to admit there was an op set in motion already, Battle Orders showing their names. So they'd have to step round and face the station again, see it busy, preparing for them.

Alfred put his hands in his pockets, because that would seem slovenly and relaxed. "We could not bother going."

"That's right."

The grass giving under feet as they walked in, closed the afternoon up after them.

"But do you have anything else to do?"

"That's pressing? No, Little Boss, I've nothing much to keep me out of mischief."

"Will we just go then?"

"On the op? Oh, I should suppose we might as well. It would please them, wouldn't it—if we did."

"Yes, it would please them."

"And if someone has a notion of something, you shouldn't ever stand in their way."

Circling in from the north-west came a single Lanc, big-chinned, blunt as a whale and open-armed and singing. When you heard them like that, far off, you could think they were trying to speak, words hidden underneath the roar, and if you could only work them out, you would understand everything, you would be saved. Except you were always too near to your own, half deafened with her, and someone else's Lanc would never quite talk for you. So you'd never know.

Alfred watched her, listening. She would land now, air-tested, and wait for the night. They'd all wait for the night.

It was enough to make you laugh.

"Vasyl."

It made Alfred laugh, anyway.

"Vasyl. Is there something with which I can help you?"

The Ukrainian was halted beside a bunk, his hand lifting the mattress—as if any bloody fool would hide something under a mattress. Wasn't even Alfred's mattress, the man was just snooping, chancing it.

"Vasyl?"

He must have hoped to sneak in and ferret about while most of the bods were required to go vaulting over the horse, or pretend to be occupied in choral singing—the film people were keen on singing, because it suggested high morale. Alfred hadn't fancied vaulting or the choir and so he'd disappeared. He did remember how to disappear. He'd been doing some sneaking of his own and had noticed Vasyl going where respectable Displaced Persons shouldn't be.

"Mr. Alfred. Good morning." A little temper showed in his face, fear and the press of appetite. "We haven't talked for some time, yes? I come to find you." He'd been looking for the Luger, naturally, not Alfred. "I am so happy if you are well. You *are* well? You have suffered no more fainting." Chap like him, he wouldn't let a Luger go.

Then again, neither would Alfred: they weren't so common as they used to be. "No more fainting. No." Strolling in slowly, carefully, getting a good, firm thump with every footfall. "Perfect health. Must be the fresh air and exercise—does a body good. I'm *bostin*. Thank you kindly for having asked."

That'll fox you, you little bastard—you've never been bostin in your life. Don't know what you've missed.

Vasyl flitted his hands down at his sides and made himself bland, irreproachable—which was still very far from bostin. "You have a good place here. Comfortable?" He backed up a step, couldn't help himself, as Alfred made sure to seem angry, keen.

"Oh, this isn't *my* hut. I'm next door." Both aware this is a lie. "They do take care of us quite nicely, though." Then Alfred let the silence lap out between them and liked that his hands felt restless and his spine alert.

Took me a long while, cocker, but I learned how to fight in the end and slow learning is deep, the best kind, and we didn't quite finish our business together, did we?

Vasyl was still unsteadied and rushing in to fill the pause. "You know, I have thought that I might actually want to buy that . . . that old pistol from you. I have some money—not much. English pounds."

You don't want to buy a bloody thing. You want that little knife of yours stuck in me—aerate my ribs. Can't say I have any very good reason to stop you. Still, I'm in a funny mood, these days. I might not fancy having you do me damage, or else I might mind finding out how little I'd notice. I have trouble feeling, you see—a complicated proposition, damaging someone who doesn't feel. They might not be afraid of what you'll do.

"Don't want to sell it, though, Vasyl, old chum. I like my gun. Wouldn't be without it. So sorry. No thanks. Have you seen everything you wanted?"

Inside we could be in trouble, outside we could be safe—don't know which I'd prefer.

"American dollars."

And who would miss me? Best not ask. Depressing answer.

"I have a sentimental attachment to it, old man. We can't be parted now." Alfred ridiculously happy simply because his life has started banging through his forearms, is thick and impatient in his neck—the thought of risk waking him—and also because the Luger is perfectly hidden, he hasn't lost the knack.

Time was, I could have hidden you anything. Dummy cashes, hollows behind hollows: food, equipment, history, memory—I'd tuck it away. Once laid a whole false trail of wire for the joy of seeing Köllhoffer snuffle it out and pry and tug and follow it clear round the room until that beautiful last moment when he pulled back a piece of board and found only the end of the wire attached to nothing but a piece of shit. Didn't improve his temper, that. Got his one hand filthy. Remember he wiped it clean across one completely innocent fellow's breast pocket, which was uncalled for. No shouting, though. It was the shouting I couldn't stick.

Vasyl coughed: a small, courteous noise. "There is anything else I could . . . obtain for you? As a trade? Certain objects have been thrown away by men who have a bad conscience. But these can be located."

"I can't think what you mean, Vasyl."

"Medals, perhaps." Disappointed when this doesn't interest. "A knife. The special type—"

"You're rather a fan of knives, aren't you?" Alfred walking forward in a way that troubles Vasyl, begins to back him towards the door, shrinking the time he has left to manage a deal.

"Perhaps you might suggest. I would enjoy to help you." His neat English breaking down.

"And how do you think you could help me?"

Vasyl firming suddenly, halting, a genuine, hard surprise in him and Alfred not quite prepared and too close.

"You know you shouldn't be unkind to me, Mr. Alfred. This heath is not a safe place."

Which is when Alfred decided that he would drop his palms, cuddle them into each other as if he could hurt no one. He sank, tucked his head forward and met Vasyl's look, stilled him without a touch. "You know, when you'd been aircrew for a while, you could tell things. You'd see a man take his seat in the briefing room, or pet his dog, or pass by a doorway, perhaps, and this kind of heaviness would spread inside you, unmistakable, and even the very first time you'd understand—they were dead. They were already dead. The following morning, someone would say, or in a few days we'd hear, but everything would be settled long before. I could tell."

Vasyl uneasy while he hears this, not sure if you're crazy, if he should laugh. And you may be crazy—after all, you're mainly thinking that *stilled* is a lovely verb, old-fashioned. You bite on, though, keep at him. "So do you want me to tell you?"

He's puzzled here, unsettled. "To tell me?"

"I can say if you want me to, Vasyl. As a favour. I can say if I see when you're dead. Or do you think I can see it now?"

He flickers his eyes to the side, glances down, and then winds out a smile when he raises his head again, but you have him worried. "This is superstition. I am not so interested in this. Children's stories."

"Well, if you're not interested, we'd better just go and have lunch—it is time." You take his arm and it's easy to move him, his thinking elsewhere, not in his limbs. "But I was never wrong. You might want to consider that, old man. I never got it wrong."

And you steer him down the steps and into the sunlight which is harsh today, bitter on the skin, and he twitches round to you, but then reconsiders, shrugs out of your grip and hurries away.

It isn't true, of course—I could be wrong. There were times when I didn't know.

And then all of those mornings when I wouldn't quite face my reflection while I shaved. In case I saw.

Should have joined the navy—could have grown a beard.

And what's so different now?—Messing about with your top lip, trimming and fussing. Anything rather than meet your own eye.

Vasyl ducking himself round hut seventeen and out of your line of sight. There is nothing of death about him, naturally, beyond the sense that he's been too much in its company.

"Certain objects." Ar, I'm bloody sure you could get me certain objects. Selling off your iron cross, is that it?

And for a breath the camp snaps shut and the uniforms are serious and your hands are sliding and your stomach hollows and if you walk back to your hut it will be older, it will be the way it was, and her picture will be on the wall right where you put it: Joyce looking out to the left and hugging her knees and you'll wish again the sadness in her face is for your sake. The last photograph you had left of her—you couldn't tear it up.

Then the sand veers off under your feet and you have to lean over, drop, sit straight down for fear of fainting.

They're ringing the bell for lunch and someone runs past you, and someone else laughs, but after that there is more and more quiet and you're left to yourself, as far as you can tell, and so you close your eyes and lie out flat, the ground rushing beneath you. Your spine tingles and you wonder if this isn't an echo you're reading, if so many bombs haven't changed the earth, haven't left it always shivering and taken away its rest.

This gives you the idea that you would be wise to get yourself better fixed, more reliably attached to the surface. You're tired of flying, you don't want to face any more of it for now, but who can be sure that you might not be shaken loose, made airborne.

And you're crazy at this point, you know that: bomb-happy, wire-happy, round the bend: but this means that your problem's solution ought to be bomb-happy, too.

You start with breathing, heaving in great slabs of dusty air and jamming them down beneath your ribs, but this barely makes you heavier. Exhaling is difficult and you want to shout instead, so you permit that, allow a round, dark noise to push out of your mouth. This improves matters. You shout more loudly and discover it beds your skull down slightly.

And this is an old problem, you recognise it, remember—when you'd landed, taken those final bumps, engines off, the silence roaring at you, then you'd start to be unsteady, too light. You'd leave your guns safe, disconnect your oxygen, your intercom, you'd run through the drill and then let yourself out of the turret, swing round in the space that was no space and slide feet first over the tail spar, work yourself back, land on your feet by the stink of the Elsan toilet, your legs clumsy under you when you stand in the fuselage, duck through the door and step off down the ladder, climbing out to the friendly ground and the morning: the day:

the true beginning of the day reached in the moment when you're walking, walking solid ground—flying boots connecting oddly with the concrete, giddy, still stunted a little in that Lancaster crouch, a deaf rush in
your head and only the weight of your gear between you and rising clear
away. You would have no substance and you would hope this was only
joy, only the peace and the ache and tired delight of being here again,
but maybe that wasn't the truth, maybe you were gone already.

It did scare you: the thought that you hadn't made it, weren't moving alongside your crew, that you were caught in the dream beyond
your death and would turn lighter and lighter until you were lost
completely.

You'd have to sleep and wake again before you believed in yourself.
Or sometimes there'd be nothing for it but to sing.

"And did those feet in ancient time"

Pluckrose peering round at you that morning.

"Walk upon England's mountains green"

Balancing the whole of yourself as you push on, drifting up when you
step while the words are shaking out of you, so loud that you can hear,
and he's nodding, and you can see the way his mouth is yelling, must be
braying out the next line with you. Tone-deaf, Pluckrose, but it doesn't
bother you.

"And was the holy lamb of God
"On England's pleasant pastures seen"

The pair of you bellowing, looking for pastures and Pluckrose bolting
into a run, you following, airborne in spasms, but sinking, settling, and
the last of the Benzedrine burning out through your legs.

"Bring me my spears, oh clouds unfold
Bring me my chariot of fire"

And that's too much, too sharp against your job, against the burning you remember tumbling open under your feet, and so you halt and
bend over and catch your breath, your living breath. Feeling ashamed of
something, of all of the breaking you have done—it must prove you're
alive.

And singing "Jerusalem" weighed you down like armour plate.

So Alfred stretched his spine against the bared ground of the phoney
camp and yelled out the old words, the imagined country.

> *"And was the holy lamb of God*
> *On England's pleasant pastures seen"*

He shouted it up, over and over: the bow, the arrows, the chariot, all
of the kit: he repeated it word for word, for comfort, for steel in his bones.

The only thing I care to recall from that fucking school—when Mr.
Colear caught me singing in the class, thought I was getting above myself,
showing off, when I'd only been singing, hadn't meant anything by it. But
he sent me to the head and he hurt me.

Alfred aware of small sounds around him, of men coming back from
their meal, hearing him, pausing, men being near.

> *"I will not cease from mental fight*
> *Nor shall my sword sleep in my hand"*

He wasn't mithered, there was nothing they could do to him.

And they thought it would be a funny punishment if they made me
sing the whole thing at assembly. They were wrong, though—I wasn't
mithered then, either. I just sang.

But I think I didn't ever go back to school after that.

Alfred stopped when his throat was sore and he was thirsty. He sat up
slowly and then opened his eyes, glanced round at the men standing.
One of the film people started to clap, but nobody joined him, so he
stopped, folded his arms. Alfred stood, as heavy as he needed to be and
fairly balanced. He brushed off his trousers. The men waited, as if there
was something they wanted, or that he might know, but none of them

would face him, not exactly, they wouldn't entirely admit he was there, and he didn't suppose he would have enough voice left for telling the whole bloody shower to bugger off.

Alfred put his hands in his pockets. There was a moment when it seemed no one would move.

Time was, I could have hidden you anything.

But hiding for yourself is different, harder, and then you wonder after a while if the good things you've tucked away are still there, or if they mightn't just as well be off with someone else, for all the use they are to you. There were things, in the end, that you didn't even want, that were intended for a person you couldn't be any more.

Like when the camp was breaking up in the snow: the goons had emptied out the stores and gone through the filing system and suddenly everyone got back the valuables of a man from years ago. Alfred had his fountain pen returned—the one his mother saved to buy him. She knew that he'd want it, although he'd never said.

About to march out into frostbite and Christ knew what, and Ringer looking fraught beside me and suddenly I've got a fountain pen again—most useful.

Holding the fat weight of it in his hand and keeping away from the thought of his mother dead now, or himself sitting up to learn his lessons, caring about prepositions and tangents and collecting certificates.

And letters.

That had been his letter-writing pen. His lucky pen. Notes to his ma: tell her where he was, give her the happiest version of how he was getting along, and then suddenly more, needing words that hadn't been invented, words he didn't know were already hiding, ready in his skin.

Letters to Joyce.

Real letters, and a fight to make them carry what they should, not to scare her, but to keep her, not to love her too plainly, but to touch her enough.

Apologise for the terrible handwriting and check on the spelling of everything and the commas, apostrophes, all the punctuation, practically each fucking chicken scratch that made it to the paper, he'd study and puzzle at because she'd be sure to notice his mistakes and think him stupid, half soaked. She wouldn't say so, but she'd know he wasn't right for her.

Joyce.

The finest thing you hide the longest.

But what am I hiding now? Only that she's gone.

Off with someone else.

I think.

Didn't want me, anyway—with or without someone else.

But it had seemed that she did.

She'd been there before the crew, before the skipper. Back when his days were full of unfamiliar pawls and pins and springs and learning silhouettes, stripping mechanisms, feed opening components, judging wingspans, angles of attack. The bod who taught them aircraft recognition gave them slide shows—Me 109s and FW 190s and girlie shots mixed in to hold their interest, which Alfred didn't think much of. There you were trying to be quick, knowing you had to be, concentrating, and then you're studying some dancing girl's tits, or some Jane Russell–type of bint smirking past you, it muddled your feelings: that restlessness to do with firing and your memory already too tight and thinking of the magic-lantern shows in the chapel Sunday school and a sweat rising under your knees at so much flesh which you had never seen in life and did not think you ever would.

Except in London—everyone got everything in London. You'd heard about that. In gossip, in jokes, in personal health and hygiene lectures, you'd heard about that. It was all on offer there—hooch and private clubs and dreadful diseases and women selling it in the streets, professionals and amateurs out round Piccadilly Circus and dreadful diseases and Soho—God help you in Soho—and dreadful diseases and nicer girls in dances and maybe WAAFs—you were slightly used to WAAFs—and when you were a man in uniform, you could do quite well. If you didn't worry, if you didn't think about guilt and the dreadful diseases and imagine you might be doomed from the very start, then you might let yourself be talked into going and even be hardly surprised when you stroll off the train at King's Cross station and really are there—in London, with a bit of money and looking quite fine for a short-arse in your Best Blue and not everything about you is so very short, as it turns out—another thing you've learned in uniform—so you've no cause for dejection and there you are, all equipped for most things you can think of—which isn't much—and up in bloody London.

Which meant Alfred, with his forty-eight-hour pass, had gone with four gunnery training mates to his nation's capital and seat of government, because they all had to go and try their luck.

Looking for an easy way to test it—no harm meant and no ammunition required.

Although two of the lads had girls there and family and they pretty much disappeared once they'd supped a pint and made everyone come down Putney way because that was convenient for their houses, even if it meant that Alfred didn't see the sights—or not so that he noticed—only bombed-out buildings here and there and a patch of the river.

Once the Putney lads had gone Alfred was left with a bloke known as Ditcher—although he'd never ditched—and a quiet type called Blamey, none of them sure of where they were once they'd walked a bit off from the pub in London's odd, charged dark, a fat moon lifting overhead. They'd walked back towards the Thames, they hoped, in a chilly night and had gone far enough to be highly browned off with not finding it when Blamey hailed a cab and a car did stop—but maybe not a cab and in got Ditcher and Blamey and then, before they could do a thing about it, some other chap had climbed in after from the off side and everyone shouting as the doors slammed and the car drove clean away.

Which left Alfred in the dark and sobering rapidly. He gave up on the river, then found it, crossed it, wandered along by himself fretting he should have used this time to see his ma, check that her letters weren't phoney and she really was doing all right.

He'd not been clear about where his party had hoped they'd spend the night—the YMCA, a French madam's boudoir and requesting a serviceman's discount at the Ritz had all been mentioned. He was beginning to feel lonesome, childish, tricked, but then Goering took a hand and the sirens went up for a raid, the hot columns of searchlights starting to topple and sweep, ticking round for bombers.

They look for our boys, we look for theirs.

He'd stumbled on the right way for a shelter: one of the brick-built ones that looked a shoddy job, materials skimped, which was funny, because the area seemed presentable from what he could tell in the whining black. He remembered thinking one direct hit would knock down the whole lousy effort. But maybe serve them right—maybe they'd demanded a local shelter—could you do that, if you'd got the money, influence? Seemed you could do most things if you were that kind—the five courses at the Ritz and bugger the rationing kind—so why not demand somewhere for yourself, or maybe for your staff, if you didn't just run for your country house and stay there in a funk?

Count on a war to bring out the finest in people.

He went inside anyway, perhaps out of curiosity—and because if your number's up, it's up, and you could be sitting in a fine, deep Underground station and have a sewer blown apart above you and then drown as easy as anything, choke in shit, or maybe you'd only fall on the steps going down and crush yourself, crush everybody, no matter what you were worth.

He'd turned through the blast protection and then been knocked against the wall. Couldn't work out for a moment why he'd never heard the bomb—then realised this bundle had swiped round and clocked him when he wasn't expecting it. This bundle carried by a woman's voice.

"I'm so sorry. Did I hurt you?"

But she hadn't hurt him, he was only surprised. "No, I'm—"

And the bundle unravelling then and dropping: a quilt, a book in a plain paper jacket, a glasses case, a packet that suggested sandwiches.

I wanted to know what book. Already trying to know people by their books. Stupid habit.

She'd managed to keep hold of her Thermos. "Thank the Lord." Joyce. "Oh, dear." Standing close, almost against her—like being, all at once, in a warm room and happy. Joyce.

Green coat buttoned to the top and her hair not exactly brushed, very deep black, and the largest eyes, these huge dark eyes. Joyce. He sees her and feels untroubled, slowed.

She was a place to live. My place to live.

Joyce. And already he's looking too much and can't stop, but she hasn't noticed, is busy with flustering over her things, so he'll just keep on. Even when he crouches to help her he keeps on, takes in her shoes— good but scuffed—and her ankles, her legs, the start of her legs, the calves, the way they take his thinking out of words and into a panic: thin, thin, dizzy air.

He hands up the case for her glasses but doesn't lift his head, because he is blushing and appalled. He wants to run somewhere with her. And he wants a few days to consider, to gather himself. And he wants things he cannot say.

"Oh, that's—You're most awfully kind."

Felt like a creature, a wammell. Heat and shame and enjoying the shame. Hotter because of it.

Raising the quilt that is warm from her arms and heavy and sweet-scented, he stands and he folds it and can't think if he should hold it tight or else far away from himself, because both of the choices would seem rude.

And you're a good boy, remember. Hold hard on to that.

And now that he's standing, it's her turn to bend at his feet which staggers him again, the glimpse of her bared neck, while she gathers up her book. He worries that he smells of beer, of the twist in his head, of this new, marvellous burning.

And then because he's a fool and he does want to know what book, "That's a long . . . a big . . . What are you reading?"

Shy about it when she answers, "Oh. It's, you know, *The Odyssey of Homer*—new translation. I never really paid attention when I was at school. Bit of a dummy. I'm up to where Circe turns them into pigs."

And his face dying, abandoned out there in front of his thinking, because he cannot nod as if he's read it, cannot move, and soon she will raise her eyes, stop staring at the wallpaper cover she's used to protect her book—she takes care of books—and she will see that he's just an idiot and they've nothing in common at all.

"Anyway, I remember he gets home safe in the end, gets the girl and so forth . . ."

The end of her sentence tingling in his spine.

And not sure if she was making it sound simple, because then I'd understand—her being kind—or if that was only her way of talking. She seemed kind. Always kind.

She clears her throat neatly and begins edging further into the shelter, chattering on as she draws him in behind her. "I don't usually come here—been using the basement, because it lasted through the proper Blitz, so why not. Only then the house two doors along caught it last week and their basement didn't come off very well." He thinks, hopes, she hasn't noticed he's so much a bloody fool.

And they're walking together after that and finding a space, sitting, this old dear frowning at them sideways and put out, a kiddie starting to whimper elsewhere, people fixing themselves for the night while a man in a long, grey coat gives out Communist leaflets, lots of praise for Uncle Joe and how they're still holding out at Stalingrad after so long. Alfred takes one because Joyce does—except he doesn't know she's Joyce yet—and he folds it up into his pocket.

"Do you approve?"

There's this shine about her, as if she's a magazine picture, or something religious and he doesn't know why people haven't noticed and can't think why she's bothering with him—not that she truly is bothering, more like passing the time, and there's something about her that's nervous, upset, and it seems that she's speaking against her will. In those astonishing eyes there's a type of question, or a request. He can't read it exactly and maybe his want is making him find what isn't there, but he has the idea that he might be able to touch her hand and that it might calm her if he did and that he should do something to mend her: that should be his job. Of course, he'd forgotten—so tickled with his idea—that she really *had* asked him a question out loud.

"I said, do you approve? I mean, it doesn't matter if you don't." She's dipping her words, nearly murmuring—the old dear staring sharply, trying to overhear. "I always did think the Blimps and so on could do with getting a good old shake. We'll need things to be fairer when this is all done with, people won't stand for anything else. And we're used to sharing by this time, mucking in. And meeting each other." She frowns at herself, at her quilt which is resting on his knees. He raises it, but she stops him. "If you can bear to keep a hold—I've nowhere else to put it." She glances around at the shelter, the dim, musty packing of strangers against strangers, grubby bedding, a shady fellow knocking his pipe out and laughing as if he's told an off-colour joke, elbowing his shady friend.

"Oh, God." She gives a shiver, very small. It clatters his bones.

Alfred's stomach fluttering and, "What's wrong?" Sounding too loud to himself and not quite respectable. "That is . . . is there something the matter?"

She shakes her head, "No, no," as if there was water rising to meet her and she hadn't expected it. "Would you like a sandwich? I have some. There's spam, or there's jam. My mother made the jam. No way of telling who makes the spam—some Yank, I suppose. Oh, Lordy. You must think I'm cracked."

Alfred wants her to stop and has cramp in his arm from needing to reach across to her, only then he wouldn't know what he should do—even if she didn't slap him—which she would—and also that aircraft recognition feeling is seeping into him again like sin. It's tearing him: trying to seem presentable and this nasty eagerness, a bad want of her that breeds more of itself and tricks his breathing up and what kind of man can he be that he likes his going wrong, loves that it springs him up, leaves him hiding his lap under her quilt.

It had a gold satin cover, her quilt, very smooth. His hands were ugly when he set them down against it. He seemed to himself a very ugly little man.

"I'm sorry. I don't know your name, Sergeant. Did I see you were a sergeant?" She turns slightly and this presses her shoulder into his, covers his stripes, strips his heart back to the breech.

Saliva so thick in his mouth that it gets in the way. "Yes . . . I'm a very new sergeant. Air gunner." Better be honest from the start. "But I haven't done anything yet. They make us sergeants just for saying that we will." Be honest in what you can.

"But you have a name, too . . ."

He looks for how she said this and she's smiling a little. The biddy in the corner almost growling, finally getting something worth her disapproval.

"Alfie, I suppose." His voice muffled by pressing down against so much.

"Hello, Alfie you suppose."

"Hello."

Then a horrible silence and some kid coughing as if he's swallowed a button, or something, and the distant thump of things starting up out in the world.

"You could ask *my* name, if you wanted. As we'll be spending the night together. It's quite all right, these days. Everyone's very modern and no one comes to any harm. Not much from that, anyway." She doesn't sound modern herself, or casual about this—more as if she's pushing into somewhere she won't like.

And now you have to make her happy, have to help and that means you can be a good boy really, a good bad boy and that calms you. A bit. "Well, I don't know . . . I've never been in London . . . At home we had an Anderson out the back, used that." Understanding she'll find your old life unattractive, but you can't stop. "Wouldn't have been any good if my sisters were still at home—not enough room—I've got a whole wing of sisters, but they left years ago—married. Apart from Nan, she's in . . ." Can't say she's in service, not with someone who probably has servants. "I'm the youngest: the babby." Sounding soft as shit, but it matters much less than it ought, because of how safe you seem, how well, how comfortable she makes you.

She felt like home—gave me that.

Then stole it.

And when he'd finished, finally run down, he turned and discovered her watching him, apparently pleased, but also surprised in some way—

as if he had opened a door on her while she was busy with something else, a duty she didn't like.

"Sergeant Alfie, you still haven't asked me what I'm called."

"Maybe I shouldn't." Because he knew he had to. This feeling that he could die if he didn't know.

"I'm Joyce."

Landing like a hot stone in him. "Oh." Rippling his breath, rocking what had only ever stood before, some place in himself he hadn't known. "Hello, Joyce."

The city outside the shelter louder now: desynchronised engines worrying in and the dull shake of bombs, ack-ack doing its best. Not a big raid, but enough.

The batteries firing up always seemed inadequate, thin. Never like that when you got on the other end of the German flak, had to ride across boxes of the bastard stuff, pretend you didn't mind.

But when you were busy, you didn't, that was the marvellous thing. It was a mercy. Like her.

He said her name again just because it tasted lovely. "Hello, Joyce."

"Hello, Alfie."

His breathing all shallow and helpless, making him babble at her. "At the back of Ma's house there was an ack-ack emplacement—three lads and some sandbags and a Bofors gun. Ma used to bring them mugs of tea. I think everyone did." He didn't know why he was telling her this, it wasn't the right kind of thing, not witty, intelligent, not any use. "Then one morning after a raid, she went out to see them and their heads were lying in the lane. Blown off. There in the lane . . . She shouldn't have had to find that." Joyce was still watching his face though, listening. Brave girl. "I was away by then. Training." He tried to swallow and didn't quite. "Finished now, though. Well, the basics. Not operational, but I've got the brevet." He wanted to shut up. "Would you like to see?" He wanted to start again, be a man she would like.

But it truly did seem that she didn't mind him and so he angled himself to let her see his wing—and his pretty lousy sewing—while her concentration, her attention felt enormous, like a kick from Sergeant Hartnell, only deeper and wonderful, like a strange recoil echoing in his chest. He felt it, the breath when he split open.

"Alfie, I came here — " She faces straight ahead now, falters. "Alfie."

She is so, she is too much. She hurts him with being Joyce, even when she seems not quite concerned with him, is preoccupied. She is the first good hurt he's known.

"Alfie, I came here because I wanted to be with people, but I don't think I can stand being jammed in like this all night . . . This will sound awful . . ." She checks with him now and he shakes his head for her before he knows why and maybe she's going, maybe he's leaned up against her side too hard and she's offended and their having met is over and no more of it to come and perhaps now he has to be shaking his head because he can't let that be true.

"This will sound awful, but I don't want to go back alone."

Alfred's mouth hasn't got a clue—his mind, likewise—they can't help him. He is beyond wanting her, lost in a splendid, shining fear.

Joyce clears her throat. "Look, I wouldn't ask. And I also shouldn't. And you ought to know that I'm a married woman. I really am terribly married and I don't want there to be misunderstandings."

She says other things after that, but he doesn't hear them. He thinks he might still be shaking his head, because here is something else that can't be true.

Then she is quiet, tense.

He hugs the quilt. Doesn't want to give it back. Perhaps he is shaking his head about that. It would be very simple if this could be all about a quilt.

She brushes his hand, which stings, or lights, or twitches, he doesn't know which without looking and he doesn't look and she tells him, "You really don't mind? I do realise it's an imposition."

His head still swinging back and forth without him and that blasted old woman tutting and acting as if she's outraged, when there is nothing to be outraged about.

Joyce again, insisting gently, "Because I'd probably get out now, if we were going."

And he stands and his legs are unhelpful and he follows Joyce, because he can't do otherwise.

Should have stayed where I was. Stayed safe.

But I couldn't.

Not in a million years.

So they'd gone out beneath the edge of the passing raid, rushed out before anyone could stop them.

He'd stumbled through the streets beside her. The moon apparently swollen, watching: at its highest and very naked, very bright for them.

Thinking all the way that what she said was one thing and how she seemed was another and you believe how someone seems, don't you? That's common sense.

The reek of fires as they went. The harsh, the sweet, the rotten: another lesson war would teach you, the way there could be such variety in waste, the infinite variations of fire.

They stepped across the head of a street, something leering at its end: a squat, red threat and a bell sounding, a fire engine going somewhere and a whistle blown, three blasts. Funny how you heard the detail and not the guns any more, not the Heinkels, not the bombs: the larger noise of that more like a grip around you, a heaviness you moved through and learned to ignore unless it pressed too sharp, came down and bit you.

Alfred saw the muffled street lights changing and pausing, showing their signals in the proper order, as if anybody cared. The scent of her quilt and of her hair were so much the only urgent things.

A little dog ran past, upset—yipping and snapping, which made Joyce draw in her breath and then what sounded like a shell fragment dropped down quite close and she held his arm. And he let her.

And they went on like that.

Otherwise, he might have said goodnight when they found her doorstep. He might have tried to.

"This is very decent of you." She struggles with the lock in her front door while you look at nothing and her arms are pointlessly full and the glasses case drops again. "Damn and blast the—" And there are tiny noises from her that make you think she's crying, so you rescue the case and follow her into the darkened hall of a house that smells expensive, officer class.

"Mind, there are stairs." Something lost about her voice and you don't know this dark and so there is only her in it and your idea of her and your clinging on round the gold satin cover of a quilt. Together you rise and turn with the curve of the staircase, fumble your way.

When they reach the second landing, she's easier with her keys and another door, but she pauses in the hallway beyond. Alfred hears himself a long way away whispering, "You didn't need to say, you know." Whispering to Joyce. "About being married. You never needed to say. I wouldn't do anything . . . not because I was in your house. I only . . . I'm not . . . I wouldn't have done anything."

"I'm sorry."

"Well, I had to tell you."

"I'm sorry."

"Well, I think I had to tell you that."

And she is most likely crying again—sounds like it—and hurries off up the passageway and he hears a clattering, confusion, something heavy tipping over, but just waits, leans against the wall and puts his hand on to the paper, thinks he is touching her wall—there will always be this place where his hand was and he touched her house.

He closes the front door and the dark becomes a little darker.

He waits.

"I'm, I'm sorry." Her voice rather distant, calling. "You should . . ." Then a spill of light ahead and to the left, the shapes of little tables now along the corridor and a clock, door frames. Officer class. "Do—Ah, do come in."

For a diving moment he wonders what room she is in, because different rooms have different meanings and this will be important and he wants and does not want to know what he will be supposed to do.

"I forget if I put up the blackout and then I . . . I mean, I must have done it this time, because it was dark before I went out, but sometimes . . ."

Then he moves himself forward, lets her talk him forward.

"So I'm in this habit now. Crashing about through the dark. I broke a vase yesterday which Donald's mother liked especially . . . I . . . I'm not very good at this war. Maybe when they have another."

And there she is in an untidy kitchen—not a bedroom, or a parlour: a kitchen—sitting at the table, wearing her coat. Her head is dropped and her fringe hides her face. There are two nice cups and saucers set out and two plates and that would be for her and for him. Her hand is holding a teaspoon, turning it over and over. There is no sugar bowl. She has perhaps forgotten it. There is a smell that is faint, but not clean, stale.

Alfred blinks. "Do you, would you . . . This quilt."

"Oh, my goodness. I am a BF, aren't I?" She darts up, wet-eyed, and snatches away his bundle, almost runs to another room somewhere to his right. He thinks he might sit down and, after a while, he does and holds her teaspoon and turns it over and over. No sugar bowl. No milk.

He hears when she steps back in, feels a line taut in his neck.

"There, that's . . ." She pauses until he glances round. "You're very kind."

"I don't think so."

"I think so. I think you're very kind."

"No."

She is a little more collected, slower—he heard water running while she was gone and imagines that she must have washed her face. Carefully, she pours him cocoa from her Thermos and takes out her sandwiches from the packet and puts them on the plates—two sandwiches each. Then she reconsiders and gives him three. It doesn't matter, because he can't eat them, can barely sip the watery cocoa.

"Don't you want to be in your basement?" Although the raid seems a good way east by this time, not their concern.

"I couldn't. I mean, sometimes I don't. I mean, there'll be my neighbours and if you're here—"

"I can leave." Which is his first lie to her.

"No." Which is when they look at each other.

And there is nothing to be said. And Alfred sits and believes what he sees and allows himself to be in love, cannot prevent himself being in love.

Then quietly she turns the lamp out and takes the blackout down and they stand side by side and, in the window, Alfred watches the swipes and smears of warlight, the way it searches, judders, bleeds. The night cracks and heals and cracks again, while he feels it tremble, his own lost skin taken in with the shake of everything and he sees the little garden below them apparently undisturbed, but made out of some dark metal, precisely engineered, mysterious.

Thank you, Ditcher, thank you, lads. Thanks, God, if You're up there. Thanks for my night. My burning night.

And Joyce told him about her husband who was Lieutenant Antrobus—Donald—and how he'd been out in Malaya and then withdrawn to Singapore and then no word from him since the Japanese overran it. No word for months.

Standing there like a bastard and hoping this Donald Antrobus was dead. Pretending it wasn't unlikely, was already settled and thoughts could do no more harm. Wanting to push a man out of his bed.

Changing the subject after that, "We ought to move, you know," because you would rather not hear any more of Antrobus and rather not think any worse of yourself than you already do. "It's not safe here." Although this doesn't change the subject, it only means more than you want.

She nods for a while, drifting, then pays you attention again. "What?"

"It isn't safe here . . . the glass could shatter. If you can't be in the shelter, or the basement . . ."

Very soft, "I don't really care. Do you? That is, I don't think it makes any difference."

"If your number's up . . ."

"Yes."

"You think we can't change what happens to us."

"I used to. Not sure now. Or maybe that's the wrong way round. I don't know."

Then she's saying how she married Donald quickly—their mothers being friends and having known him for years and suddenly being his wife: this married woman: changed into his wife just a fortnight before he went away.

And why would you say that, why would you tell a stranger that you didn't understand your marriage and were glad that you hadn't a child and why would you invite that stranger up into your home and be with him and talk and then hug him very quickly, a flinch in the end of it, a kind of regret, but anyway you hug him, you do that to him.

"It isn't safe here."

Why hug him then leave him alone?

"No, we shouldn't stand by a window. It's silly. And it's very late. You should sleep."

All of his blood confused by this, jumping in him, straining. "I—"

"The spare room is all in mess." She backs into the shadows at the side of the table, fades beyond him. "But there's a big couch through here. Do you mind a big couch?" Walking ahead, becoming brisk. "I'll find you a pillow. I do have nice pillows—someone gave them to us. Wedding present." Alfred following blankly, the hurt of her kindling something all along his arms until, by the time she has made the couch ready, he is shivering.

"Are you cold?"

"No."

Needing her to bring him the quilt, let him lie under that. But he doesn't ask.

"You look it."

"I'm not."

Room full of broken furniture, chairs bleeding horsehair and the iron pieces of a bed stacked by the fireplace.

"You're sure?"

"I'm not."

A breath between them and the room swinging underfoot. "Well, I'll let you rest. The bathroom's second—no, from here, it's third on the right. I mean . . . you'll know it when you see it. That kind of idea. I really need to . . ."

"Of course." Words coming out of his head and dropping round his feet, as much sense in them as gravel, fag ends, bullet casings. "Of course. Thank you." For the first time realising how much he would seem to her from another country, how silly and alien he would sound. Talking about equality was one thing, touching a man like him as if he was possible, that was another.

"Sleep well, Alfred." Calling him by his Sunday name as she closes the door.

I should have worked her out from that—hugs you then runs away— means it, then doesn't mean it. That's how she is.

Except I still don't think so.

I believe she was kind, that she still would be kind.

He'd turned out the light and lain under her blankets until he smelled all of her house, already covered in holding her, and no chance to sleep, only to feel that she would be lying now in her bed, the pair of them lying in their beds, and he didn't know what he should do.

So he did his own running away before she could wake. Washed in her basin, gently, gently, washed with her soap and readied himself and then ran away. Never tried to see any more of London's sights.

But I remembered her address, repeated her address, went straight to the station for the usual chaos and hanging about—bought cheap, grey notepaper and hoped that wouldn't be a problem, because there was a war on, after all, and I wrote to her, sat on the platform and started to write.

Dear Joyce

The way to break your heart from the beginning. The first pieces shivered off then by how dear she was.

But it was only what you always put. I didn't expect her to know what it meant. She didn't have to. I think I could still have been happy if all of the feeling had been only mine.

Liar.

Bloody liar.

Fucking liar.

Yes, I know.

There were days when Alfred liked the filming, when it suited his temperament which mainly needed rest. Time was, he'd have loved the phoney drills, the displays of gymnastics, physical skill. And there had been that genuine hope in his mind that he'd come over here and get fit again, into condition—he could still do a handstand, or almost—but he was maybe too old for that, or else his mood was wrong, because now he was happiest when they told him to lie down. Possibly this was because when he fainted lying down, no one would notice, but it could be he'd become a lazy bastard, a pit-basher.

And if he couldn't lie, he'd hope to sit, so this morning he was jolly, comfortably seated with a dozen or so other bods, tapping away at tin cans and making dummy ventilation pipes for the film's supposed tunnel. Although he'd got bored with that quite quickly and it didn't much matter what he was actually making, so he was slowly in the process of converting two splendidly clean and shiny Carnation tins into a miniature cooking stove with added blower to give it some punch. He was just cutting out the blades for the little fan. The lad next to him paid no attention, but over the way, a chap smiled, recognised the contraption as a Kriegie standard and then made a point of averting his eyes politely. Alfred decided the chap might therefore be all right, but also thought they needn't ever speak.

As Alfred tinkered with the cooker the cameraman and hangers-on stopped and shifted, adjusted and started, but Alfred hardly noticed. He found himself glad to be busy, humming a tune and as mindless as he could have wished until he recognised the melody he'd chosen and then the words tripped him, brought him down.

"Tho' the days are long, twilight sings a song,"

Pluckrose had picked it—partly because it took his fancy.

"Of the happiness that used to be,"

Partly to shut up the Bastard who always sang dreadful trash.

"Soon my eyes will close, soon I'll find repose,"

Partly to tease Alfred.

"And in dreams you're always near to me."

A sleepy tune to it and clinging in a pleasant way and he'd listened for the first time while Pluckrose, like the elongated boy he really was, frowned into Alfred's face, studying him hard as any chart to be sure they were enjoying the same thing and to the same degree, that somebody was sharing his enthusiasm.

> *"Tho' the days are long, twilight sings a song,*
> *Of the happiness that used to be,*
> *Soon my eyes will close, soon I'll find repose,*
> *And in dreams you're always near to me."*

And Alfred did like the song—vaguely recalled that he'd heard it before—and especially appreciated the teasing, because *his* happiness was still there, impregnable—by this point, he'd sent letters and received them, Joyce's words layered, soft and bright in the back of his head—and there wasn't a love song that didn't seem new and indecent and lovely and the blush that rose over him when he gave in to the lyrics and listened properly was something he didn't mind happening with Pluckrose.

"It's all right—I'm ghastly with our fair sisters myself. As organised and successful as the BEF. I may become a nun."

"You mean a monk."

"Not giving up my last chance yet."

While Alfred thrummed with the knowledge that he *did* dream her, loved dreaming her and the rare, deep mornings when he'd wake with the touch of her clear and focused, as if maybe she was leaning on his arm, or had pressed her hand up to his cheek. All imagined, all wishful thinking, but more than that, too—like a promise, a message, a contract. You couldn't feel something so perfectly and not have it arrive in the end. He'd been so certain about it he was actually pleased to wait, enjoyed the sore way it made him.

"Will it do for us, Boss?"

"Hm? Oh, yes. At least, I think it's nice."

"Nice? Nice? It would tear a virgin's underthings into tiny, delicious threads. Spin her round the dance floor to that, shoot her a line about risking life and limb for King and whatnot . . . and all would be well and all would be well and all manner of things would be bloody well, I'd say."

"I wouldn't know."

"Certainly they would. Pick your secluded nook, get all cosy, then breathe on her glasses."

"You what?" Worried that Pluckrose somehow knew that she really did wear glasses to read.

"Breathe on her glasses, old man—so she won't see what you're doing . . ." He widens his eyes, winks. Then waggles his hands, placating. "But no offence intended, just . . . Oh, to hell with all that—d'you think the boys'll like it? The tune?"

As it turned out, the crew was very much in favour. They played it on

Pluckrose's gramophone, or any other available gramophone, at every permissible hour. They grew fond of it, possessive. Intent on preventing pilfering, breakages and loss, they all found they'd finished up buying one or two or maybe more records of "I'll See You in My Dreams"—with Pluckrose's assistance.

Whistling to it in the sergeants' mess, the Bastard had dabbed and slid his horny grubby hands across a tabletop so they sounded a little like brushes on a drum skin and he'd been quite amenable for a while. "It's not half bad, is it. Not too shabby."

Alfred, Pluckrose, Miles, Bastard Hanson: they'd all sunk back in the battered armchairs and the sergeants' mess had become very slightly golden to them in a way they enjoyed.

> "*Lips that once were mine, tender eyes that shine,*
> *They will light my way tonight, I'll see you in my dreams.*"

Pluckrose had leaned across and knocked his knuckle delicately on the back of Alfred's copy of *Tee Emm*—asking to break in and interrupt his reading.

"Enter."

"Damned civil of you, think I shall." Pluckrose mimed drawing on a pipe. "Gad, sir—it's a grand life, ain't it."

"I suppose."

"Oh come on, though. I've found you and your star-crossed sweetheart a loverly ditty. You can croon it to her when next you meet. Results guaranteed."

"Thanks a lot."

"You do like it? Honestly?"

"Yes. 'Course I do. It's very—"

"Enough. Before you even start. Not another one of the Day artistic and critical lectures—education's an awful thing—and my life will be short enough as it is: no time to waste." He paused for a beat to be sure he had Alfred's entire attention. "But may I discuss a fine plan that I have?"

"I suppose."

"Wise choice. First of all—did you ever hear of a fellow called Cardini?"

Hanson sucked his teeth. "Who's he, then? An Eyetie admiral?"

"Shut up, Hanson—the adults are talking."

"Yes, talking all over the bloody music." He'd got hold of some toast from somewhere, possibly his pocket, and started gnawing on it frighteningly.

Pluckrose sighed and rose up like an extremely long-limbed dowager, beckoning Alfred away to the window where they stood and examined the drizzle and heavy cloud that meant they'd be flying nowhere tonight.

Alfred didn't usually have to prompt around Pluckrose, but, "Cardini?"

"Yes." As close to a whisper as Pluckrose ever got. "Served in the trenches: '14 to '18: and while he was there, to stay sane he taught himself card tricks, magic. Turned professional in peacetime. I saw him once—amazing. Did remarkable things in all directions—while wearing gloves. Magic was how he stayed sane." He leaned his head over, blinked at Alfie, hesitant.

"Well, go on, you big, soft article. What's your plan?"

"More of a theory. Yes. That would be more accurate." He paused again, but then grinned at Alfred and patted his arm. "You see, I stay sane imagining people like Cardini—or Rob Wilton, Tommy Trinder, Jasper Maskelyne, old Maxie, Max Miller—I run through a great, long music-hall bill: wonderful turns and plenty of dancing girls between, loads of leg. Keeps up the morale. D'you see?"

Alfred didn't want to disappoint the pink, affectionate face looming in at him. "Not . . . I don't really . . . No."

Pluckrose sighed. You could see him wondering whether he should go on.

Alfred elbowed him gently. "Because you're no bloody use at explaining, you barm pot. Have another go."

"Suddenly, you suit those sergeant's stripes."

"Get on with it."

"Precisely." Pluckrose beamed, buoyant again. "Any road up—I was reflecting on a bit of business I'd seen old Cardini do and then . . ." He grinned with significance. "I *got interrupted.* Had to jump off the blood wagon and climb aboard D for Doris and drop HE on the widows and orphans—"

"Don't joke about that. I've told you."

"Only being realistic. But as you wish. The point is—I *got interrupted.* This is on Wednesday last, you may remember—our first little visit to Germany . . . So all the way out to Happy Valley and all the way back with the natives decidedly hostile, chucking pots and pans and fuck knows what— for the whole of the op, in the back of my mind, there's this idea that I have to get home, because *I wasn't fucking finished* with what I was doing. Cardini—I hadn't thought through to the end of his turn. I wasn't done."

"You're not seriously—"

"No. I'm not. I'm just saying it maybe could do us no harm if when we left on our next outing, we had something unfinished."

"You want us to learn card tricks?"

"*No*. You dreadful little troll. I want . . ." Pluckrose halted, drew in a large breath and hissed it out while he folded his hands behind his head, stretched the length of his back. "Tell you what, I'll show you."

"Show me what?"

"I'll show you."

"When?"

"When the time is right. When the time is right." And he strolled back to the armchairs, sucking at his imaginary pipe. None of which made much sense to Alfred.

But he did understand when Pluckrose set up the gramophone and started "I'll See You in My Dreams" playing when they'd already run out of time, when their third op was ready for them and the dark outside busy with trucks and flying boots and murmuring.

"Tho' the days are long, twilight sings a song,"

Edgar Miles softly quizzical. "No point in doing that now, is there?"

"Of the happiness that used to be,"

Pluckrose staring straight at Alfred, wanting him to understand. "Oh, there's every possible point, every possible point."

"Soon my eyes will close, soon I'll find repose,"

And he bolted right out of the room before the rest of the song could reach him. Alfred waited a breath and followed, wished for unfinished business, a key that would open the war, bring him back safely—bring him back for Joyce.

It had worked. They had a genuine milk run down to Turin—the Alps turning and folding and glimmering under his heels, the furrowing and cupping of moonlight, and then flak that didn't reach them, didn't really try, and an uncomplicated target: docks and cranes and industry: things that you wanted to hit.

"I told you."

It had worked. The easiest possible op, and the debriefing almost intoxicated: boisterous and short.

"Didn't I tell you?"

It had worked.

After that the crew would rendezvous on the running boards of Pluckrose's Austin 10, inside it on the driver's seat, Pluckrose's gramophone. He would wind her up, lower the needle, close the door and the pack of them would listen, the skipper always eye-rolling slightly. A few lines in, Pluckrose would nod his head and away they would trot to break the melody, collect themselves, dress—being sure to take it easy once they'd got layered up for the night, careful not to sweat: it lets the cold in later, leads to frostbite. Then they'd make their final preparations, climb into the blood wagon, heavy with kit—Alfred thinking hard that when the day came, when his work was done, he'd do his best to still be living and whatever had been left unfinished would be there for him again.

There was one other habit they developed. It was a night-time thing.

"Ow."

This one, Alfred gave them—his baby.

"*Bleeder!*"

Boots in the grass and breathing—everyone circled together at the back of the firing range—the crew not especially stealthy. Stealth being alien to its nature.

"Ah—ah—*buggerit.*"

In fact, the more they needed to be quiet, the noisier they got.

Bastard Hanson, *"Fucker."* And a sweet little impact cracking just before he spoke. It sounded as if he'd been clipped square on the forehead. *"Fuck."*

Like each of them, he shouldn't have been speaking. The point was, Alfie's idea was, to wait until dark and then go by sight when there wasn't any sight, to have no clues—why else be freezing their bollocks off out here?

"Shit." The big shade that was Pluckrose complaining now, shifting, and after that the noise of his arm as it swung.

Somewhere to port Alfred heard a thud, a stumble, had the sense of something crouching and then elongating when he stared towards it. His fingers were numbed already with the slicing Lincolnshire breeze and his head was starting to get that familiar, gun-turret sting from looking at nothing, reaching ahead into nothing, and looking again. A rind of moon, a glimmer of ice on the turf, but the rest only blanks and him raising his head, straining towards graded thicknesses of doubt.

Another thump to starboard, and a round slap of skin along with it, too—someone had made the catch. Torrington, he thought.

Then something like a swoop and an exhalation and a marvellous, slow moment when Alfred could see a dark tear apart from the dark, grow and find him.

"Buggerit."

His hands had reached up, but didn't quite stop the cricket ball neatly: he felt a jarring run through his thumb. "Bugger." He couldn't afford to have a damaged thumb. And he'd meant to stay silent and set an example.

He could hear a snigger over where the Bastard would be standing and so Alfred let himself cheat, looping his arm back, getting a whip into his wrist and aiming at the sound, the part of him that was gunnery making him glad.

"Fucker!"

A sigh came and Alfred knew it was the skipper. "Look . . . if we're going to do this at all, then everyone has to keep their bloody trap shut."

There were coughs in the gloom and other sighs, the crew ashamed now—they hadn't been trying their best.

"Sorry, Skip." Pluckrose smoothing, calming, the way he liked to sometimes. "It's that bloody jam sponge they fed us this evening—don't know about the others, but I can hardly stand." Always binding about something. "There was fucking whale oil in it, I swear, and fucking big collops of snoek tucked away in the custard . . . in a world where cream is made from pig fat, how is a man to survive?"

"Well, even so. If we're to do this, we have to do it properly."

"I was, Skip." The Bastard lying his head off when he'd been catching the ball with his face ever since they started. "Getting the hang of it, I was."

"And squealing like a Chelsea tart." Molloy blowing on his hands as he grumbled. "Are we going to get on there, or are we going to stop, or what are we doing?"

"Another thirty minutes." Skipper with a laugh in his voice, but solid about this also, near to losing his temper.

"What?" Molloy squealing himself. "Then can we step back inside and get on our Irvin suits, or I'm going to lose extremities to which I'm partial."

Skipper using his intercom voice to reply, the one you wouldn't argue with. "Another thirty minutes and then the Duck's Head."

So without being told they shuffled themselves softly, moved to new places, paused. Alfred with that small gleam behind his ribs, the one that indicated he belonged here, with his crew, while they drew one breath, angled themselves into one intention and started again.

Because all of them had to learn a way to see where you couldn't see. Because holding up silhouettes on sticks and shooting clay pigeons wouldn't be enough, no matter what the squadron gunnery leader liked to say. And because they needn't just rely on the gunners—anyone might catch a sight of something, if they knew how they should look. And because the more they were together, the more they would feel together and work and think and act together. And because if they kept on doing impossible things—even something as small as catching and throwing a cricket ball in the dark—then maybe they would last out thirty ops.

It was cold and very light. Alfred sat on the damp of a little bench and watched his breath drag away from him slowly and sink in the grass. Back at the station, dawn would have been a while away yet, but up here, so much further north, the day had started and the tall hedge behind him was layered with birdsong and the rattle of last season's leaves while a press of new green rushed out among the twigs, so hard and certain that it disturbed him, brought up a gladness he would rather not have.

He'd come out for peace and stillness—Pluckrose's shaggy garden stretching ahead of him like a park, like too much for anyone's family to have all for themselves and with flower beds and lawns and vegetable plots to the sides—the plot dormant now: he was proud of the suitable use of *dormant*, enjoyed it—everything too generous, or too greedy, and the Pluckrose house leaning up against the sky, huge at Alfred's back: three storeys and two staircases and plenty of doors and then more doors and then far too many doors and you had to keep from thinking of it sometimes, because it could seem alarming. Left to himself he could feel uneasy—as if he were a poacher or a thief.

But he couldn't be in company yet, either—not this morning, not inside with the crew and the chatter, the hours of tea and breakfast they'd cook up. In there they were building something like a family—the kind they'd have asked for, if they'd ever had a choice—and that meant they were also betraying their own. The guilty comfort of it wound him in and he knew he believed it, trusted, understood it wasn't only a war thing, that it was permanent. They were his crew.

This couple, the MacKenzies, would come by with loaves and rashers and eggs and butter and sausage and God knew where they got it— out of the country people and no questions asked, he supposed—this *was* the country—and you could tell there was some kind of rule that MacKenzies looked after Pluckroses, no matter what, and this was how things worked. He was in a place where people looked after people and never an order in sight, no orders needed, this other odd system in place, and where even Hanson smiled in passing and said, "How are you, mate?" nothing but chummy and gleaming with gunnery brotherhood.

Alfred couldn't recall how long he'd been here, had stopped wearing his watch. The mooching about and grazing made him sleepy and too relaxed and then he'd try to annoy himself by wondering which people anywhere were supposed to look after the Days.

Our bloody selves—that's who.

No, not any more. Not with a crew. You're the first Day you know of who got himself a crew.

And Alfred and his crew kept mainly to the kitchen and the stove where it was warm, the rest of the place really closed up for the war and the paintwork something shameful: a brokenness about things and the northern windows shuttered, the attic rooms with peeling paper and full of other people's memories and the wreckage of gone children, maybe of their very own Pluckrose in earlier years, and soft, dark blooms of damp spreading in and down.

But I can't stick the kitchen. Not just yet.

It wasn't that Alfred wouldn't be heading along there soon and eating to waste, stoking in the grub until his breath was tight. It wasn't that he didn't love it. But kitchens could seem so alike and you'd go there and you'd sit in the hard wooden chair and lean your elbows on the table and maybe a crumble's set ready for the evening and Mrs. MacKenzie moves past you with her soft, tidy look and the way she smells of Cuticura and there's tea in the pot and then you think of your mother and your cup seems a bit unwieldy in a sad way and your toast should be nice, but the bread isn't as it should be and you get this hopeless, childish want—this need for the wash of wireless music in your own house with your ma and no one else and listening while she does her mending and talks to the cat, makes up these great, long stories about him going Out West and fighting Indians and wearing little cat-sized moccasins—soft as shit, the nonsense she made up, but she'd always told Alfred adventures about the cats— even called one Mix, after Tom Mix.

Your dad, the fucker, he used to hurt Mix, frighten him. Catching him at night—drunk and holding him so he would squeal and wake us up. As if we weren't awake. Mixy, he got smart, though. He got fast and sharp and wary, which was good. But you couldn't pet him after that: he'd only relax so far and then he wouldn't let you.

And here was Alfred, burning up a ten-day leave in the wilds of the North when he could have caught a train back home and seen his ma. Instead, he was here putting fat on and having fun, because he had to— this running away was the best he could do.

Anyway, Wingco sent us off together: generous with the leave suddenly after the bad night over Essen. And he needed to wait for replacement crews, replacement planes.

There was never a doubt about leaving as a crew—even before Pluck-rose said we could pack up and bolt for the Moray Firth, see Family Seat Number Two.

Pluckrose property in London, Pluckrose property in Cornwall, Pluckrose property up here—but you couldn't dislike him for it. Or if you maybe did, he'd notice and talk about how it was old and pointless and needn't be kept hold of and he'd tell you that he was the only son—the way Alfred was the only son—and that when he'd inherit, he'd give every-thing away. Or sell it. Do something. Live in the woods, like Thoreau.

Alfred hadn't asked him at the time who Thoreau was, but he might yet. Diogenes lived in a barrel and Simon Stylites sat up a pole: he knew that much. Perhaps it would be an idea to learn a list, memorise a few more places where historical types ended up—it seemed they weren't predictable with housing.

A herring gull landed behind last year's raspberry canes, tipped up its head and cried about something. It paused while Alfred stood and rubbed his hands together and then, as he took his first step, it ran and unfolded up into the air, wide and white and silent. That was the way you'd want your take-offs, as if you were stretching your arms and then slipping back to life—simple.

Which was the thought that he shouldn't have started, because now when he blinked he could see his dream, the one with the gashes and spatters of fire—you don't look at them, don't blind yourself, but you know they're spilling out beneath you, eating your mind and leaving it the colour of dirty flame as the flak comes up and tries to take revenge.

I'll see you in my dreams.

Going in with the third wave and this sense there's something more there when the shells start kicking near—that something amused is winking at you: closing, spitting up hot metal while the lazy curves of tracer stitch round towards you and are suddenly fast, suddenly blurred with the race to find you and you're ready to fire, sweating to fire, hiding for now, but you'll get any fucker that comes to call, squirt off your own rounds when you have to, lay a path in light and bullets that leads clear back to you and to your skipper, but that only means you have to get them, you will, you must, you're ready, you're swinging your guns and swinging your guns and keeping them from freezing and your head caved in with roaring, and inside you're keeping the song, you're holding on to pieces of the song.

"*Lips that once were mine, tender eyes that shine,*
They will light my way tonight,
They will light my way tonight,
They will light my way tonight,
They will light my way tonight,"

The nearest you get to a prayer any more and far away you can hear Torrington, gentle and stupidly, madly slow—"Left, left . . . Steady . . . Steady . . ." Never have a Cornish bomb aimer, he'll take all bloody night. "Right . . . Steady . . ." The skin under your hair, you can feel it creaking, and your shoulders locking up. "Steady . . . Left, left . . . Steady . . . Steady . . ." And another scarecrow bursting low to port, like a door swinging open on somewhere that has no word for itself, the colour and leap of flame. You recognise every angle, detail of a ship just like your own, but you do want it to be a scarecrow that the Jerries have fired up and not a plane and you stare away from the shine, you concentrate, but you're sure there was a shape against that first hard rip of light: the shadow of a man, his legs slightly bent, as if he was walking, but lying on his back in the air, in the very thin air, and that's something you can't think of—that so many planes have caught it and the route was a dud, too straight, and this is a mess, is a bloody mess, and the bombs not gone yet and the city and the Krupps works and the people hating you below and you're swinging your guns and swinging your guns and let the fuckers come.

He'd woken with his shoulders sore, as if he'd been leathered all night. A cold in his stomach, too, that made him remember his mother and how she'd been quiet when he'd seen her last and tired.

I fixed him, though. I bloody fixed him. Showed him what I've learned—that fuckers like him can only be stopped by force.

He'd even told Pluckrose—because Pluckrose made you tell him things. Sunk in splitting armchairs dragged up to the kitchen stove—the last two awake and both of them fuddled with Scotch, genuine Scotch.

"You are appearing thoughtful, Boss. What is it you're frowning about? Tell your Uncle Pluckrose."

"I ay frowning."

"That, I will presume, is a denial, but I can see it in the blessed and familiar fizz—our Day is unhappy . . ."

"Was remembering." His father's face, the barm-pot grin for the customers and everything nice as nice. That bloody fish smell—crept out halfway up the street, made you gag.

"You were remembering. Good start." Pluckrose's feet enormous in ragged layers of wool sock—something Russian-seeming about them as he leaned one on the other, long legs aiming them straight for the warm. "But I may have to fetch the oyster knife if you're going to take this long."

"Not an oyster."

"Indeed. Let it never be said." Pluckrose swivelled his long head over and made his most serious face. "But if we are both to stay pals, I'll be needing the whole story. Now. Is there a broken heart involved?"

"You wha'?"

"Not the lady friend?"

The thought of her juddering the rag rug under Alfred heels. "No, no."

"Good." Pluckrose punched Alfred's arm with a good deal of knuckle. "Can't have a broken heart for little Alfie. Couldn't stand it." And punched again.

"Ow."

"Well then, talk, damn you. Not made of patience."

Alfred letting himself walk into the shop again, past the blackboard with the whitewashed offers in his father's curly printing—a feature being made of eels. The bell ringing over the door when it opened and let the stink rear up and greet him. That moment when his father saw the uniform and not Alfred, gave him a fawning leer and under it the obvious thought—wondering if a serviceman might just fancy something extra under the counter, hoping there was money to be made. A woman, old Mrs. Archer, reaching up towards some little package for her and her sister and Alfred had vaguely noticed the display seemed sparse and greyish, not much there to sell.

Father calling out, acting the loud and jolly fishmonger, trying a wink, "Not a lot I can offer you, sir—if someone's not registered with us . . . but if you're visiting . . ." And this when he met your eyes and knew you. His hands fell at the sight of you. He dropped his guard.

Pluckrose punched again.

"Ow."

"Then tell me."

"Went back last leave and saw my ma."

"That's nice."

"She's nice . . . Saw my father, too." Washing the sound of him out of you with a mouthful of whisky, burning him away. "Went to the shop when he wouldn't expect me."

"Ah."

"He's a cunt."

"Ah."

"Walked in on him." The same dart of blood in your hands now as when you'd walked across the shop, leaned in past Mrs. Archer, so that she would hear as well. "I told him—you leave Ma alone. I kept his eye until he had to look away. You leave her alone. Think they haven't taught me how to look after myself? Think I couldn't take you now? Feather-weight champion now."

"A little bit of a lie there, old man. But a good one."

"He believed me. Told him I knew how to fight with a knife and if I had to I'd bring home a pistol and I'd end him. There shouldn't be a night when he came home in the dark and he didn't think I might be hiding in the blackout and waiting to blow off his head."

Pluckrose sad-looking, frowning at his hands. "Good for you, Boss."

"He had to leave her alone now. And if he didn't, I would know. I would fucking know—and Mrs. Archer giving me a look and then giving him a look and he couldn't say anything back—only trying to grin again, like I was somebody asking for lemon sole, a special treat, and the bell going off behind me when somebody comes in, so I said again—yo fucking lay a hand on her, that woman yo never bloody deserved and I'll hear on it. The sisters'll tell me—the ones yo drove out of the house—they'll tell me, wo they?—and the others I've axed to watch yo, they'll tell us and yo'll be chopped, yo'll teck a shit before yo know. 'Cause I'm sick fed up on it.

"And then I turned—very parade ground and neat and I walked past Mrs. Caulfield and her boy—both of them rockin' like they was kay-lied—and I left 'im. Fixed 'im, day I?"

"Oh, you did, Boss."

"I fixed him."

And sitting then and staring into the opened stove and the fire in it—a very small, kind fire—and Pluckrose had reached and held Alfred's forearm for a while and then let it go and filled their glasses again and smiled at Alfred and rattled at his hair for a moment.

"You're a quiet one, aren't you, Boss?"

"Doe know."

"A good one, too. Have to always protect the weak. No matter what."

Alfred rushed another hot swallow of whisky, couldn't find a reply.

"I try to make that my job, you know? When we fly out, I like to think that's what we're doing."

Alfred patted Pluckrose on his shoulder. "Suppose."

"I'm happy when I think that."

"S'what they ax us to do, ay it?"

"Yes, Boss. Of course. That's what they're asking us to do."

For a while they listened to the fire.

Then Pluckrose shifted in his seat. "The thing I do consider . . . I'm not a bad navigator."

"Yo'm good."

"Thank you." He sighed. "Trouble is, even when I'm on the ground, I can get a fix that's accurate to maybe five miles, possibly one or two." He spoke softly towards the flames. "A mile's a long way, Alfred. And if I'm out by a mile, who else is out by a mile? What am I dropping my bombs on? Am I right? How often are we right? And if we're not right . . ."

"We do our best."

Pluckrose rubbed at his hair with both hands. "We do."

"Do what they ax us. Buggers on the other side, I bet they don't worry."

"Not much use if they do."

"Not much use if we do, either. No point gooing a game with ourselves about that. We'm doin our best and God's with us and all that."

Pluckrose let out a small, coughing laugh.

"Wha'?"

Pluckrose shook his head, but then began, "Remembering what my uncle told me. Story from Gallipoli. He said the trenches were very close there and the lads used to yell at each other—the two sides: the Turks and our chaps—they used to yell back and forth, and the Turks, you'd hear them saying *Allah* this and *Allah* that, calling on their maker, and we'd yell something back in return and on it would go between the shooting. Turns out, the Turks, they thought we were like them, that we'd be calling on our maker. So they thought the name of our God was *Bastard*."

Alfred started to smile at that and then didn't feel right about it. "We'm doin the best we can. It's the Nazis, they're the bastards."

"No argument there."

"We'm doin our best."

"I hope so, Alfie. I do very much hope so."

And then they sat quiet for a while.

At the film camp Alfred had restarted his habit of walking around the perimeter—this didn't constitute vigorous exercise, but it made him seem more useful to himself. Not that the circuits did have any point, only the memory of one—of Kriegie Alfred working to harden his feet, ready for marching, or running, or whatever awfulness might come to pass. You needed to mind your feet.

Proper boots I had, looked after them, too. Had a pair of lousy clogs to slope about in and stashed away the boots, kept them greased up, in good condition, with God knew what, it didn't bear thinking about.

With every day's walking the place grew more defined, the garden plots settling and thickening, the hut windows showing curtains, mugs full of wildflowers, stacks of books.

Shouldn't put books in a window—the sunlight foxes them and then when it's wet the damp catches hold and makes them bloat and warp. Silly blighters.

His tour this morning brought him to a quiet crowd, mainly of film people, huddled in away from the fence and highly interested in something. Once he'd stepped close enough to see, he realised he didn't want to—they were watching a demonstration of tunnelling.

A couple of chaps who'd written books—personal reflections on imprisonment and so forth—they were down on their knees and showing how they'd dug. Alfred knew about the books, they'd been in Ivor's shop at times, but he hadn't read them and didn't intend to.

One fellow was hunched on all fours and acting out a crawl underground, holding his trowel and moling forward beneath an invisible roof. The director was kneeling beside him and peering in that half-soaked way he did, while the other invited expert was pressing batons down into a shallow hole he'd made—the result of neat work with a little entrenching spade. Standing to the left in what looked like a proper Luftwaffe uniform was a genuine German—well spoken, quiet about his war, and playing the camp commandant. Oscar Vonsomething. Rumour suggested he'd been a navy boy, or an opera singer, or a political refugee, although Alfred didn't much care. Of course, being an actor as well as a German, he didn't mix much with the average bods, wasn't one you'd see kicking a ball about, or mucking in. But Alfred had almost spoken to him, had walked up and nearly started to tell him a sentence that withered as soon as Alfred thought of it, that left him only staring and then dropping his head and hurrying on.

Just now, Vonsomething was sinking, crouching on to the sand and blushing, unwilling to have someone lower than he was and working in front of his feet, their body in a frightened shape, even if they weren't currently frightened. You could see it in him, the way he was embarrassed by himself, his uniform—happiest after the scenes where he was outwitted, where he could find humiliation.

Maybe that's what I want to talk to him about—maybe it's nothing to do with the war, only that I'd like him to know he should fall in love. Then he'll be humiliated soon enough.

Busy in his excavation, the expert worked at shoring up his five or six inches: too happy, too intent. Something in his face reminded Alfred of London, of the men—see them working as bank clerks, or on the tram that takes them to an office, a school, a shop, some job they can't keep, can't get, can't want in a country that is brown linoleum and saving money for the meter and war surplus and making do and the blood pressed out of you years ago, everything seeming small and cheap for ever. The man was digging himself out.

The actors—even Vonsomething—they were different, had some life, a bit of health about them. Three of them were studying the diggers. But they'd only be trying it out back in England, lying inside pretend burrows in a studio somewhere—safer for all concerned. Queer how people got so fussed about themselves when nothing much would kill them any more—not beyond the usual.

Alfred left them to it, quick as he could: trotted on, turning the trot to a run, a chase, eventually stopping himself against the wall of the equipment store, enjoying the small impact, the dunt of his heart, the kick of breath. Inside, old Jack set down a coil of cable and then gradually sauntered out.

"Sorry, Jack."

Jack spoke around his cigarette. "S'OK." He picked up the cable again and put it in a box. "They after you for something?" Decent sort, Jack—the only one whose name you could remember.

"No. Just . . . felt like a gallop." Breath hard in him, shaking things loose.

"Mm-hm . . ." Jack withdrew to a little table, sat and began to dismantle a mechanism, some part of a camera, stripping it down to mend it, to find it out. "Twenty minutes and they'll need you in the crowd." Jack had been in an army film unit, front-line cameraman. "And on we go."

"No rest for the wicked."

"Nor anyone else." Examining an invisible piece of metal. "This bloody sand gets everywhere." Some types, they went this way—only calm and more calm and slowness, nothing else left.

"Suppose it would."

Jack pondered him for a breath. "You all right?"

"Yes."

"That's all right then." He went back to studying the broken nothing between his fingers, let Alfred be because that was what Alfred wanted. "The gentleman is all right."

Or the gentleman is buggered, what's the difference either way?

Alfred pushed off, steered towards the parade ground, admitting—because he might as well—that the shadow beside him should have been Ringer, his good friend. He had been running to get away from his lack of Ringer—because digging, that couldn't go on without Ringer. Nothing could.

Mooney had been his name outside the bag—David Mooney—an amount of suspicion and bother at his arrival, because he was such an unusual bod and couldn't explain himself. There had been an idea that he was a snooper for a while. But he'd been on a British Stirling all right—only to see the sights—his first and last op ending in a cack-handed parachute drop and a broken ankle. And for what he'd been told was a milk run, he had worn a dispatch rider's helmet—swore the thing had saved his life and they must not be parted: its padding and thickness making his head seem even larger. And the Germans had let him keep it, maybe thought that he wasn't quite right in his mind and wearing the helmet would help him. He took it off to sleep, but even then he'd cuddle it. Superstitious.

And maybe he *was* unusual in his thinking, sometimes slow, and you couldn't always teach him, but he wasn't daft. Called him Ringer because in private life he'd rung bells—*campanology*, the sound of a peal inside it, tumbling. Farm worker in the fen country, bloody awful life, but on his Sundays he'd walk for miles with some other lads, go from tower to tower, ring the whole day.

"To get a good tower. You like that. Sweet bricks, they make it sweet. For hundreds of years. Ringing sweetens the bricks sweetens the bells." Gently spoken—because when people heard him they made fun. "You're something that keeps on after hundreds of years—what they put in the ringing books, that's years of raising bells and Pleasures and Superlatives and Surprises. Once we rang a peal of Treble Bob Major, that's 6,144."

Not exactly an expert at writing, but he'd scrawl you out these long chains of numbers, patterns, had thousands of them packed in that monster skull.

"12345 then 21345 then 23145 then 23415, d'you see?"

And him almost tearful once, Alfred thinking some bad thing had happened, but it was only that Ringer was worried the bells were quiet at home and that after the peace it might be too late, what they needed might be forgotten.

"40,320 with a peal of eight—that's how many changes you'd get. Would take you seventeen, eighteen hours to ring that many. 40,320. You see? Eighteen hours. And I've never."

"Never yet."

"Christmas Day in '41 and when we won at Alamein—victory peals, that's not enough. That don't let them sing."

"It'll be fine."

"The lads'll forget. They'll be in the services now and the old uns'll die. It'll all be forgot."

Alfred with no idea if this was true, but not wanting Ringer to cry, not wanting him to be publicly weak, because some bastard would always notice and take advantage. "They'll remember. I'm sure they will. You will. So they will." Rubbing his hand between Ringer's shoulder blades because when his ma did that to Alfred, he'd feel calmed.

"Accomplishing the extent. They'll paint my name up on the board if I do. Me and the boys, if we do." Rain banging off the dirty hut windows. "Accomplishing the extent." His eyes so scared they hurt you. "Will I, Boss?"

"Well, there's time enough." Alfred lying the way that he might to a child, if he ever had a child.

Not that he was like a kid, Ringer. He'd try and fight you if you said so—would lose against anyone, but he'd still fight. No sense of direction in his fists, just head down and flailing, useless length of arm. The thing was, you didn't understand him if you thought he was daft—it was just that he'd get so scared and he wouldn't hide it, not always, so you'd need to calm him. For yourself, you'd need to make him steady—then you'd be steady, too. Got him the bunk under mine. Kept him right and close.

And Ringer kept everyone right—because he never did forget. Not anything. Whatever got into him stayed and he could read and tell the pattern of the camp—the passage of guards, deliveries, times and days, alterations, substitutions—he carried everything.

Out walking, it was Ringer you missed. Long stride he had, but he'd rein it in for you, head nodding with that mad helmet and his soft eyes flickering at each movement, each new detail and always an angriness or a sadness in his face, a sense of some feeling that made him hurt.

My friend.

My crew.

My girl.

You were some kind of mug to bother with any of that.

Because where did it get you? Here. Just marching round and round inside a daydream.

He halted, crossed his arms — hugged the sum and substance of what he was meant to look after: Day, Alfred F.

As it happened, he'd reached the assembly point for the first scene of the day.

Might as well stop where I am, then.

So while the others mooched and trotted, scuffed and marched up to join him, he watched the technicians fiddling, Old Jack setting up and making good, methodical. And finally Alfred permitted himself the comfort he'd had through too many bleached-out waits, the privacy he'd built in too many crowds — he remembered her, he searched out the full, high rush of her, stepped inside it and closed his eyes.

"Hello. Hello? This is me . . . Is that you? That's . . . I . . ."

He'd not done well the first time. He'd known the number for a while: it was printed on her headed notepaper along with her husband's name and their address: another wedding present, no doubt.

"I'm sorry, I can't quite . . ." The line so bad that he might have been back on the Lanc, her voice only barely defined. "Is that . . . when you say 'me' . . . Is that Alfie?"

Not that hearing even this much of her didn't make his neck sweat immediately. He couldn't tell if she was pleased, though. "Yes, it's —"

"God, I'm . . . You're a surprise. I'm . . ."

"Well, I didn't intend to be." Or not a bad surprise, anyway — a good one, please a good one. "It's only me." As if he spoke to her every day.

"Where are you?" She did sound mainly pleased. "Are you here?"

Didn't want her scared — it was easy to scare people. "I am. Here. Or there. I mean, we're both here."

Molloy, packed into the phone box with him — and Pluckrose also —

prods him under the ribs, hisses so she surely must hear it. "Jesus, make sense, willya."

"Well, I *am* here." This meant for the lads, not for her, so now he has to try again, "I'm in London, sorry . . . there's . . . things going on here." Pointing at Pluckrose, warning, no room to point at Molloy, both of them being no help to him, in any bloody way.

But he *was* in London. Which meant this was very last minute, but his leave was his leave and couldn't be changed in any case and he'd rung her before, quite often, you could say repeatedly, and got no answer, started to think that the line was out, misdirected, or she'd moved house, or been bombed out, or hurt, or worse, and he wouldn't know—there really wouldn't be a way that he could know—or else she'd maybe guessed that he would call and was just ignoring him until he'd stop. He couldn't tell. How could you tell?

"Alfie? You're in town?"

"I . . . yes, I am. I'm sorry."

"Don't be sorry."

"I would have said before. There wasn't time to write. The post is so . . ." He swallowed and realised that he was smiling, that his whole head felt loose. "Are you busy today? I don't really have much more time than today. My crew, they're . . ." One of his crew was currently banging the back of his knee while another sniggered—the rest were in a cordon just outside, the Bastard licking the glass in the little windows and winking whenever Alfred looked his way. "I only have today."

"Well, that's . . . Shall we go to the pictures? We could do that . . . see something? I have to fire-watch later. Making myself useful—I'm a mass observer, too . . . Donald would never have allowed . . . anyway. I'm keeping busy. You're lucky. I mean, lucky that I'm not working today. I work ever such a lot now. That is, not as much as you, but—"

"I'm glad I'm lucky." With all his heart, unbroken and hot and big between his lungs. "I'll meet you . . . I don't know where, though." Hating that he had to shout and Pluckrose grinning at him and nodding, while Molloy blows smoke in his eyes, makes him blink.

But he keeps listening, keeps on willing her voice to come in, catching it, holding.

"Oh Lord, I'm hopeless with directions . . . what about Hinde Street?

I have to be there for . . . There's a church in Hinde Street, you could get the Underground to Baker Street, could you? Then it's not far."

"I'll find it." He didn't for a moment think he could.

"At twelve?"

"I'll be there."

But you found it. You did. Ran all the way.

You met her at the bottom of the steps, still ruffled with the nonsense your crew yelled after you as you escaped, a solemn little handshake from the skipper before you made the dash and a kind of embarrassment still on you—as if she might see what they'd suggested, what they thought. What you thought yourself, that was another matter, that was something you should keep at bay because this was just meeting someone, a girl, a woman, a married woman, and this was just everything, but also just meeting, seeing each other after letters where she's said that she thinks of you often and so it's not a bad thing if you say you've thought often of her.

"Oh, and I've got you this." She pushes a flat, soft parcel into your hand—her fingers touching your knuckle, cool.

"What?" It's something wrapped in wallpaper. "I mean, you needn't." She seems to have a lot of wallpaper. "I don't have anything for you . . . If you smoked."

"I don't."

"No, neither do I. But I could get you cheap cigarettes—out of the NAAFI. Would you like to start?"

The rubbish you talked around her—every time you'd collapse into trails and heaps of words, be lost in them rather than realise you were beside her, rather than have only silence thin between you, transparent. And that first time probably the worst, while you watched her move, the lightness in her—even with those big, scuffed shoes—and the blue hem of her dress beneath the green coat that you know, duck-egg blue dress and her face that wonderful oval, tiny chin and the neat mouth, soft neat mouth you can hardly look at because it makes you jumbled and the eyes more than anything—eyes of some creature, something marvellous— never seen them in daylight before now, never let them ease inside you and not stop.

"I don't want to smoke."

"I know. I don't want to smoke, either . . . because . . . But if we *did* smoke."

"Then we'd need cigarettes."

"Then we'd *have* cigarettes. You could note that in your mass observation." Wanting her to note him. "Along with me wanting to dress you in parachute silk." Struck shy when you say this, but it turns out all right.

"Yes, I could." A smile in how she says this, lovely smile, while you trip yourself up a little, because you are almost stepping backwards so you can face her, or because you have forgotten how to walk.

"Maybe I've noted it already." She catches your near arm softly and you almost drop the parcel. "Careful, Sergeant Alfie—I have to give you back to that crew of yours without anything broken."

"Thank you."

"Well, otherwise it would be sabotage, wouldn't it?"

"No, I mean thank you. For the . . ." You wag the parcel. "For this."

"Gratitude might not be quite the thing, you know. You haven't seen it yet."

So you unwrap the string and unfold the paper and there is this woollen thing that you don't quite understand.

"It's a hat."

A woollen thing which is red.

"It isn't regulation, but then I couldn't get the regulation wool."

You both pause and study it where it lies across your hands like a fillet of something unpromising.

"It's—"

"Terrible, I know. But I wanted to try and I did manful work—see, there aren't any seams—it's all on four needles and terrifically complicated and one has to keep count for the ribbing—and you can wear it under your flying gear when it's cold, that was my thought. It's rabbit wool—like they use for babies—so it won't itch."

"Under my—"

"It's a *hat*, you chump. That much, at least, is obvious and I refuse to believe that it's not."

And you are halted on the pavement—this broad street with surges of people tramping along it and this little reserve policeman in a helmet that doesn't fit and he's only really the same height as you, but seems small today, seems a bloody dwarf because you are so grown when you're with her and there are fine, high shopfronts behind you that would be impressive, might even have something to sell and there are quite possibly sights nearby and you don't care to see them, don't care in the smallest way, are only sure that you will wear this terrible rabbit-wool hat until you die and that it will be as if she is touching your head, is putting her hands over your hair.

Spent all day with her.

Strolling and sitting in Lyons Corner Houses and not letting her pay for anything and you didn't make it to the pictures.

Like her to promise and not deliver.

Only at the time, you didn't want the pictures, because that's to do with being back at the station and watching *The Lion Has Wings* again — it's all they bloody show you — or thinking of the fleapit back home and being someone else and Humphrey Bogart up there in *High Sierra* and hearing the couples at your back, believing you'll never have anyone like that — a girl to touch.

Not that you touched her. Not in a bad way.

No, you did worse.

"I . . ." Over another pot of tea — this time in one of those old, square teapots — drips like buggery only you don't want to complain. "Joyce, you know . . ." Half of your cup spilled on the tabletop and no taste in it anyway — you suspect these are leaves they've been using for a while. "I . . ."

You were comfortable and happy and you told her, "I like seeing you."

"So do I. Like seeing you. I see *me* all the time. Well . . . in the morning in the mirror. Not all the time — that would be ghastly."

And she's veering you off-course, so you have to correct. "And I like the letters, your letters. I like them a lot." You like correcting.

"You write good letters back."

"No, I don't."

Then this bright, lifting pause that you're both inside and the scent of roses. There's the bombsite reek as well — charring and plaster open to the rain, woodsmoke, something distantly sickening underneath — but you have roses mainly, because you are here with Joyce.

"I like knowing you, too, Alfie. I like it very much."

Nothing simple about this and perhaps everything hopeless, but you don't mind that, because your doing the impossible is no more than what she deserves. Love requires the impossible, you understand.

Joyce looking out of the window at the street that's fading now, bustling into darkness and shuttered headlamps. You realise that you have made her sad.

That bandage smell: he'd never liked it. You wanted them to smell clean, but they didn't, there was always a sourness about them, as if they'd been used before, were bringing you something to do with decay. They weren't healthy.

So why volunteer to wear them, cocker? Never volunteer, you know by now.

The film people had wanted injuries. A little crowd was organised to stand and be saddened by a few other chaps got up as casualties who'd totter in through the gates as if they were new to the camp and fresh from some unhappy time in the sky, or on the run. Alfred—as always, in favour of lying down—had said he'd like to be a stretcher case.

The bandages, they taste of fear and church.

Three women were doing the make-up. Odd to have a woman touch his face. A woman to choose what damage he'd have, how it would look.

This dry, disinfected perfume that you'd think would make things bet-ter, but only turns them strange.

Alfred had sat on the edge of a table, beside him a man with his hands swaddled up as if he'd been burned. There was nothing wrong with him, of course—in fact he was an irritating bleeder, knocking and clapping his big parcelled mitts together as if they were the funniest thing out, asking if anyone would light him a fag, scratch his nose, wipe his arse.

"Be all right going home to the missus like this, wouldn't I? Wouldn't I?" Laughing his stupid head off. "I'd finally get a proper handful. Wouldn't I? Wouldn't I?" Peggy brown teeth that you'd rather not see—too deep and narrow a mouth.

Alfred with a gauze pad plastered over his left eye, three or four yards of binding round his head—like a kid's idea of someone wounded. The binding made him slightly deaf.

But not quite deaf enough.

"Turn out the lights and I'd think she had a pair. Wouldn't know where to start. I should say so. Wotcha reckon, mate? Eh?"

What do I reckon? What do I reckon? I reckon septic articles like you never should have made it through the war. I reckon somebody should have bombed you, bombed you flat. I reckon if we'd known you earlier the crew and I would have happily volunteered. I reckon the wrong people die. I reckon that happens every fucking time.

Alfred remembering his mother, the burn on her leg where his father scalded it with tea. She'd dressed it herself, meticulous, and taken care, but there'd always been marks left after that. A woman, she wants her legs to look nice, they're something she's meant to be proud of. His father had made her ashamed.

"I'm planning to keep this lot, mate—take it back home. Make meself think that I'm lucky for once. Might as well."

Might as well.

Alfred remembering how they tended him in the German hospital. He'd worried about scarring to his lip: if Joyce would ever see it and be upset.

Might as well.

And then Alfred remembered nothing and reckoned nothing and had only a pink-grey light in the back of his head, a comfortable sense of warmth, before he realised his eyes were closed. There was a funny noise from somewhere near his feet—like a dog being sick. He glanced down.

It surprised him a little that the man with the bound hands was lying on the sand and that his nose was bleeding entirely convincing blood and then Alfred noticed an ache in the knuckles of his right hand and realised that he had punched the man, hit him very hard: wound the idea of it up from his waist and twisted it out with what might have been anger, or could have been joy—he seemed purely still at the moment and happily relaxed.

"Jesus!" The man was upset. "What the bloody hell . . . ?" Browned off, but too nervous to get up yet. A shock would do that, a blow to the face. People cared about their faces.

"Sorry, mate." Alfred settling in behind his best Kriegie expression, the inoffensive blank. "Can't see a thing with this bloody eyepatch on. Didn't know I'd caught you. So sorry."

"Here though—"

Alfred stepping out. "Sorry, mate. Honest." He could see a make-up woman staring at him, deciding whether she approved. "Don't worry, they'll patch you up. They've got all the kit for it. Handy."

And he walked off for a turn or two, circled the nearest hut to keep from laughing, to keep from thinking.

It bothered me when I first saw it, that one scar. Half the length of my top lip—swollen and stitches in it—something most women wouldn't find too pleasant. But I'd thought Joyce wouldn't mind it, because we were ourselves and no alterations could bother us.

Otherwise, I'd have covered up, I'd have grown out a moustache for her back then.

So why grow it now, when she won't see you?

You do know she won't see you.

So why are you suddenly bothered about how you look?

You are sure she won't see you.

So why end up taking yourself down into London and living where she lives?

You are almost certain she won't see you.
How much of a fool are you planning to be?

"I'm not a complete fool." Pluckrose with the boys out strolling by the sea.

"Oh, really—and what parts are missing? Do tell." Miles with his milky, big face as placid as ever, just chipping in.

Pluckrose gave a delighted great howl of affront and barrelled himself into the wall, bouncing along it while staring at Miles. "Well, I'm bloody glad that you're on our side."

Miles just sucked his pipe, the flicker of a grin escaping him before he could smooth it away.

Last evening of their leave and all of them out here, straggling into the wind along the dimming shore. The gusts punched at them and rubbed their mouths with salt, caught in their greatcoats and generally made them feel lively. Alfred thought that he would recognise the particular crack and drag and scuffle of his own crew's feet no matter what. Years could pass and make no difference: he would know them.

Eventually, the skipper halted, turned out to sea and they all gathered alongside him, watched the yellow-and-silver end to the day, the clean shine on the wave tops, the splitting and shaking of lights where water lay among the rocks. Alfred understood they were simply ignoring the rolls of wire staked out between them and the firth, defending the closed up houses and emptied hotels from a Nazi attack.

"How's life, then?" The skipper nudged Alfred gently, murmured, "Ready for it all again, Boss?"

"I suppose."

"You suppose?"

"Well, the gunnery leader would miss me if I didn't go back. And the sergeant armourer—he told me that he'd cry."

The skipper's hands, when Alfred looked at them, were cupping round his fag as usual. "And I'm sure he meant it." The part of him that always showed the strain. "Always very sincere, your armourers."

Alfred waited, because he knew that's what his skipper wanted.

"You're a . . . you're a fighter, aren't you, Boss?"

This meaning that Pluckrose had told him about Alfred's father, which was fine. No secrets in the crew.

"That is—if you wanted to talk about anything with your trusty skip, you would?"

"Yes." Hoping this can turn out to be a promise he needn't keep, because the skipper is a Sunday Best person, he's class, and shouldn't ever see Alfred's home, shouldn't know his family—even though he'd like Alfred's ma, because everyone did and because she had proper class herself and maybe after the war things would be so shaken up that she'd get to lead the life she ought to.

"You've gone quiet on me, Boss . . . You know I don't like that." Another nudge. "Are you sure you understand that I would help—that we'd all help with whatever you needed?"

Alfred studying a patch of sand very hard now, his forehead hot and a great, precious kind of brightness in his spine. "It's . . . that's . . . I would ask." But thinking of Sergeant Hartnell, of asking him how to fight and win.

Hartnell had agreed, given him a tight, sharp glance, a frown, and then agreed. And they'd met up for three or four evenings and done their work: the Japanese stranglehold, the hip throw, the waist throw, breaking and making grips, disarming attackers, the sentry hold, striking with boot and hand and knife: around them the empty gymnasium making their movements echo and grow.

But it did no good.

"Look, son." Hartnell taking Alfred's arm in a way that required no violent response. "You're not the first. Happens quite often in fact. Lads come along and they ask me for help . . . help with an argument they've got to settle back at home . . ."

Alfred didn't shake his head, didn't do anything beyond standing and feeling slightly sick.

"Part of growing up—knowing how to handle things. How to stop the bastards messing you about. But you . . . you're a gunner, mate. That's the thing you're good at. I'm not saying you'd have to shoot someone to sort them out. I'm not saying you should show them a gun and that'd wake them up and bring them round to your way of thinking. I can't suggest that and I haven't."

"No, Sarnt."

"Forget that sergeant business, we're just talking here."

Alfred glancing up at this and seeing Hartnell's face, having the chance to take it in fully and noticing how he was quite old and tired-looking: a fit man, but tired.

"Day, if you have a problem with someone, you come up behind them when they aren't expecting it and you hit them with a bit of pipe, or a bloody big piece of timber, or a chair, or whatever you can find. In a fair fight, I wouldn't back you. You understand it with your head, but there's no conviction. Now maybe you'll get that. But I wouldn't risk it myself. I was you?—bloody big piece of pipe and hit 'em so they won't get up. All right?"

"Yes, Sar— Yes."

"That's us finished with this then. Won't waste my time any further, nor yours. And no more to be said about it. That clear?"

"Clear."

And they shook hands in silence, Hartnell seeming fatherly, like a father should.

"Thanks."

"We've all done it, son. We've all gone home and sorted them out, or tried to. We've all done it." He smiled in a grey, small way. "Now bugger off out of it—I'm gasping for a fag and cup of tea."

Trotting back across the grass to his barracks, Alfred had started shivering. He'd stayed cold the rest of the night and seemed too young to be where he was and clumsy.

So it wasn't true that he was a fighter, not the way the skipper thought.

"Skip?"

"Yes, Boss."

"I'm not . . . I . . ." But he was a gunner. That was true. "I'll always do the best I can."

Pluckrose breaking in here. "Lord—you pair. You look as if you've both lost your way to the mothers' meeting." He punched their kidneys lightly. "Cheer up. Mrs. Mac has promised to bring us a real cake for our leaving, possibly two—with fruit and booze and God knows what impossible delights—a garter from Jayne Mansfield, who can say?"

"More like a garter from Doris Waters. And anyway it's too bleedin' dark to keep on strolling." Hanson chipping in with a rattly cough. "Unless we're supposed to be waiting for local skirt."

"Military Objectives Already Attacked—seen any?" Torrington drawling this out while he tucked his arm in through Pluckrose's.

" 'Fraid not, old dear." Pluckrose swinging about and beginning to lead them home. "Not a Self-Evident Military Objective within miles. Unless they've been keeping things from us."

Hanson coughed again, then spat, then spat again.

"Well, I can't imagine why." Miles muttering round his pipe stem. "Us is lovely, us is. You can't beat us."

Once he'd calmed himself, the being a stretcher-case job was not half bad. Alfred was bumped about and clattered down here and there for the best part of the day—with tea breaks now and then and lunch. He lolled his head when he was told to and even groaned a little, although that wasn't actually required.

Towards four there was a sudden shower, the air filling with the tang of wet dust and running. He'd flung off his Red Cross blanket and then watched as the film people hurried their equipment under cover and his people scattered to take in their laundry. Amazing how much washing got done in the camp—partly to balance the lack of new clothing, but partly, Alfred thought, because cleanliness made you respectable and gave you something to take charge of. Not that your bunk mates wouldn't bind on appallingly, anyway, if you were slack with your personal hygiene.

And we all wanted the wash-day smell: the one about being back home and taken care of.

Alfred still did his own washing, ironing, wherever he was.

You can't beat a well-pressed shirt.

As if anyone bothered about it beyond you.

The rain hardened, raked across the roofs while Alfred still sat on his stretcher, slowly unwound the bandage from his head and set it at his side, the fake blood in it weakening under the downpour, becoming a general, salmon-coloured stain.

Then the first impact of thunder started off to the north-east.

Only weather, nothing bad.

A thin slash brightening and closing, another couple of detonations—the storm was coming to them.

Alfred made sure to get up slowly and then walk towards what they called Pall Mall—the lane between huts that led up to 27, which was his own. Hail started and another barrage from not far beyond the trees, it seemed, but he kept to an even pace. To either side, shutters were being fastened, windows closed, from a half-open door he could hear slightly nervous laughter.

A lot of us don't do well with bangs, not now.

The sky lifted above him and slammed shut, blitzed him to his knees in spite of his better intentions and he knew he was shaking again, badly. A tearing raced above him like shellfire, before the air burst and then slammed shut again.

Bastards.

Volley followed volley and he pressed his fists into the sand, tried to rise up, stand under it. This took him some time.

Bastards.

His thumbs cramped, and when he finally rose to his feet he couldn't help reeling over towards a hut wall, finding cover.

> *"Lips that once were mine, tender eyes that shine,*
>   *They will light my way tonight.*
>   *They will light my way tonight,"*

The rest of the route would take two or three minutes. That wasn't long.

"They will light my way tonight."

The hail subsided, rattled to an end, and left him back under simple rain.

"They will light my way tonight."

He was sweating, greasy with it.

When he passed the end of the hut a movement to his left disturbed him and he dodged back before he could think. Under the receding thunder he could hear something wet and heavy. Crouching, peering out round the wood, he saw three grey figures hunched under the downpour, an arm looping, casting off water as it gathered pace and then barndoored round, made contact. Three men grouped in a dead end, tucked between the blank wall of the latrines and two empty huts, dark-windowed. They were Ukrainians in their Jerry get-up: two coal-scuttle helmets running with rain, another upturned on the ground. One man was holding a skinnier chap from behind, while the third lamped him, methodical, something practised about the beating, considered.

Alfred couldn't see them too clearly, they were crowded in with their backs mainly to him, but then the man striking took off his helmet, wiped his face and he was plainly Vasyl, could not have been anyone else. He seemed very out of breath, but happy.

A last crack of thunder sliced down between the huts and Vasyl's target was allowed to drop, to curl on his side. Alfred didn't recognise him, nor the man who'd been holding him up and who now patted Vasyl on the shoulder. They leaned in together and exchanged a few words before nodding, slipping through the little gap that would lead them out to the football pitch and the tent where the DPs waited and were given mugs of tea and sandwiches and their instructions for the day.

Alfred waited once they were gone, stayed watching, but they didn't return. After a few minutes, the man on the ground shifted, rolled. He was covered with dirt, but also bleeding, that red sheen on his face. It took a good while for him to roll again and lift himself enough to crawl. He would have broken ribs maybe, concussion, damaged internal organs and fractures, fear. That's what a proper beating was meant to produce. He did look afraid, crawling there, dragging himself up the steps and into an empty hut where he might hide, or sleep, or gather his wits, or die.

Alfred could have helped him, but didn't. The man wasn't crew and he looked like a German. So there was nothing to be done.

On the train back from Scotland the crew occupied a compartment, filled the luggage racks, lit up, removed its boots. They hadn't slept much, not really at all—talking and singing their last night into tatters before a far too early start. Alfred, snug beside the window, glanced round at his family, his people: Miles asleep already—was he ever entirely awake?—and his snoring desynchronised with the engine, the Bastard nodding, Torrington eating a sandwich—one of the many dozen Mrs. MacKenzie had supplied—Pluckrose sitting opposite and gazing out through the glass, something slightly misty in his expression, Molloy slowly courting a bottle of beer, then going in very quick but gentlemanly with his opener, and the skipper glancing back at Alfred, winking. Alfred couldn't quite return the wink, it didn't seem respectful, but he grinned, let himself believe what it seemed the skipper wanted—that they were set, every one of them set and a good, good fit and ready to go and do their work again.

You'd always remember Skip's hands. After the first few ops, you could see the bone in them, the tendons, a sense of grip. Hauling a Lanc about, it changed you. Said it gave him forearms like Popeye—but that was no good cos he'd always favoured Betty Boop, not Olive Oyl. Skinny girls were never any fun.

Without discussion, they'd happily commandeered the compartment's eighth seat, sat bottles on it, two fruit cakes and a small deer's head (with antlers for the use of), a dilapidated object which Pluckrose was bringing down for the sergeants' mess.

Dilapidated—more appropriate for buildings, it being to do with stones, but you'd liked to have the thought of it in your mouth. You'd let your first sip of beer in to melt it through you, a word you might never have met, would probably never use, but it was there in any case, swallowed down and warm, slipping under your chin.

Put it in a letter—try and make her laugh. Tell her about the deer. Joyce would want to know about the deer.

Of course, any civilian or even a service type could have come in and spoiled the arrangements, but Molloy said he had a plan ready for just such emergencies.

Alfred was travelling backwards because he now preferred it—liked things in the turret direction—the pools and streams and tawny slopes of moorland sliding away from him as he looked, being replaced by mountains: real mountains with snow on the top in Britain, he'd never have thought. And he watched the fat, white backside of a stag as the animal turned in fright, headed up over a slope in a punching, stilted run and disappeared. He'd never seen a live deer before, but didn't want to mention this when Pluckrose seemed so fond of his little dead one.

And Alfred didn't feel like talking, anyway—holding this stillness under his skin while the heather skimmed along beside him and he edged down his beer and started a Philip Trent mystery to go with it. He'd fancied a bit of crime, seeing wrongdoers get what they ought always made him glad.

When they jolted into another dusty wooden station, he discovered he'd lost an hour. A handful of people boarded, one of them a stout, older lady with a carpet bag who quite mistakenly supposed that they had a spare seat and she should claim it. Molloy intervened.

"Ah, Freddie. Mind your feet now." Molloy staring directly above the bottles and clutter in the empty place and yelling fiercely. "You'll be in the lady's way when she's come to talk to us." Molloy wagged his finger at no one. "You just be polite now and remember the last time. That brought shame upon us all." He beamed at the woman. "Lovely of you to pay us a visit and can we do anything for you, or shall I come out and speak with you privately?"

The woman hesitated. She looked at the empty seat. She looked at the faded deer's head with its one remaining eye squinting glassily back. She looked at the Bastard who occupied, in all his dingy glory, the next space along. The Bastard smiled at her as only he could. He crossed his legs and wiggled his feet, both of them mainly hidden inside contagious socks. The woman appeared disheartened but still likely to protest, or point out some kind of entirely irrelevant fact.

Molloy forced her hand. "Freddie, you mustn't do that. It's not right." Molloy shook his head sadly at thin air and then focused himself on the woman. "Is there some assistance we can give?" He stared as if mildly unhinged.

Pluckrose decided to aid the process. "We're terribly well trained. Could pitch in at a moment's notice. What we're meant for. Do let us help, we'd love to." The innocence and eagerness of his expression suggested all manner of accidents waiting to happen.

The woman's shoulders dropped, she frowned and then quietly offered, "There isn't anybody there."

"Ah, but don't we love him all the same?"

She contemplated Molloy and the deer and the crew and they contemplated her until she understood she was defeated and gingerly worked herself and her carpet bag out of their doorway, as if she expected some further uncertainty might arise, more trouble from present or absent men.

Hanson fired up another Players. "She'll complain to the guard. I've seen her sort before."

Molloy was still pleased with himself and said only very gently, "Let's hope she hadn't seen *your* sort before." And Hanson smirked and shrugged.

Alfred wondered if it was altogether lucky to make themselves a crewman who wasn't there. But Freddie kept them undisturbed and cosy and, as the miles passed, they dozed contentedly and drank more beer and ate more sandwiches, enjoying the peace they had come to need. They offered some of what they had to Freddie, but he apparently declined.

Between connections there was further beer and they played cards— Hanson, Torrington, Pluckrose and Molloy—or read newspapers—Miles and the skipper—or fuddled through a book of crime yarns—Alfred. On a blurry, country platform Molloy borrowed Miles's *Times* and this for some reason led to Hanson easing in and stealthily holding a match against the paper's bottom edge. The effect was not unspectacular and there were hardly remains worth stamping out by the time Molloy had flung them down.

Eyebrows were raised among the station staff and Alfred was bundled, along with the rest of the crew (and the small deer's head), into a stuffy, wavering room with very bright paintwork and floored with the bloody brown linoleum he'd already learned to hate and questions were directed to them regarding bottles of beer consumed and the validity of travel warrants and routes chosen, during which both Molloy and Hanson were most strenuously respectable and sober-minded.

"High spirits, sir, that's all. No cause for alarm. My companion here, Mr. Hanson, he's recovering from shell shock. We've been off in a flak house. There's no harm done."

"All crew, we are, mate. Crews are pals. We has to be." Hanson put his arm around Molloy while two disapproving porters remained grim and a chap with enough polished buttons to be at least a station master, if not an admiral, sat behind a desk and looked to be nursing savage indigestion.

"That's it—*pals*." Molloy pronounced the single syllable as if it were a password. "We're *pals*, sir. On our way back from leave."

"What with the disruptions and delays, it'll be a bleedin' miracle if we're anywhere near the station before lights out."

Molloy, believing this might be construed as criticism, rushed in, "Ah, and I've just thought—*you're* a station master and here *we've* a station commander and we're all doing what we must for the empire, aren't we? We're all on the same side."

Alfred was trying to remember how many bottles of beer he had drunk and only slowly realised that mentioning their station commander might mean that someone would telephone their station commander and harsh words would be spoken in the direction of their station commander and they'd all put up a black.

But the admiral softened slightly and the skipper was placating—while kicking Molloy's shin firmly to shut him up—and no constables were summoned and praise was lavished upon aircrew as a species and the admiral expounded theories on taking the fight to the enemy and the frailty of German morale.

After encouraging mugs of tea but no toast or biscuits, they were carefully escorted to their next train by the porters—one a pale lad too young to be called up yet, and what could have been his grandfather behind him.

Once the crew was safely underway again, "He was eighty if he was a day." Hanson was bucked by his brush with authority.

But the skipper had decided to rein them all in, declare their leave over, "Which was why watching an Irishman burst into flames was something he found alarming." He gave them his commanding glare and this was a serious proposition. It made Alfred flush. "Never mind looking shamefaced, Boss. Or you, Miles . . . Bloody hell, we're a total shower. *No more beer.*"

Pluckrose almost agreed. "Well, *nearly* no more beer, Skip. There's only four bottles between us—that's all that's left."

The skipper sighed. "Then get it inside you now and the rest of the journey's tea and cake. That way we might have a chance of arriving sober. No more for me."

As it turned out, with other abstentions, Pluckrose and Molloy ended up drinking two bottles each, which everyone else agreed could do no harm, because they'd hardly notice, being already more drunk than even Hanson. And the whole crew started in on both cakes they'd been given—the one that was meant for the journey and the spare. They ate them to waste without being hungry, ate themselves sick.

Alfred tried to sleep, but couldn't. He hadn't liked the way the porters treated them—slightly repelled and slightly craven, the way men had always been around his father.

· · ·

Ivor Sands, he wasn't the aircrew type, not the pal type, either. Too much of a temper.

"Get your fucking workman's little face out of my shop."

The first time it happened, Ivor had leapt up and screamed at the end of a brooding morning. The couple who'd been flirting between History and Modern Verse shifted out of the door and the shop was cleared before Alfred could break off from shelving and know it was him Ivor wanted to insult.

"Well! What are you waiting for, you shit?"

"I . . ." This wasn't good, this shouting, you never knew where things would go from shouting.

"Jesus Christ!" Ivor's scars seemed to limit his mouth, to make the effort of yelling painful so that he scratched at his cheek compulsively. "I didn't ask for you to come and fucking hide in here. Run away to somewhere else, I'm sick of the bloody sight of you!"

And Alfred had to think about this, calculate: should he hit Ivor and leave—should he hit him and stay—should he leave and not hit him— stay and find out what he meant? It wasn't clear that Ivor knew what Ivor meant, so Alfred didn't think that was important.

Hit him or don't, then—leave or stay.

"Do I have to kick you? I'll do it. I'll kick you out into the street."

"No you won't." Because when they threaten you matters become simple—because no one can do that. Not any more. So you're standing in the smooth place now, the one where you're sure. "You might try." You don't shout. "But you shouldn't." No one ought to shout, you could be quite vehement on that point.

"What?" Ivor blinking a lot and puzzled and he isn't drunk, only maybe crazy in some way. But you've made him quieter. "You—"

"Are you giving me the sack?"

"Well, not—"

"Because I won't go. I like this job. It took me a long time to find somewhere I could be. This suits me."

"I—" Ivor turns his back on you which you don't like and is also stupid, opening up so many ways that you might kill him. It's not that you normally think such things, but he's made you annoyed.

He walks a little figure of eight with his hands in his pockets, then sits on the edge of his desk. "I wasn't about to dismiss you. I only . . ." He watches his feet as they twitch a little in their grubby army surplus desert boots. "I should be very grateful if you could take a turn outside for a while. An hour or so."

"You want me to take my workman's face out of your shop." Because you can't let him hide this away again—it would make you both cowards. "My fucking little face." You have to push him. "One to talk, aren't you—about faces." Shake the rest of the threat in him free.

And somebody pushed will push back, including Ivor. "Oh, yes. What did *you* do in the war? Because I was on the ground, cleaning up after bastards like you, putting out the fires, lifting out the bodies and the bits of bodies." His hands shaking, which you recognise, but ignore. "You ever carry someone melting?—they'll drip like a candle sometimes, runs all over you."

"You were cleaning up after Germans, not bastards like me."

"And your bombs were different, were they? When they landed? Opened up and rained down chocolate for the kiddies, did they? Nylons?" Pulling one hand through his thickness of hair—always seemed odd, his having such a solid, dark head of hair, glossy, when the face was half wrong and no need to shave the scarring. "I didn't want what happened. I was trying to change things, my mother—"

"Yes." Your own hand going to the scar across your lip. "What about her? She in the fire brigade, too, was she?" Not that you're making comparisons, it's just a habit you have.

"She had a heart attack in '41. Couldn't stand the bombing." Looking at you, blue eyes flecked with something like sparks of metal and you want to ask if that's to do with the burning, too, or has he always had it, did his mother—the way things run in families. "Before then, she dragged me round every holiday, visiting people like you. The less fucking fortunate. Taught me how guilty I should be about what I'd got and you hadn't and, in the end, there would be a turning point and everything would be more equal and no one would be wasted any more. It was going to be marvellous. Remember that? The balls everyone talked before the war?"

"No, I don't remember. I was too busy being working class."

"Fuck you."

"Fuck you."

"We were all supposed to be civilised together, we were all supposed to be elevated. Well, we're not." He's standing again, forgetting if he was frightened before, whatever pain there is in him rushing out at you. "I can only tolerate so much. We are not all the same, we should not all have to be together, we are not we. The whole fucking place is fucked!"

He's shouted again and it brings you in, craning up to face him, the way you've faced so many others in so many pubs and streets and lodging-house dining rooms, because there are so many places where stupid, stupid fuckers will say the wrong thing, will be the wrong thing, will be wrong. "Fuck you." Standing with your chin near his chest, Alfred Francis Day, the little angry man.

He surprises you then, tucks his head low and whispers to you, "Last night I met a girl, a nice girl. And she didn't mind my face. Only then I found out she didn't mind it because she thought I'd been a fighter pilot and walking out with me on her arm was just the thing she needed to feel noble."

"Try telling them you flew in bombers. You won't be so popular then, either."

"Fuck you."

"Fuck you."

But Ivor almost smiling, squinting at one hand and shy like a kid. You patted his shoulder and you let him have his way, spun on your heel and wandered out, caught the bus into town and walked where you shouldn't walk, because he'd made you raw already and some of your defence was missing, broken, so that you ended up tracking it: your love, pursuing the path of every impact, letting it group in around you, tight. The part of St. Martin's Lane that sang with her, the comfortable rooms where you'd taken tea—your time then so constricted, the edges of it ripping and flaking away while you sat, but the two of you held inside what you were and safe and firm—and you're stupid, allow every detail to blaze in, penetrate, so that now when you cross behind the Palace Theatre and face north you can hardly move—everything altered and everything the same, no sign or hope or chance of her, but the air expecting that she'll come, that she's trying to meet you, the drag of it enough to leave you swaying by the kerb. Crying. Grown man in the street, crying.

This is what happens when you don't hide, this is what happens when you go looking for your life. The one you never had.

You take a beer somewhere quiet and low-ceilinged, leave when a man tries to sell you his watch and says he was at Anzio. There is a little rain when you go outside again, but the street was looking huddled before it started, and you a part of it, too, trapped in a flinch out of habit, watching the pavement at your feet.

Which means you find money sometimes, coins people drop.

But you're always too embarrassed to pick them up.

In the end, it actually makes you want to go back and see Ivor. Because he'll be there. Because he has nowhere else that he could go. Like you.

And when you trip the bell on the door, it's past six and he's waiting inside a deserted shop. You suspect the place may have been empty all day—he does not look inviting.

And he fires off the line he's got ready for your return, "You have no moral high ground, not with me." Sitting behind his desk as if he'll be your teacher, except his pullover is holed at the elbows, and his shirt, too.

"And I have none with myself." Which he didn't expect. Sometimes you give the person whatever it is they wanted to fight you about. Sometimes that defeats them more than you could.

Ivor leans his chair over on to its back legs. "All right then."

And you wonder if this is the way a marriage goes, this delight in drawing blood, just a drop at a time. "And you have none with me." Was this how you would have ended up with her? Was this how she would be with Antrobus? Were there happy marriages?

"Fuck you." He seems happy as he says so, in control of himself, except for his hands which cling to each other, clasp too hard.

You sit on his desk, claim his territory. "Let's not start that again. It's nothing to do with me that everything's buggered. Jerry didn't win the war and we didn't win the war. The spivs did. They were bound to. The spivs and the Whitehall Warriors."

"That little shit Attlee and his mob—worse than what we had before. They're all the bloody same. Promises, promises."

"And you were here at home and could have stopped it. I was busy."

He lets the chair clump forward again—loves doing that, has dented the wood of the floor all about himself with years of doing that. "The shop's finished, you know."

"I thought we did well this month."

"Oh, we'll be fine for a while yet. But not the way it was." He sips his tea. That'll be all he's managed today—made a cup of tea. "People read in the war. More people than ever. They understood it, all the things it could give them, the way it lasted out anything else. They appreciated it. You—you're the perfect example." He points at you—officer class, they're always ones for pointing—as if they might buy you, or might want you taken away.

You point back, the way a gunner does, wishing you had your hand full, felt a trigger. "Thanks ever so. I'm still reading. I always will, it's mine."

"And it gives you somewhere nice to go at night. I know. We are not unalike. And I'm not saying they'll all just jack it in next week. It'll take years. And more years before they notice they never got their nice new world and their welfare state and by then people will be busy with the things that keep people busy, the unimportant things."

"Wives, lovers, families." You can say this, because you can't hurt any more today and it's worth the sting that it leaves in your teeth to see him twitch.

"The unimportant things." He clears his throat and glances at you for a moment to find out if you'll hurt him again, really argue, or just stay and be company for him and have him be the same for you. "You'll see. After a while, they won't want what's here, then they'll think they don't need it and then they'll forget what it is. You'll see."

"I won't forget."

"It won't be up to you. Or me. We won't be relevant."

"You're a depressing bastard."

"You're no sunbeam, yourself."

You stand, take off your coat and throw it into the back room. Something about the way it smells reminds you of Joyce. "You said I was hiding."

"I hope you're going to hang that up."

"Earlier, you said I was hiding. What did you mean?"

"You know what I meant. We're both hiding. We're the kind of people nobody needs any more and so we end up here With the kind of things no one will need any more."

"I'm not hiding."

"The pot's still warm." Smoothing his hair down with both hands. "Have a restorative cup of tea. Of course you're hiding. Would you like to make toast? Why wouldn't you hide."

You start to go through to the back, pick up your coat, because you are orderly, hanging it up on the peg by the door. "I'm all right for toast. I don't have to hide."

He calls through after you, "Really? That's a relief. Well, let me know your embarrassment of other options . . . colonial administrator? One of those lads with medals who open doors at the nicer hotels? Or a Chelsea Pensioner—they get those crimson uniforms, lovely—could you do that? Not too handy for *me*, having been a conchie and all that, but would they have *you* . . . ? Don't take air force, do they? Bombers? Or what did you have in mind?"

"Tea. I was thinking of tea." Tea and toast—the operational diet. Tea without end and toast. "Tea the drink. Not the meal. Tea's not really a meal you'd ever eat, is it? It would be dinner to you, or supper?" He's left the milk right by the stove and it's turned with the heat—only bloody place where there is any heat in the shop.

"I'll have a refill while you're in there."

"You'll get your own. I'm not a bleedin' servant."

"I'll get my own."

And he comes to lean in the doorway, watching you stir in your sugar. He looks scared, but not of you. You hold out your hand and he gives you his empty cup.

When it finds you out: your bad news, your bad luck, your bad life, there's maybe a second before the pain starts when you realise all that hiding had no point. However skilled you are at tucking what you care about away, however low you lie, however trained and fine you make yourself, it doesn't matter—you are a small, soft thing and the world is full of fire and hardness and if you are scared, alert, distracted, bored with your job, the bullet hits you all the same. It doesn't mind.

Piling off the farm truck near the station gates, the pack of you roaring about something and then thinking you ought to be quiet, but not quite fast enough, because out comes Chiefy and a ginger sergeant and they're looking not wholly amused and there's the small deer's head peering out under Pluckrose's arm and you are a shower and the leave has made you worse and wounding remarks may be expected and Chiefy's hauling up that final breath he needs before his wrath descends, but then it doesn't. He nods the crew in and, as you pass him, says you should see the chaplain, have a word, and he treats you as if you are ill somehow, delicate. This puzzles you. Skip and Pluckrose, both of them glance round towards you, but you shake your head to show that nothing's wrong and you quietly pass Molloy your kitbag and walk off, too light without it, under-equipped, and you go and present yourself as requested to the vicar.

Never took to him: Anglican and soapy, yellow teeth and a way of talking as if his tongue was sticking in the cracks between words, as if he enjoyed himself licking at the cracks. Some kind of dirt always on his glasses, smears—you'd have no way of spotting anything through that.

"I'm afraid I have to tell you."

But he wasn't afraid, you could see that. He probably hadn't ever been afraid, not the way he lived: boxed up and peering out at ordinary people and telling them he understood and that there was a sense and the presence of God in everything.

"I'm afraid I have to tell you."

You knew what it would be. You knew from his face, maybe from Chiefy's face.

"I'm afraid."

You wanted to put him up against your sandbank, fire a few thousand rounds in close beside him. That would help him be afraid.

"Your mother unfortunately."

Didn't want him talking about her. Didn't want her name in that mouth.

"I am most dreadfully sorry."

Felt like his saying so made it his fault. Felt like he wanted this all to be his business.

"You can see Wingco at any time about leave, the funeral is, I think."

They read your letters—in and out, they read them—stood between you and Joyce, between you and your mother: they are always in the way. Burned-out cases do it: penguins: nobody wants the job—censoring correspondence, getting in the way.

"I am most."

Hating him after this, every time you see him, shutting your head when he gave you out a blessing or a prayer, wished you well before you bombed. Not his fault. But hating him, all the same.

And you shouldn't have been in Scotland, not when you could have been home with your ma. So that was someone else to hate—yourself.

"A very unfortunate accident."

You could have been there.

"With so many houses so badly damaged, one can't be too careful."

"Are yo sayin she wasn't careful?"

"No, I merely—"

"Are yo sayin she was daft? That she day know?"

"I think perhaps—"

"It wor her fault. Are yo sayin it was? How could it be her fault?"

"You'll need time for reflection."

"It wor her fault."

And he slides out and leaves you to know it was your fault. Yours and the fucking Germans. You let the fucking bastards murder her.

Duisburg.

Day after you got the news and you could have gone home, they said so, but that wouldn't have been right. Your crew fly a mission without you, then you're lost. If you all go on together and you make it, get right the way through, that means they'll have worked out their time when you haven't, so you'll fly your extra mission without them at the end. You wouldn't want to deal with that.

Or they could leave you, not come back. You wouldn't want to deal with that.

And there's nothing you can do at home now, because she's dead.

And you want to bomb, tonight you need to bomb.

Tonight you want to kill the fuckers very much.

You don't wait to hear your music, you don't speak to the lads, only layer yourself up for warmth—the soft hat from Joyce, you leave that off: you can't let it see you as you are tonight—collect your gear and then ride the wagon with them out into the dark and the engines waking, speaking all around you and the flares of light.

And it's not so bad.

Not so bad going, rattling on through numb banks of cloud into the climb, gathering and stacking before it's time and Pluckrose calls the course and you're in the stream, you are the stream.

You're trying a new American oil and 50 per cent paraffin—meant to be just the thing to stop you freezing. Talked a lot about it this afternoon with the armourer Bestwick. He knew about your mother and said nothing, which is just what you'd have asked. Talked about oil, talked so much about oil—more than really anybody could—he even went and got the can to show you—see what a Yank can looked like. Almost went for a walk after that with Molloy and then couldn't face it.

And it's not so bad.

Water in veins on the Perspex.

When you tested your guns they jumped for you, lit out your will in whipping arcs and you told the skipper everything was fine, listened while Hanson did the same, the faint din from Torrington.

All the tests were fine.

So you're set up and ready to fire off rifle bullets at armour plate, watch them bounce. Need a five-inch gun. Don't have one. Need a bloody cannon. Don't have one.

Like shooting peas at a nanny goat's arse.

Watch them bounce.

What larks.

Depression, elevation, rotation, nice and smooth.

Flying in Q for Queenie—a bit of a bucket, but you're too new to be trusted with anything else. You've had her once before and came home and perhaps you like her and besides you know a turret is a turret is a turret and that keeps you right. Leastways it's best to think so.

Not nervous, only packed: something strange, fierce, wound down into you and waiting. It feeds you, tires you, eats you, feeds you through the night. But you're not nervous. Miles is sick every time before he climbs aboard: fine once he's underway, just chucks up like a pup while he's still on the ground. You're good, though. The shaking is in everywhere but you—Q for Queenie trembling, rocking, shuddering and you trying to rest yourself against her, leaning back on her big breath—the ache, the shiver, the rattle, the ache, the shiver, the rattle.

Although you do want to shout sometimes, scream yourself free across the Channel, yell while you have the chance and there's nothing you can see that's come to hurt you.

Thinking that back on the ground Chiefy has your wallet and your photograph of Joyce and the letter from your sister, from Dorothy, the one that said how falling slates had killed your mother, hurt her head, some ARP stranger finding her in the street. Your mother lying in the street and this makes you see her curled up on her side, as if she's resting for a while the way she did sometimes: sneaked a minute to herself and you sitting at the end of the bed and quiet as quiet to be a help and because then you know she'll let you stay. Always her eyes covered over by one hand.

Smelled of lavender and Cuticura, lily of the valley—no metal, no cordite, no fish guts, no fucking pain.

Judder through the second turn—France long gone, the goldish rim cast up from it far behind you, no blackout there—and a sick sweat hits you.

You haven't been paying attention.

No way to be totally sure of how long you were dreaming: scanning without scanning, betraying everyone.

Take another Benzedrine and breathe. Check your oxygen. Breathe.

Cover's too thick, visibility zero. Good to keep inside it, cosy—but you'll never see the target. Hit 'em with dead reckoning and guesswork— what a way to fight a war.

But it's not so bad.

The kick when the bombs are gone, the airframe jumping up in the love of it, the last spring in her lifting under you, flexing—bombs tumbling, diving to nothing, swallowed, a pale bloom spreading here and there, flushing the haze, but inconclusive.

"That's another field of Nazi cows gone west, then." Pluckrose— always sounds younger on the intercom and very far away.

Skipper swinging you round from the bomb run, the turn hauls and creaks behind your back and you are going home. First to take off, last to land, but you are going home.

Left foot getting chilly. The electric's gone US. Better remember to wriggle your toes. Wouldn't want to be without them.

And you're up in the dawn, in the start of it, the great, bright roll of tomorrow peeling wide. Should make you feel naked, but it cheers you — the day reaching out to find you, call you. You've been slow: headwind shoving at you, but you're almost there. It will still be dim when you're landing, everything layers of blue.

Unhook the oxygen mask, breathe some proper sweat- and Elsan-smelling air.

Funeral on Wednesday — get your Best Blue in order for that.

Except when she saw me in uniform she cried.

A quiet run. A milk run. Piece of cake.

Cover clearing slightly as you reach the Channel — typical, now it's no use — and you can see waves, the blades of them glinting.

Wrong.

A shine too high and then away again. Forty degrees.

Watch for him, watch for him, watch for him, the fucker.

Again. Not wave tops. Forty-five degrees.

"Skip. Company. Eight-hundred yards. In the cloud, but he's on us."

"Tell me when."

Snapper, there's a fucking snapper trying his luck.

Don't want to go down in water. Fuck that.

Then you're uncovered, caved in a dirty white that he breaks through coming after, his yellow nose first and then his body while you sing it, sing out, *CorkscrewportGo* — thumbs firing and arse over tip into the corkscrew, thumbs firing and more noise than you can hear, thumbs firing and the gleam of tracer and churning at angles you don't understand, falling as if you will die and a bitterness filling your lungs and the belt cutting into your hip and doing no bloody good to hold you and the fit of the turret is close and you think of coffins and down Q for Queenie runs and surely you'll hit the water before you tear up, flat out, sick and staring.

But you talk, don't yell, you talk in among the other talking. "I don't see him." Talking that might be thinking. "You see him?" As if you think your Lanc. "Astrodome caught it." Understand how it is beyond yourself: blood and glycol feeling for you, knowing, telling you, "I don't see him."

As if you think each other, *are* each other, all one, stinging low above the water, then up and cloud gaping and slamming shut against you. "What caught it?" All one.

"Shut up." The skipper cracking in. "Now tell me. Any more sign of him."

There was none.

"And everyone OK?"

You call in, tell yourself you're all still there: Torrington, Hanson, Molloy.

"Alfred here, Skipper. Fine."

"Rudder feels sluggish."

And Miles sounds strange, confusing.

And you wait for Pluckrose and he doesn't say he's fine. And you ask yourselves if you heard, or if you saw anything, and Molloy is going back to take a look and you need Pluckrose, especially now you need him for a course to pancake quick, get down anywhere big enough, get help for him. You need him to help himself.

And Molloy, you hear him very clear, "Jesus Christ. Jesus Christ. Jesus Christ."

And Miles, "It wasn't a big noise. I wasn't sure."

"Jesus Christ."

And then you know.

What you remember is the smell of him, hot and something filthy about it.

Out of the turret before you're down, as soon as you see the runway rear up close, you clatter through your set of doors, slide back, slam your elbow into something and try to see—Molloy there on his knees and tugging something ragged across the wing spar—Miles with his back to you helping and this red mess with them. No face. Stumbling up towards you along the fuselage, dragging this mess. Trying to reach the first-aid kit, as if anything could be done with it. And then all of you by the door, all of you: Torrington, Miles and you are sitting, kneeling in the blood and doing nothing.

Recognise the trousers, the shoes. Pluckrose no longer Pluckrose.

You see without wanting to where they've hauled him and his pieces have come loose. Look at him once properly and, even then, you can't make out what's happened—a clotted hollow above his collar, a curve of bone and this glistening dark where he used to be, where he used to talk and look at you, and the one shoulder hangs and is ruined and big pale hands—his two hands but odd and messed with blood. He's all messed with blood.

He messes you, too.

Hard to let go when the door is opened and they try to take him, these strangers try to take him, take it, more pieces being lost—you don't like it, what he's turned into, but you don't want him to be with strangers.

Then they put you in a wagon—couple of sleepy corporals usher you up, keeping back. Miles, Molloy and you are all wrong with him on you and the others, even Skip, they don't want to see, they sit at the opposite side. You notice, though, the way Pluckrose is on them, too: their boots, their jacket hems, their trousers, because—swinging over the wing spar—they've rubbed through what he left, or they've walked in him down the fuselage—he's marked them. So you're together, the six of you messed.

The wagon starts to pull you somewhere else when you don't want to go, not anywhere else.

And Hanson, you're facing Hanson, who is now cleanest of the crew and he gives you this queer smile and a cigarette which you only hold, because you don't smoke and you don't want your hands near your mouth and then he leans his head back and lets himself sing.

You want to hurt him when he does, but then he stares at you again and you sing also and, by the time the wagon stops and the corporals come to get you, your whole crew is singing, what's left of your whole crew is singing—corny tune, a navy song.

"All over the place"

Singing and laughing while the corporals swing down the back of the truck, singing and laughing and grinning and holding each other, grabbing at cloth, and covered in him and singing and singing while the corporals watch you: the crew that laughs.

"He's there for a day and then he's away,
He's a-a-all over the place."

That afternoon the fake prisoners were being filmed picking the locks on their fake handcuffs. Back in the war, old Hitler had given the order to handcuff Kriegies, because some bloody fool had tied up a dinghy full of Luftwaffe types, or because there were nasty rumours to that effect. Penalty for non-compliance, one hour in the sun with hands up. They'd be filming that next: trembling British arms and British sweat, very dramatic—lots of sympathy you'd get with that—now that it wasn't happening any more, now that it was a story.

Although Alfred couldn't recall the cuffing lasted long. It hadn't turned out to be practical, what with the lock picks and complaints. And the camp was like anywhere else—it had its own patterns of cruelty and kindness, its own methods—the handcuffs had simply been superfluous.

Meanwhile, in the current scene, Alfred was required to sit still and look gloomy with a small eyepatch in place—suggesting his (as shown previously) head wound was getting better. He had no problem with sitting, or looking gloomy, and he liked to imagine the eyepatch would draw attention, seem dashing, mysterious.

And why would that matter, our kid? Think she'll go and watch the picture, do you? Think that'll do the trick—Joyce'll see you, way off in the background—eyepatch and a new moustache—and then she'll have to come and seek you out. When she never has before. When she wouldn't know where to start.

Which was probably rather more gloom than they'd asked for. But he couldn't help it, wasn't having a comfortable day, had the sensation of something burrowing in his chest.

Every break, he'd leave the hut and try to breathe, drag some life from the motionless, burning day. This time outside he saw a Good German working at one of the gardens. The chap had been hired to play a stern but ridiculous *Unteroffizier*. Right now he was in his shirtsleeves with a hoe. Roughly the same age as Alfred, something old about him, though, in the way he stood. "Hello. How are you." English-looking, wearing good corduroys and giving a small, shy wave of his hand.

But Alfred didn't want to chat with a Good German.

The Good German kept at it, though, leaning on the hoe, overfriendly. "It's too hot honestly to stay out here, but I like to be with a garden." A gentleness in his face that pressed for a reply, for some acknowledgement.

But Alfred didn't want to chat. Not with anyone.

The bloke had a funny accent for a German—a mix of Liverpool and something Northern. "A grand day for it, if we had a seaside we could go to." Red on the bridge of his nose from the sun. "You caught me in Africa." A panama kind of hat set far back on his head, so it gave him no shade. Silly bugger.

And then Alfred couldn't help it. "Caught you?"

The Good German straightened, eased out his back as if it were a little sore in a pleasing way. "Yes. Your Eighth Army. Near Mareth." He grinned, maybe being pleased by something else: by having been a desert soldier and getting sunburned now, by Alfred giving him his answer, or maybe only nervous. "Then I was a prisoner in Yorkshire. Do you know it? Very pretty. But not always so warm as this." He paused as if he thought Alfred might go away, might have heard enough. When Alfred didn't go, the Good German cleared his throat and then began. "After the war, we were kept for a while by your Mr. Attlee and there was more farming to do, which I liked—always enjoyed plants—and some road mending and moving about a lot. We would make a garden for ourselves wherever we were sent."

Alfred jerked up his chin once in agreement.

"They help."

"A garden is nice."

"And keeping clean."

"If you can."

"We could. People were mainly very kind." The Good German nodded. "I was classified as a grey—not white, not black—a grey person. You know what I mean by this?"

As soon as they could, they all had to confess. Everyone. If they wanted to be innocent, to never have gone wrong, then they'd have to tell you, talk it away. It made them happy.

You looked at him being happy, deep inside, how it glimmered in the colour of his eyes: him so chuffed that you were going to listen. "They showed me photographs and films—what had happened, what we'd done." He made a point of facing you, hardly blinking, not breaking out in a glance to the side. "In March of 1948, they said I was allowed go back home, but there was nobody alive there." He cleared his throat. "Excuse me. My aunt there, only gone mad. She recognised no one. And it wasn't my home." He paused again. "*Aus der Traum.* Except we hadn't been dreaming. We had been awake. In all we did. Very important—not to confuse sleeping and being awake. When you are asleep you might do anything." He paused to let Alfred understand this, in case he didn't already. "So I stayed with you. I live in Hawarden now. Do you know Hawarden?"

"I don't."

"It's near Chester. Quite near Chester."

Without noticing, Alfred had edged up to stand beside the Good German and after a little silence they both seemed easier, able to study the haze of carrot leaves, sweet peas and real peas. Alfred thought aloud, "Will this all be ready before they make us go?"

"Maybe not, I think."

"Seems a shame."

"Except the flowers."

"Yes. They won't need the flowers."

"They're for us."

"We can enjoy them."

"Yes."

"And somebody will have it after us. The DPs. Somebody. It's proper to leave something for strangers when we're gone. It's a good thing. As if we have children."

An ache growing in Alfred's forehead. "Do you?" Must be the sun.

"Do I?"

"Have children."

"No. My father was . . . misleading. I could be the same." The Good German wiped his mouth. "I have a garden."

"A garden helps."

"You have one?"

"No." This tightening Alfred's throat, his lips. Eyes letting him down and becoming awkward.

"You should find one."

Alfred's turn to clear his throat, doing it a couple of times to keep steady. "Maybe. But you should have a kid, a lot of kids. It would suit you." Knowing that was probably untrue. "You'd be all right." Knowing most hopes were misleading. And knowing that Day, Alfred F., would not be all right, that nothing suits him.

The Good German setting his hand on Alfred's shoulder. "Maybe."

For some reason the contact shook him, as if it were a blow. "No." Alfred put his hands up to his face and pulled them down again, sheened with the way he was losing himself. He felt the Good German watching. "I should really get back. Work." But Alfred didn't move. He stared at the earth, at how poor it was and dry. A wonder that anything could live. A wonder that anything ever gets to live. "I should. I should ask your name."

"Does this matter?"

"No."

"Because we know each other."

"Yes."

"*Ach, was man aus mir gemacht hat* . . . You understand? I think this often. And what I allowed. I allowed them to make me what allowed them to make me. You understand?"

"We made a bloody mess of it." The Good German saying nothing in reply, although maybe nodding—Alfred had the idea the man was nodding, but couldn't look because he was busy preparing himself to ask, "Where were you from? Before."

"Hamburg. In Borgfelde, that was the distict. I was from Hamburg. All of my people were. Do you know Hamburg?"

"I don't. No. I don't."

Alfred left after that.

Two funerals in one week.

The whole way on the train getting through to Wednesbury it was in your head—that one grave was more than enough, that if God was upstairs and arranging matters then He'd found a bloody funny way to do the job. But you didn't think there was anybody upstairs, not any more—or not anybody but pilots and crews, crews and pilots, poor fucking bastards.

People smiling when they see you're aircrew, but you can't smile back. And they forgive you that. Because you're aircrew. They think they know about you. But they don't.

Heading down from the station towards the Patent Shaft where cousin Ray worked and there's nothing different here, no change that you see, and this puzzles you, rattles and clings around your legs and makes it difficult to walk.

The air tastes of metal, iron dust, steel—no wonder you're a gunner, it's in your breath.

Back at the house and the curtains are drawn against the street. That's the only way you'd tell. No sign in the front gate being not quite shut, or the hard shapes of the roses in the narrow beds behind the wall— on either side of the little path. Your father always pruned things to nothing, the only bit of gardening he liked. Not much growth back in them yet. And brick everywhere: an almost glossy blue, like when there's too much blood: the way it changes, passes beyond red and that same faint iridescence, if you look—and you can't help looking, it's already happened before you can know you don't want to.

Brick wall, brick path, brick set around the roses in their beds, brick house.

Iridescence: shifting with colours as the observer moves—from the Latin for iris. Which is something you can't understand until you've seen the ruin of an eye, when it's out and split and the iris cut and wrong and shining by your boot. That's the trouble with education, it never stops. It is too much. Too much everything.

It makes you feel buried.

All that brick.

And two doors along—you keep your head low and don't check— there's the mess where number 7 and number 9 used to be. Where the Corleys and the Thomases used to be. Mr. Thomas once scared you with a frog, held it out in his hand to show you and it had jumped. The Corleys you didn't know well, because they weren't fond of boys—wanted the house kept neat, always washing the net curtains. Made them seem silly now: wasting their time with frogs and curtains when they'd been going to die all along. Hit by a lone raider, no warning.

They can't have been a target, only a mistake: bad navigation, or maybe aiming for the works, a secondary target, or maybe a crew just jettisoned their bombload because they were lost, or in a funk, or lazy. One night, the orphanage went up—probably nobody meant that to happen, either. But it still did.

Slates from the roof at the end of number 7, from what was left standing, that's what fell and hurt your mother. But no reason for her to be up there. The shops were the other way—and what friends she was allowed.

And she wouldn't have liked to go nearby the damage, it would have scared her.

Two funerals in one week.

You knock at the door where she won't answer and when it opens you can smell her, you can hear her step, but it's only Ruth standing there to bring you in and Nan stepping up at the back of her, seeming tired. Nan calls you *the babby—here's the babby back wumm*—and brushes your hand and the pair of them are leading you into the parlour where you don't want to be.

The coffin is closed. Your mother now something that no one should see. The box looks like furniture: polished, dark—looks like a mistake, looks so much like a coffin that it can't be, that it ought to be a joke.

And there aren't so many people at the house, should have been more, should have been the fucking town—sisters there and a couple of neighbours, woman from the bakery—nobody knows why she came— and not many flowers, what with the war on, and then carrying her, the box between you and your father, the two of you leading the rest, right shoulder, you won't forget the weight, staining into it, down.

And the chapel waiting full, and you're proud for her then, and words from the preacher, words that no longer apply, never did, pretending, and you can't sing, but you want to because it's like shouting and that would help you, but you can't and then you carry her again and then there's nothing that you can remember after: not the earth, not losing her into the earth, and your father in his suit, thinks a lot of himself in the suit, you can tell, and the woman from the bakery is crying, but no one else, no family, the family's crying done with years ago, your father saw to that.

And there aren't so many people at the house, should have been more, should have been the fucking town. Sisters fussing with what little food there was, knowing your father could have shown better respect, could have provided, God knows, shopkeepers will always help shopkeepers: keep in with each other, they do: know each other's secrets, they do, he would only have to ask: for a special occasion, for burying his wife.

And you wouldn't stay the night: rather sleep on the railway station, rather sleep in the street, rather be anywhere, because you won't sleep.

And you stood in the bedroom, her bedroom, just before you left and you sat on the bed and you reached to her pillow, but didn't touch it, and then you stole her hairbrush—it was still on the dresser, still in the place she gave it—and you put it in your pocket and walked out, strands of her hair in your pocket.

And you never spoke to him all day, you never met his eyes, until he was standing in the hallway, ready to open the door for you, see you gone. Then he fell still, something so sudden about it that you stared round at him and he'd got you, made you watch as he started to smile.

And you knew then. He did it.

No slates. No accident.

He did it.

You hadn't stopped him.

He did it.

While you were playing somewhere else.

He did it.

You'd pushed him and he did it. This was how he'd pushed back.

He did it.

And you'd run from your music and the crew, broken your luck and lost Pluckrose, angry with the Germans.

He did it.

Not even thinking of him.

He did it.

Made you lose them both. Made you to blame when you lost them both.

He did it.

Swinging the door open for you now, flick in his wrist at the end when he lets go the wood, and that suit a good fit, new, he must have fiddled extra coupons, it's braced around the size of him, the block of him, and still he's showing you his teeth while you sweat and you are not you and the walls are bending back behind, they are disturbed, and you have to do nothing, step away, move your foot and then step and then again and do nothing, because this is important, this is all you understand— that you promise when you kill him he will not expect it and he will not smile.

Awkward to the last. Struan Macallum Pluckrose, never let it be said that he left them without complications.

Alfred sitting by the window in the sergeants' mess. "What?" Failing to understand while Miles explains again.

"He's entitled to one officer and twenty airmen. Escort—in attendance, that kind of idea. At least I think that's right."

Alfred has only been gone for three days, but Miles looks thinner.

"Of course, we'd be six of the twenty—so that's only really fourteen. Unless it's twenty and us. I don't know." Miles rubs his forehead.

"He's . . ." There was an op last night and Alfred missed it—only nine missions and everything spilling already, getting out of shape. It was impossible work, holding on to your crew.

Good scarf and driving cap to Pilot Officer Edgar Miles.

"Except that it won't be a funeral. Bloody man, never could be simple about anything. Family tradition and all that—he has to go up North." Miles stumbling under the weight of talking. "Has to go back . . . The ancestral plot. They want him . . ." He is grey.

"Back where we were." When he was out among ordinary people, Alfred forgot that shade of aircrew grey—particularly since he dodged most mirrors, most of the time.

"Yes. Or thereabouts. Somewhere unpronounceable." Miles folds his hands and gives a tiny shrug. "So we don't get to tell him goodbye, not really."

"Who does."

"Good job we pancaked where we did—let our own ground crew off the hook."

"Yes. Wouldn't have wanted them having to hose him out. Much better the way it happened." And you don't think of flying back home in the afternoon with water still lying in the fuselage, pink water and the smell of bleach.

Two pounds to our ground crew—for beer and fleshpots.

And Miles nods and is quiet, because he understands you, is a man of your crew. "Didn't think much of the gunner they gave us last night."

Alfred knowing they won't talk about the replacement navigator. "Well you didn't have to fall in love with him, did you—not just for one night." The new navigator will stay—the gunner they probably won't see again. Unless maybe Alfred buys it, or Hanson. Then he might be back.

Clodhopping in, here's Hanson, "Less of that dirty talk from you." He claps Alfred on the arm. "Bugger me, though—he was a fucking dud . . . didn't know what he was up to." Fantastic pimple the Bastard's growing underneath his bottom lip. "Couldn't coordinate his scanning, then he's not scanning at all. Stripped the paper seals off the ejector openings— said he didn't approve."

Alfred getting that lift back, that rush of his crew running near him, of being back inside the stream and the good, cold madness that lets you laugh when there's no laughter in you. "What—d'you think he didn't like the colour?"

"I think 'is bloody guns froze is what I think and then he bloody lied about it after. I told him before we unstuck—you get thirty degrees of cosy out of that paper, I'd wrap my balls in it if I could."

Miles chipping in softly, the way he does, "Then why don't you? Unless you'd rather not rustle when you walk."

"It isn't that." Hanson making a big Stan Laurel grin. "It's just they're not so big, your sheets of cellophane paper." He twiddles his fingers together across his chest, hamming it up. "Wouldn't want to crush anything vital. There's some things I care about."

Which is enough of a reminder and the dark seeps up again. Alfred gets a sudden taste of that morning, the one Pluckrose didn't see. "Tell me again, will you?" The metal smell of blood.

Miles gives Hanson the nod and it's the Bastard who explains that you'll rendezvous at 1500 hours and there'll be a kind of service before they take the last of your Pluckrose away, boxed up like cod.

Five pounds to my crew, all to be spent at
once on getting stinko.

He couldn't be an easy airman, follow the standard procedure: blow apart in the air, fly to earth in another country, stay out of sight. Had to come home and be our problem.

He'd upset people, that was the trouble—made himself noticed and liked which meant he'd be missed when no one could stand to miss him—the ladies came out of the NAAFI and got wet-eyed, when all that he'd ever done to them was bind about the food, and some ground crew were there, which you'd expect—only more than was necessary—and Bestwick and Chiefy and Wingco and the squadron leader and the fucking padre and the guard of honour and too many bods, just standing about with nothing to do but feel, because Pluckrose was stupid and smiled at them, asked after their popsies and gave them lifts in the little blue Austin and was a visibly pleasant man. No one should be like that any more, it was only cruelty.

Gramophone and records to Pilot Officer Sandy Gibbs. Also my
programme from the Folies-Bergère.

The crew, the unfinished crew, they stood with each other and saluted and they did as they should, carried the box to the hearse: lifted the coffin full of pieces. Alfred behind Torrington and Molloy and thinking how neat it was that one man dying left six behind to shift him—three each side—and thinking his shoulder was used to this now and thinking himself down into the beat, the drag and slip of step, the slow march, that respect, and imagining he might hinge down his jaw, open his face and try to scream, but certain not a sound would come from him, not a song.

Alfred knew they were being stared at, this crew—small glances, people wondering if they weren't lucky, if they weren't safe any more, and their fresh navigator—Parks, Cyril Parks—watching them send off their last and new bods wanting to understand what nobody fucking could, or should want to, and old hands fretting against that terrible outrage, the rush of happiness and guilt that took you when the squadron had a loss.

Wisest thing to do was just get on—standing about like this with your dead, it didn't help anyone. And Pluckrose would never have liked it and now Pluckrose couldn't care.

The chaplain talking fucking nonsense—"lighten our darkness we beseech thee"—well, who wouldn't ask that and how could it possibly be that we'd all get our way?

It was balls.

Then the hearse pulled away with him loaded inside. Pulled far away.

My Austin 10 (Reg HU 8962) to Sergeant Richard Molloy. Keys left in Briefing Room.

Funny little bloke that drove the hearse—motored the full distance from Scotland, Christ knew how he got the petrol, and going straight back up again. Didn't say much, but he seemed all right. You'd trust him. You'd let him take your friend. As if you could stop him.

Too quick at the end, the leaving. Felt wrong.

Alfred had run for the phone box after, called Joyce, and she was there and he'd had to ask her, couldn't explain, simply pressed on and asked her. "Could you come here? Do you think? I mean now."

"What's—Alfie? What's the matter? I . . ."

Her voice softening him, bringing him close to losing his own. "I'm sorry, I just. I shouldn't have, only I—" A silence sweeping out beneath him like the bomb door's gape while he swallowed and breathed and kept his feet. "I shouldn't have asked."

"No, I'm just thinking . . . would tomorrow do? I could come tomorrow. I mean, it's nearly six o'clock now. Are you all right? Are you hurt? Is there something—"

So wonderful to hear that she was worried, wanted him not to be hurt.

"You don't have to. I'm sorry, I just—"

"Well, of course I have to. If you ask and it's important, then I have to." The way she might sound with a child: brisk and bright and a care set under both. She would be a good mother—to someone else's children.

"It's important."

"I'll fix things up here and horribly offend three dreadful ladies I'm meant to play bridge with, which I do hope will mean they never speak to me again, and, and . . . someone else can dole out the tea and sandwiches for once. I'll fix things up. I'll come to Lincoln and then get word to you. Do you know of somewhere I can stay?—no, don't bother with that, I'll work that out. You don't bother about anything, Sergeant Alfie. Are you all right, really?"

"Yes . . . I'm . . . Yes."

"Will you tell me when I'm there what the matter is? Alfred?"

"I will."

He'd been right, he shouldn't have asked, but he left the phone box with the smile she'd given him, the one that he had to tamp down, eat, because it wouldn't do, not today.

Inside your skin, though, behind your teeth—she was lovely there.

He wandered towards the mess, needed their company—walked in and found a small cluster of chaps, all lurking about near the door and watching a bod he didn't know—fellow called Wilkins—taking great handfuls of newspapers and *Picture Posts* and *Tee Emms*, crumpling them up and dropping them round his chair. He was doing it with a funny kind of precision, almost ceremony.

Chess set to Warrant Officer Bill Torrington. Also two pairs marcasite earrings for which he may find grateful owners.

Finally, a little wall of paper built up on every side, Wilkins sat, took out his lighter, fired it up and threw it down between his feet.

Alfred and the others ran at him, hauled him out of his seat, stamped on the flames which were spreading remarkably quickly, petrol spilling from the lighter as Wilkins had intended.

"Silly bastard."

Someone chucked their pot of tea in a helpful direction and the curling ashes hissed, smoked appallingly.

"Let me go." Wilkins not shouting, not sounding too interested, but still repeating, "Let me go." While a lanky W/Op frisked him as if he'd searched people before and took charge of his matches.

"Let me go."

"He's ruined that bit of bloody carpet."

"Christ, it takes you enough time to get things decent."

"Fancy" lighter to Sergeant John Hanson.

Alfred—not wanting to look at Wilkins, or hear him—had started to scoop up the charred papers but then couldn't think where to put them and just stood reading an item about a plucky submarine crew—sixteen ships sunk and 40,000 tons—two VCs, one DSO. That and an advert for Barney's pipe tobacco, an overseas flying officer saying how fine it was—*The Barney's "EVERFRESH" Tin has conquered time, distance and climate. In the desert of Sind Barney's opens out as sweet, fresh and fragrant as when it left Tyneside.*

"Let me go."

Miles appeared soon after that with Chiefy and some burly chaps in tow. They didn't seem surprised, only highly keen to get Wilkins out.

"Clean that bloody mess up, will you." Chiefy in a rush. "Don't just stand there. Inspection at 16:30 tomorrow." And he two-sixed their man off.

"Let me go."

The mess adjusted itself with chatter. Kicked about the ruins and lit new cigarettes.

"Poor bastard."

"Poor bastard nothing—I was reading that *Picture Post*."

"Reading nothing—you were eyeing up that bint with the bathing cap in *London Opinion*."

"Bugger me. He hasn't tried burning her, has he?"

"He'll be cleaning fucking toilets for the rest of the war."

"Quite bloody right. If he's ruined page seventeen. She was all that got me through."

"Oh, yes. Poor sod." Hanson dropping into an armchair with the air of a man who intended he should stay. "Scrubbing away at that porcelain, while we have all the fucking fun. We're the lucky boys, we are." He yawned, scratched inside his shirt and pulled out a *London Opinion*—opening it carefully and then licking his lips. An unscathed paperback was flung towards his head, its previous owner protesting as it flew.

"Oh, now look, you bleeders—I was reading *that*."

A couple of bods laughed, Alfred heard them. Last week, he'd have laughed as well.

My books, what there are, I give to Sergeant A.F. Day.
He's read them all, anyway.
Other effects to family if crew don't want them.
With apologies for any inconvenience and my thanks in advance.

Vasyl caught Alfred about nine o'clock, ran across the junction between huts that a bright and patriotic spark had christened Charing Cross—but after the one in Glasgow, apparently. "I saw when you were talking to that German cunt." A kind of anguish in the Ukrainian's face and the evening falling down at his shoulder—colours heating, deepening.

"Seemed a pleasant type." Alfred sure Vasyl wanted to take his arm, so he drew off to one side, which would seem defensive, but never mind. "What's it to you?" Alfred had wanted to watch out the end of the day, be undisturbed.

"He tells you he suffered?"

"Not particularly, no." Now he could see it coming. Vasyl was the type who'd want to have suffered, whose suffering was special, who'd want to tell that kind of story. "Have to go, now, Basil. Spot of tin bashing to get on with. Trying to make a coffee pot. This time, if it works, I can take it back home." Which would be pointless, given that no one in London—not even Ivor—would care for a tin-can coffee pot.

Vasyl pushed at his Jerry headgear, some kind of thought going on, then made a tiny lunge forward. "Please. No." Hands up in surrender, but preventing Alfred moving off, eyes attempting to be gentle, innocent. "You should know. People should know."

"All right." Alfred sighed, folded his arms. "What is it I should know?"

"I was prisoner, too. Of the Americans. I was mislaid for a while and caught and then put in the Rhine Meadow. I ended in Remagen and the Amis took my watch."

"You poor thing."

"But no, this isn't right. Some Amis with five watches, six. They steal our watches. But they give us no food. It rained. In that April it rained. And we were sleeping in holes—no tents, no huts, they put us in fields like animals and some they were drowned like this in these holes."

It was odd, Alfred almost believed him: the way his palms waved in front of him, helpless-looking, and his voice wavered. It was somebody's true story, anyway—even if it wasn't Vasyl's.

"We could see the boxes of food, but there was nothing for us. Almost nothing. I ate grass. You ever eat grass?"

"As it happens."

Vasyl ignored the interruption. "At night sometimes they fired tracer over our heads, so we would be down all the time, on our hands and knees—to make us crawl. Why would they want this?"

"I can't imagine."

"Policemen, firemen, postmen they just take everyone in a uniform. I was in a good uniform. They could tell I was not SS. I had a good uniform."

And you could see then a little tick of truth and Vasyl paused for a moment and blinked at you. He'd got himself a *Wehrmacht* uniform, or a policeman's, fireman's, postman's, and he'd tried to hide and been taken anyway. He'd been SS.

Alfred grinned at him. "Well, none of us enjoyed ourselves too much. What with one thing and another."

The hands rose again. "They keep me ten months like this. Men dying everywhere—men have the *Ruhr*."

Ruhr—you haven't heard that for a while—the German slang for dysentery. A sense of humour there—all of that heavy industry in the Ruhr Valley making its river the colour of running shit. All of that heavy industry making you bomb it, bomb the Happy Valley, night after fucking night. Some places have no luck.

"Very bad *Ruhr* among everyone, you understand."

"Dysentery."

"I—"

"Yes, that'll kill you, often as not. By the way—that bod you gave the third degree—that man you beat. What had he done?"

Now it was Vasyl's chance to grin. "I don't beat anyone. I could never do such a thing." He sloped his fists down into his pockets. "But there are bad people here—ones who have done terrible things."

"I'm sure there are, Basil. And I'm sure there are other people who want to say so." Alfred began walking, Vasyl staying with him.

"Perhaps."

"How did you come to be a DP—that's for civilians, isn't it?"

"But I was forced. We didn't wish to be soldiers, we were just glad to be free from Stalin when the Germans came—and then—and then I was a kind of slave." He made a different, softer smile, as if such a bad lie was a disappointment to him, an amusing example of human frailty, and so he would disown it as he spoke. "They have to keep us as DPs—if they don't we are sent back to the Russians, the Communists, and nobody loves the Communists any more. Everything changes, Mr. Alfred, and one must be on the clean side when they do. A man must be clever."

"I'm sure. *Sehr schlau.*" And rather than have to put up with this any longer, Alfred stepped up into a hut he didn't know, hoping that Vasyl wouldn't follow.

Although they hadn't seemed to be there a moment before, he found himself walking into a pair of quite large gentlemen—"Hello there"—solidly made. "Can we help you?" They were friendly enough—in a brick shithouse kind of way. "We're busy in here, you see." But Alfred knew they wouldn't mind a fight and probably wouldn't lose it, not unless he did bad things to them, and they might have learned some bad things of their own. "Yes, laddie. Highly occupied."

Alfred half turned, checking for Vasyl: but the Ukrainian was yards away now, a queer look about him—amusement and worry blended. He gave a carefully insolent salute, turned on his heel and sloped away.

"Laddie?" The voice at Alfred's side rumbling so deep he could feel it in his arms. "You really should think of fucking off."

"No, no—he's all right." Somebody calling from further indoors. "He's one of ours." A Scottish twang and a sense of authority, of matters being taken efficiently in hand. The guards shrugged, parted, and Alfred was facing a slim, restless man dressed in filthy long underwear—very blue eyes in a filthy face, filthy hand extended. "You are, aren't you?" The man glanced down at his own general disarray and let his hand drop before Alfred could shake it. "You're the boy who fainted, aren't you?"

"I . . ." An odd clank and scrape started up at the far end of the hut. "Yes . . . You . . . You're not . . . ?" The guards settled themselves down to crouch either side of the door—each of them looked like a stack of normal people. The din continued and Alfred had to ask, "You are, aren't you?"

The man clapped his knees and laughed, teeth showing white. "Yes, yes we are. Couldn't help ourselves." He scratched at the back of his head, producing a small shower of sand. "Come away in and see." Alfred followed as the man barefooted it over the floorboards. "Apologies, by the way—Gad, they call me—should have done the introductions first. The two bruisers are Binns and Duncan. And you?" There was a happiness about him that seemed too fierce.

"Ah, I'm . . ." But there it was, really there at his feet, preventing speech, "I'm . . ." Neatly sawed planking and joist, shoring—and another man, you could hear him, lost inside the hole, over his head and digging, tunnelling out a dream. "You're . . ."

"Had to be done." Gad peered down almost shyly. "Didn't imagine I would when I came here, but—"

He was interrupted by a shout from the excavation. "Gad? Who are you gossiping with now? Another bloody pair of hands, I hope. We'll never get anywhere near at this rate."

Gad turned to Alfred, all benevolent enquiry. "You heard the man . . . You being someone who was here before—you'll understand."

A hollowness spreading in everything: the walls, the chairs, the view stuck up against the window, the lies walking past alive, and you're thirsty suddenly and very tired, head pressing your neck. "I'll . . . I can't today. Tomorrow. I'll maybe come back tomorrow."

"Awful decent of you if you could." Gad's joy shading itself slightly. "Such a lot to do, if we're to put up a proper effort. And the film and that—it takes up our time so."

"I'll . . . if I can." Already easing your weight back, starting your first move for the door. "If I can."

"Cheerio for now."

"Yes. Cheerio. You take care."

"Oh, we do. We do." He pats the cut edge of the wood. "We take care." He's proud.

You nod, have to close your eyes as you spin round to leave.

"You, ah . . . you won't . . ." Gad too polite to continue.

"Of course. I won't tell anyone." Talking to the open door, can't face him again. "No one to tell."

"Splendid, splendid. Well, must get on."

And you run after that, run through the evening light that's thready with dust, run to the shower block—the one with real plumbing for practical use—also employed as a background in several light-hearted scenes. You stand in beneath the water and you wash.

Bod you recognise from Hut 26 comes in. He nods vaguely towards the wall behind you and leaves. He saw that you're fully dressed but didn't mention. Because everybody is mad here, all permanently mad.

You're sitting with Joyce and the world is beneath you, set out in a long, slow scoop that rises to the far slopes and their trees.

"This is good, is it?" You have to check, because perhaps she isn't happy and perhaps you can't make her be—something in your day feels lost and you want to mend it, ease it. "The view and the tea and everything. Isn't it good?" Tea and plum bread given you by a large-handed, powdery woman who says you should call her Dot and come back for more if you want it and smiles as if you and Joyce are a couple when you can't be. "God bless the WI." The city rolling down from you to the meadows and the wreck of the Bishop's Palace at your back, honey walls shedding the May heat, making the air seem heavier, tighter, and behind all of that the cathedral.

See it from miles off, even on the ground—the big box of a spire, calm on its hill. The only proper hill you could find on that plain, that level which did so nicely for building airfields. Drive to it from the drome in about an hour along roads the fens make too easy, too smooth—ditches hiding in reeds to either side if you risk yourself and race, misjudge a bend, stop caring. Pilot broke his neck that way—motorcycle. Can't recall his name and there's no need to since he's gone.

Joyce leans back slightly, stretches out her hand into the grass—she's sitting on your jacket. You love that she's sitting on your jacket, it makes you delighted.

"It is very . . . it's pretty." But everything about her is only sad.

You would like to ask why, but don't in case this has to do with you. "Bit too hot?"

"No, it's just right. London never really seems to get any proper weather. And I don't get out into the country any more. Sorry."

"For what."

"Complaining."

"Complain if you want to. I won't tell anybody."

She smiles at the view, but only gently, maybe tired. There's a dance tonight and you want to go with her, hold her that way, to music—if she's tired, though, perhaps she'll say she'd rather not.

But you won't think that, haven't a way to stand it and so you let yourself lean, lean further, then topple—gently, safely, control the descent—so that your head is rested up against her. Not in her lap, you wouldn't chance that, but your skull is touching, leaning maybe halfway along her thigh—something about which you cannot think too hard.

The light of her—made you want to cover your ugly face—made you want to be so much a better man.

Joyce reaching down then, setting her palm beside your cheek, the too-hot mess of your cheek, and the cool of her was perfect, the mercy of her perfect and lifting you out of your chest, your self, the touch of her gloved in the touch of your mother when she woke you—some old, unfurling memory you can't prevent—her gloved in your mother and your mother gloved in her so that you shake, so that you are terrified.

"Alfie?" The edge of her thumb brushing by the corner of your eye, finding the start of a tear that you hadn't known about, the start of something you can't finish, not here. "You all right? Alfie?"

"Glare." A wild, hot noise inside you that you should never let out. "Not used to so much daylight."

"Well then, close your eyes."

And you do as she tells you and in the red dark you are not alone because her hand is there, so near, so smooth beside your mind.

"Thank you." For taking care of you, when you should take care of her.

Close to a laugh in her voice, a new lightness, "For what, silly?"

You should have noticed that, how it worked—that if you were sad it made her happy.

But you never will know if that was true. If she's been as happy for all of these years as you've been sad.

At the time, you don't mind and she asks you, "What are you thanking me for?"

"For coming all this way. For seeing me. You'm a fine wench. Yo am." A fast, hard weariness hitting you now, a wish for sleep.

To sleep with her.

Wouldn't work.

But I can want it anyway.

And sometimes, when you want, you ask and then you get. But you shouldn't overdo it, should only try just every now and then.

It's the second time she's travelled up to meet you.

It's the second time you've asked.

The first trip was truly awful—having to rush out to Lincoln in the evening and the crew along with you. They said they would like to meet her, that she'd cheer them up, and they were your crew and you couldn't refuse them, not even Cyril Parks. But it turned out they almost ignored her and did what they would have anyway—drinking to not talk about Pluckrose, drinking his money, until they had to say he'd been a pal and a good man and a bloody fool and an utter shit and an excellent navigator and a madman. Joyce had stayed quiet, tucked in between you and Molloy, who was playing the gentleman very well.

But then he leaned across her and asked you, "I'd want to know."

"What's that, Dickie?" You stroked Joyce's arm to keep her feeling she was safe, but she was staring across the room and keeping herself beyond you. No chance to even tell her your mother's gone. And you don't know if you want to, if you can. "Dickie?"

"What they put on his stone, now—I'd have liked a say in that."

"The usual, I'd suppose." You tickled your finger across her hand. She wasn't wearing a wedding ring. But that was about not wanting any talk and should have no particular meaning for you. "The squadron crest. I don't know."

Molloy nodded heavily, agreeing with himself before he spoke. "Should put something he'd have wanted."

And because you knew what that would be—what he'd have wanted—and you missed your poor bloody Pluckrose and were slightly drunk and you fucking bloody missed him, you said out loud what you shouldn't—not with Joyce at your side. "*I wasn't fucking finished*. That's what he'd want."

Knowing it was a mistake as soon as you said it and Joyce having to leave and head for her hotel not too long after, maybe because she was offended, uneasy, maybe because she was frightened you had no chance, were a rotten bet, and you walked her along and up that bastard hill that winded you both, stopped you talking.

But it made her take your arm.

But when she left you at the door of the little hotel she shook your hand, no more.

But she leaned in and told you she'd kiss you if it weren't for the way it would look.

But you wanted to kiss her then and for her to not care how it looked.

"I'm so . . . I was going to say sorry about your friend, but that would sound useless." She folded your hand in both of hers and you started to sweat, although it was a chill night, misty. "If you liked him, he must have been . . . he must have been fine."

"Yes."

"Thanks for asking me, for wanting me—that I should come and see you."

This as if she'd punched you, or torn away something you'd used to hide your face. "Couldn't help it." You want to say about your ma. You want to cuddle her in. You want her to cuddle you in.

"Well, thanks, anyway. Even if this is—I mean, it's a shame you're so busy. But lucky to see you at all." She pressed your hand. "I . . . appreciate you."

"I appreciate you."

But there was no more to be done, not beyond watching the door close with you on the wrong, cold side and then clattering down to catch the bus—the roaring bus, the press of lunatics, the rest of your crew swept away from you in the mob, and you're sat at the back with a strange bomb aimer, just a sprog. The din was almost solid.

Because sometimes there's a chance to scream when other bods are there—don't need them to listen, don't expect it—you understand they'll all be screaming, too.

The bomb aimer beside you spoke about some girl at home when you'd rather he hadn't—although he was talking to himself. And there was crying somewhere, sobbing, and a loud fellow laughing about it and maybe you recognised Molloy's voice binding about watered beer, but you weren't sure and then somebody kicked up singing.

> *"I'll shoot 'em down, sir, I'll shoot 'em down, sir,*
> *I'll shoot 'em down, if they don't shoot at me,*
> *Then we'll go to the ops room and shoot a fucking line, sir,*
> *And then we'll all get the DFC."*

Close air and damp running down the windows, couldn't look out if there'd been anything to watch for and you needed visibility, it worried you to lose it, made you jump, and the thick smell of blue was on you, in you, and the blood under the blue, the meat, and this thing you all feel, this red, loud, hunting thing you have become.

The bus clattered you back to the station and the kites, to the oil and metal places where you now belonged.

Up by the palace it's civil, civilian, civilised.

From the Latin.

You twitch out of a tiny doze, sit too fast and dizzy yourself, blink at her grin.

"Hello."

"I'm sorry, was I . . ."

"Only for a minute or two . . . But now I know you don't snore." After this she brushes her skirt and stands—as if talking about your sleeping was more than she ought to do—and you sit for another moment, stupid with the thought of her and a sour rag left behind from your dream, a kind of mist.

Then you walk with her, lead Joyce on the milky paths and under the shade of chestnut trees, those broad-fingered leaves. A few other bods about, doing much the same—the month just tipping into summer and they're out enjoying it, wanting their year to turn forward as if it had hope, wanting to forget the lousy spring and dirty weather are probably why they're still alive, but now it's clear and dry and fine for flying and will maybe stay that way.

You don't think of flying or death, you only stroll and attempt to be dapper, be RAF beside her. This is the only time you enjoy the uniform, the flight crew wing—people are used to flight crew around here, but they still notice, pause over you more than they might and you hope it makes Joyce think well of you, feel slightly proud. That's what you catch in the watching eyes: in the other people who don't know you, who just guess—that you're something to be proud of. Or else you're their anger, the way it will be expressed. You're going to take revenge for them—because of some loss, or no loss, or nothing to do with the war, some personal hate. Or else you're meant to be their son, or their sweetheart, or their fear, or their dead.

Gets a bit much, after a while.

But you miss it when it goes, cocker. Oh, you don't half miss it when it's gone.

Back in the pale walled streets of Lincoln the afternoon is shaking with its heat and thickening, humidity pressing your skin.

Without thinking, you've wandered with her to the front of her hotel and it seems only sensible to duck inside and have a drink, some shade—the thought of her bedroom burning up above you, the guesses you can't begin to make.

You sip half a pint of shandy and watch while she rocks a sherry, then looks at you for a breath, downs it like medicine—like something to do with you, an antidote you've made her need.

"Alfie, this is . . . I so much like when we're together, or you write to me, or . . . It's all so nice."

A kind of horror in this, because she seems to have made a decision and doing that could hurt you in ways you might not be able to resist. Maybe she doesn't love you and this is where she says so kindly.

Or else she does love you, she truly does.

And you've made her love a dead man, a problem, a disgrace.

And you will believe her, trust her, love her first and love her back.

Her eyes on you, asking something you don't understand, so you take her hand and you face her.

"Alfie. It's—"

A waitress passes with little sandwiches on a tray, she nods to you when she passes, assumes you understand what's happening to you and can like it.

"Alfie, it's so difficult."

"I know."

"I was glad when you asked me to come, because I thought I could say all these brave and sensible things I rehearsed on the train, but I can't now I'm here. I want to be with you."

"I want to be with you."

"I want to be with you."

Wincing because this is where she must tell you that it won't be possible.

"And I think I should be, Alfie, because . . . we don't know what might be next."

You nodding while you corkscrew through the floor and the room pitches round you.

"I want to be with you."

Tight in the base of your spine, pulling you like a stall turn. "I want to be with you." Trying not to crush her hand, because you need it, because it is holding you to the world.

She leans back then, as if something has been decided and she'd thought it would be more troublesome and is relieved it's turned out so well. "Shall we see the cathedral? I think I'd like to."

"I—" and you kiss her hand, like an idiot out of a book, drop your head and do that, but only because you can't think, don't know if it's decided that you're pals now, or if you'll be able to touch her, have her for yourself.

Which I want.

I fucking want.

But what if I can't do it? She's married, she's been married. She'll expect things.

What if I can't do it right?

Or what if she's my pal, because we'm only pals and pals don't fuck their pals?

What if I haven't understood?

You keep your head down.

"Silly." Her brushing your hair at the neck where you're offering it to her—bad position for you, she could kill you with a stroke if she knew how. "Come on. Cathedral. We need to be elevated before the evening. And it's meant to be very pretty."

You go with her because you have to.

You had your own things to tell her that would have been troublesome to say. You will not say them.

The rain runs you inside, leaves you breathing and smiling and flustered while the height of the cathedral shrugs above you, makes you feel giddy and naked.

A church, but not a church, not the kind you've met before. Somewhere for larger people, for a larger idea of God. Gives you something even bigger to disbelieve in—Our Father who art Officer Class—while dull thunder closes in at you and the downpour rustles over the stone far above.

"Gosh, it's a good one, isn't it?" Joyce quite content to be here, to stroll. "The plain glass will be where they've put the proper stuff in storage, I suppose." She takes your hand and means it, would like it to be seen. "On we trot, then."

She is wearing her ring.

Strange smell as the storm continues—nothing of damp about it, more a kind of green, a rush in the columns, as if the whole place is drinking, growing up.

"Almost time." As she leads you towards a wall, a complication of dark, carved wood, stonework. "Evensong. Just what I could do with." Chap in a long blue shift nodding and waving you along to a side door and the church within the church, what she tells you is the choir.

Inside you can recognise the pews, the shape, but not the black oak reaching above you in spires and spires, your sense of it like the moments before take-off when the engines ask to go, strain to be higher and free. Joyce sits in the way someone does when they know what to do and you sit beside her, in among the handful of other nice, officer class people. And when she stands, you stand and watch the choir of old men and children parade in. It's a drill you've never learned and so you're slow as you follow the sitting and standing and kneeling and bowing to the east and you hear prayers for your leaders and commanders and local councilmen and find no more sense in them than in the creed. But Joyce is calm with it, soothed and so you stay and try not see Hell for yourself if you're wrong and there is Something and Hell for yourself if there's nothing beyond yourself and what you do.

It's only at the end you come towards peace, when the pantomime is over and the organ sings and threatens, shivers in the lowest notes, pushes up into the oak and makes it seem to climb. You close your eyes then and let yourself unstick, no words to offend you, just the ache you have to be out in the sky.

Joyce pats your leg and you look at her, see she's content, leave with her past the vicar whose hand you shake and who gives you the blessing kind of smile.

Not my wife, cocker. Another man's. Not what you're thinking at all. And I'm not going back to my lodgings, not tonight — tell them I was drunk, slept under a hedge, whatever lie they'd like — even if I walk about all night, or sleep in the street outside, near to her room. I'm not going back. I want to be with her.

No other wish left, no other prayer. I want to be with her.

And he was.

Alfred Francis Day was with Joyce Melanie Antrobus, née Collingwood.

No truth beyond that one, the little stone he built himself around. The one she took away.

Lying on a bunk so far from her, lost in 1949, awake underneath a short summer night and trying to be quiet while it all bursts through and hurts him — the thoughts you should never be able to find.

Writing Antrobus down in the hotel register, taking his name before I take his wife, Joyce lying about a sudden chance at leave, a nice surprise so that I can join her, Joyce taking charge.

I don't think she'd done such a thing before. I don't think it was a habit.

Turning his head and turning his head while the heath beyond him dreams, his head pressing back in his pillow and eyes closed and no clear memory he can see, only the wonder that her heartbeat was everywhere in her skin.

It had been such a confusion, being too scared of her and scared to hurt her and shaking and the dark being in his way and making him bewildered so that he had to stop and only hold her, cling on, until he could breathe and kiss her.

In the real camp he'd lain and thought of this. Not often—only when he could stand it, when he could still be confident they'd meet again. And even then, he'd learned to be careful: some memories, the ones you'd rather keep—the more you tried to look at them, the more they wore away.

Rationing her out to a kiss. The planning of a kiss. Having faith there would be kisses to come. The life in that, it keeps you well. It feeds you.

Only once a week, letting it be on a Saturday: when I'd lie with the warm of her kiss.

Sometimes things would go further—I'd try to think of talking and romance and coming home, but it would spin down into fucking and being angry and sorry and shamed and just wanting to hide inside her. Wanting to sleep, wanting a true, deep, unlonely sleep.

That's not so unreasonable.

The muscles in his neck cranking his head back further and his breathing too loud and his mind pays no attention, races on, can't wait to uncover everything.

"Alfie."

His own name touching his neck in the heat of her mouth and she'd told him nice things about how he looked and while he lay there, out of anybody's sight, he had been handsome. He had smiled. He had let her feel him smile.

It opens his mouth, this remembering, changes his shape—lets him picture himself as he really is—the twitching little man on the top bunk, bastard who sweats and blubs while everyone else has a kip, still playing their parts—being sleeping men, tired men: men who will stand at the edge of important pictures, men who will be in the background of significant events.

That night with her, I didn't want to sleep.

But the resting was lovely. And the tiny sounds when she shifted a little, or opened her lips, or sighed—and then above us and heading for the Wash, the singing of Lancs, their kind of comfort.

The evensong rubbish hadn't seemed so bad then. I'd slung it back up to the boys—couldn't do any harm.

> *"Lighten our darkness, we beseech thee, O Lord*
> *And by thy great mercy defend us*
> *From all perils and dangers of this night."*

He'd searched between the sheets and found Joyce's hand, squeezed it.

But then he'd been too happy, too relaxed and he'd drifted, dropped past her into a doze where she couldn't reach him. He'd dreamed of the Marl Hole. He'd dreamed what he couldn't tell her, never would.

Going into the Marl Hole. Father used to threaten us with it when we was babbies—said he'd chuck us in the Marl Hole, frit us with it, said horses fall in there and never get clear—they cor ketch hote on the steep of the clay to climb out, they just slip and get drownded, slither on the mustard-coloured sides and get the chop. The water a green that's black, that's terrible, such a depth: yo could tell it'd kill yo.

He watched himself walk through the trees and creep to the edge, lean over in the grass and marigolds to where he could touch the bare marl, to where his weight could almost topple and rush with him down to that cold—he knew it would be cold—right down and into the way that it stares.

I thought if I killed him, my father: then I could drag him through the blackout to the Marl Hole and push him in.

I decided.

Picking up his forty-eight-hour pass, he'd felt himself topple and rush.

Hide him in the Marl Hole.

The hiding had been very clear, the first thing he'd thought of. What came before—what came before was difficult. Not the want, the need to do it, but the planning—he'd read enough stories about crime to know he should have a plan. But he didn't. Not quite.

Lying in tight beside Joyce, he kept still, kept sealed around the night he'd spent in Wednesbury with his father and his plan.

Waited outside the pub, the fucker's pub—the Jolly Collier—no doubt he'd be in there, he never was anywhere else in the evening. Maybe even heard his laugh from inside: him being happy and on his way to drunk, proper kaylied.

Waiting was no good, though, because you'd be seen, you'd be recognised—and hanging about made him angry the wrong way: sick-feeling. So Alfred moved off, shifted up the street and on, started to comfort himself with the dark—because he knew it, spent so long in it at his work, practised seeing what he couldn't see.

His decision was still made, though. Leaving didn't mean he'd changed his mind. In fact, his mind seemed to be fading, couldn't be altered: the longer he walked, the less he heard from it until he was cloudy and numb—a dark in the dark.

Couple making love somewhere—I heard them. Hadn't ever done it myself then, but I'd heard it before. They'd be in a doorway somewhere, or against a wall—people get different in a war. They don't care like they used to. Or else they all turn into who they are, let it show where someone else can feel it, but nobody sees.

After a while, he stepped inside the shadow that had been his street, the rise and lean of its shape around him. Overhead, the stars very big, he noticed—almost a painful brightness. Not much of a moon, but so much other shine up there it could lead you astray, make you stumble.

Ended up I did trip, skinned my hands in the horse road when I landed—trying to save the trousers. Trousers were the King's. Then again, my hands were, too.

The wreck of number 7 welcomed him, let him sit as quietly as he could among the shattered bricks, the clean little ring of them against each other when they shifted.

Thought I heard a rat. Sure I did. Not close, but there.

It seemed correct that he might pray, or ask forgiveness, or say something for his mother, prepare—but his head was all cleared, and the night a high roar of nothing: no judgement, no regulations, just air rising up and chilling to the point where it could kill and the sound of organ music from a wireless—end-of-the-pier stuff—and the bang of an outhouse door and a woman's voice, quite distant, calling the way someone would for a pet.

He could almost have stopped where he was until morning and done no more, gone away without killing.

Almost.

Then the heat coming for him, filling him, and knowing what he should do.

He took a brick in either hand and scrambled out on to the pavement, headed back for the pub.

I can throw in the dark, I can. I have a gunner's aim.

Town's falling to pieces, you can't tell what might happen, what might hit somebody's head. Make it neat—give him what he gave to her.

It's easy to see the journey—remember—eyes closed, eyes open, doesn't matter much—his gunner's skin leading him—his dreams of it afterwards always the same, because from the start it was a kind of dream—driving forward inside the barrel of the night, that cover—feet careful, spine alight and ready—across the lane and further.

And then he got his gift—had the whole matter taken in hand.

Nearly enough to make you thank God. Or thank the blackout.

Because here came the slither and clack of his father's feet—Alfred knowing the noise with a jump in his stomach before he could think—the same as when he'd lain in bed a child and understood bad things would start soon, his father being home would make them.

No one else with him that night. Your father alone. No one else about. No safety.

Stand still. Picture your range. Be invisible.

The first brick leaves Alfred's hand when his father is maybe four feet away, the angle guessed at twenty-five degrees.

"Wha—?"

I missed.

Listened as the brick hit cobbles. It scared him—there was this flurry of cloth and movement and his voice breaking out from him, weak, before he could stop it.

"Wha—?"

I was laughing. No sound but laughing. Aching wide smile. Pass the other brick to my right hand, draw back, let it go, let the fucking world go, let the fucking bastard go, throw your heart, aim it, because that will kill him—your heart, yourself, that makes the kill.

Soft impact. Caught the body somewhere. Not the head.

"Ay, now. Yo . . . Wachyo doin? Ay?" While the fucker's moving, stumbling. "Ay? Yo do—" So you need to follow, go in, finish this. "See . . ." Then he tries a laugh, to be mates with whatever has hurt him. "Hello? . . . 'sonly me, though." A clumsy scuffle of feet as he darts, tries to catch you where you're not. "Just old Arthur . . . Ah—"

And a noise you don't understand, a thud and a drag after and then something hitting water, thrashing in water, fighting up for air.

Fell in the canal, day he? Didn't realise we'd been standing on the bridge—either that, or he didn't realise enough. Tipped himself up and went over the wall, dropped in the cut. Not really deep enough to drown you. Not unless you're drunk and heavy and frit with the shock of it and your feet held in the mud. Then you'd need help to get out. You'd want saving.

"Ay. Hay!" Wallowing din he was getting up—you mithered because someone else might hear and come. "I know yo'm there." Another crash as he punches at the water. "Helpme?"

"No."

Stepping methodically across the road until you kick one of the bricks. You launch it down. You hear it hit him.

"Wha—?"

Speaking quietly. "No. I won't help you." You feel for the other brick.

"Who?"

The churning in the canal frantic now, but also weakening. It has something defeated about it. A man trying to stand taller than he is and failing. A man not breaking free.

"Yo?"

You think he knows you. You would like to think he knows you now.

His voice has become tired and thin.

"Yo."

He doesn't complain when the second brick hits. You have the range now.

Then there are only noises.

Took him a while. I like that it took him a while.

Alfred leaned over the bridge and listened and listened beyond the last trace of movement, the settling of waves against the bank, the return of stillness and reflections, stars.

The dim shape, the one that used to matter, came to rest against the brickwork to the left. Alfred watched in case it moved again.

What might have been an arm seemed to reach for him when he didn't quite look at it.

There was a moment when the head appeared to turn, to shake mildly and Alfred expected eyes, the mouth to open and call him by name. But that didn't happen because the dead stay dead.

Stayed at the bridge a good while—until I heard footsteps—couple of ARPs. Told them good evening, but they hardly saw me—the first of my disappearing. A good gunner always knows how to disappear. A good prisoner always knows how to disappear. A good killer always knows how to disappear. The wardens were sharing a cigarette, talking about a dog race, swinging along. One of them said he was cold.

I was hot and life in me to walk all night, for ever. Went for miles. Such miles.

He'd woken next to Joyce with the sweat of the canal bridge on him, that permanent strange hurt. Remembering a railway station, catching the earliest train to Birmingham.

So he'd kissed her.

No mother, no father, that makes you a finished man—free. So you can kiss whoever you'd like.

She'd grumbled awake and then seen him.

Never understand yourself until someone looks at you like that, finds their joy in you like that.

Or you'll never be more mistaken.

Fuck her.

Fuck her.

Fuck her.

Holding his head in his arms while the phoney barracks slips towards the day.

Lost every letter she sent me before the camp, don't have a word of her left from any time when I was free.

Ivor listening, but also making toast as you talk.

"I was trying to find the place where it happened, but I couldn't remember the street. I thought it was Dean Street, but when I went over there, I wasn't sure . . . It all changes."

"Mm-hm." Ivor with his back to you, busy: a slice of small bread caught inside this huge wire frame he's made for toasting—he extends it to the gas fire and waits. "That's London for you." This always produces bad toast—scarred by the frame and with a peculiar flavour. But now you're both used to it. Prefer it.

"The night it happened, it was after . . . I'd . . ." Not wanting to talk about playing inside a long day of leave: fat summer hours that you could taste and going to the pictures with Joyce, walking in London with Joyce, in brief and acceptable ways, touching Joyce, being cautious—except in the pictures—being terrible in the pictures—your hand hunting up for her stockings and then the gold feel of her skin and catching the fur of her for a moment—all of this she gives you.

Had to stop before somebody noticed.

And she could touch me—I didn't mind it—liked it. Of course. I was hers. Of course. But she never seemed to want too much that way.

Almost the last time I saw her.

So much waiting in those weeks—odd delays, odd bits of leave, unexpected—the seemingly endless hanging about.

It would be Hamburg next, but we didn't know it: Hamburg and Hamburg and Hamburg. But we didn't know it, not yet.

And twenty-three trips done and everything getting scrubbed, seized up.

But she stopped me thinking of it.

Still seven ops to go, as if they were dogging along behind me and we'd never meet.

But Joyce stopped me from thinking of that.

Joyce had to fire-watch in the evening, so you were set off drifting in the city by yourself, her scent on your collar, your fingers, the heat of her in the smile you couldn't help, in your chatting to strangers, in your very happy happiness. "I ended up just wandering, you know."

"Just wandering in Soho . . . How unlike a serviceman." Ivor flipped an overly complicated hinge—design not his strong point—and started abusing the raw side of the bread. "You want this slice?"

"No, you can have it. I'm full."

But you're not full, never can be—you're only sickened, tickle-stomached over Joyce. Wanting to feed the whole time till you're sick, but then you'll remember you miss her and that's the end of it, can't face your bash. So she keeps you near your fighting weight. As near as you get.

The shop's back room was blue with the charring of more than half a loaf. It had been a quiet morning. Nothing to do but toast. No one in and Alfred with the books all to himself, he liked that—patrolling the perimeter, lining the spines up level with the edges of the shelves. "Anyway, I'd met up for a pint or two with Dickie Molloy and Miles and then they'd beetled off—romance to organise elsewhere. And I felt like a walk. Too much energy—needed exercise."

And you knew the roof she watched from. You thought you would go and be where she might see you, or might possibly just sense that you were near.

"I was by myself again and I went out in the street and there was this brown type, a commando."

The man had come up to Alfred, very serious. "You have knowledge of the working of bombs? I am trained in bombs." Perhaps a French accent, foreign anyway, and once you were close enough you could see that he wasn't right somehow, that you should leave him be.

"I know about bombs. Yes. Cheer-o, mate." And Alfred quick to get past him, but then skipping into a doorway and looking out. The commando slewing through the warmish dusk and finding another airman, the only other passer-by—closing on him, patting his shoulders, shaking his hand, the privacy of the street clamping narrowly around them, shades running into shades and breeding, night coming in.

Then the commando breaks away, fumbles in his pack, hands bigger, complicated with something when they emerge. There's a moment when the hollow fretting of London beyond you fades and he raises his arms, looks about him in a way you understand, a way that makes you crouch before you think. He throws something, the thickening blackout taking it, slowing it, waiting.

And then a pounce of noise and flame, the heart of it nodding at you, knowing you as it strips your hiding place, scoops it out with light. Incongruous burst of water, a type of rain—the explosive hit a water tank—and a shatter of windows while the commando folds his arms and nods and the RAF man half dances over to him, claps him on the back.

They hug for a moment and then caper, laugh at what they've done. Then they stroll on arm in arm and you have to follow, track them because

I didn't know why.

Thinking they might do worse and that I'd stop them.

No.

Thinking they seemed like me. Thinking they'd show me what I'd be. Thinking I should understand the flicker of infinity that's showing round their heads.

Behind you the street they've harmed begins to squeal and clamour. You feel fresh glass creak underfoot.

When they reach a junction at New Oxford Street the two men step into the road and then lie down. They settle and stretch. You cannot tell if they are tired or if they would like to be hit now by something, maybe a fire tender heading for Dean Street, an ambulance.

You see a warden approach them, careful. He tips his tin hat just a little forward as he crouches down and you know he is thinking of blast damage, of trying to shield his head. The commando, still reclining, chats to him, hands illustrating something that sweeps and darts. You cannot hear them, even when you pass close by, because they are talking very softly.

"I don't know what happened after that."

"Somebody cleared up the mess. That's what always happens. I've told you before." Ivor seated at the table, cracking his black toast into pieces without the benefit of a plate.

"Somebody like a noble pacifist fireman."

Ivor grinned and leaned forward, set his angle so he could face you with his scar, the bad eye drooping as usual—as if it was drunk and sly. "Now that you mention, we were quite remarkably good at clearing up. One colleague who shall be nameless cleared up bottles and bottles of hazardous Scotch and dangerously scattered items of jewellery and I think, once, several gross of loaded powder compacts."

"It's true what they say—war is hell."

"Apparently so. He dropped through a roof one night and straight down into a warehouse of burning sugar." The toast sounds like clinker when he bites it, talks through a mouthful. "His coffin smelled of toffee." The margarine—grey to begin with—is filthy with fragments.

"Well, it would."

You can take a lot of nonsense from Ivor because of how he looks at buildings—the same way you do.

Walk anywhere and you'll catch yourself calculating out from where the first cookie would fall and blast the buildings open, let the incendiaries in to lodge and play. Difficult to pick where you should live—too near a bridge and you've had it, too near a railway junction, too near a railway station, too near a factory, too near a harbour, an airfield, a prison, a port, a tunnel, a dam, a power plant, a refinery, a river, a road, a canal, a forest, a mountain, your neighbour who's dead already and his house on fire

Wooden floors and wooden roof beams: they'd mean you would be lost, your attic blazing down at you as soon as the tiles were off. Narrow streets and the flame would jump, would feed, would eat your shadows. Your stores of coal and petrol, your broken gas mains, they would burn and serve your enemies, the ones who were trying to kill you. Books and papers would forget themselves and turn to fuel, just like your furniture, your pets, your clothes, your hair.

And so you see targets beside targets: nothing but targets and ghost craters looping up from the earth, shock waves of dust and smoke ringing, crossing. You feel the aerial photograph staring down at you where you stand, waiting to wipe you away. You always are a target under naked air.

And sometimes you dream of the men and the bombs and the targets all learning from each other, testing and perfecting, changing—except that they really stay the same—are built around numbers and burning, which is to say, around death.

But you don't talk about death.

You only ever say you have knowledge of the working of bombs.

"You got any?" Ivor swaying his mug back and forth as if this would produce more tea, shake it out of the corners in some way.

"Got any what?"

"Toffee. I could just fancy a toffee. Or a Pontefract cake. How many Pontefract cakes to a coupon?"

"Do I look like a fucking confectioner?"

He taps his fingers lightly against his good cheek. "No." And then tilts his head again, squints at you like a starling—some type of bird anyway, an ugly type of bird. "What you look like is browned off. What's up?"

"Nothing."

"Shouldn't tell lies—they blacken the tongue. My mother said so and she was always right."

"Thought you got all your advice from your nanny."

"I think you're confusing me with someone else."

And he's right—the accent, the height of him—you're not an idiot, you have realised—there are days when you want to confuse him with someone else.

He winks his bad eye, the thickened lid, smiles in the way that he does when he knows he's right.

Pluckrose.

There are days when you would like him to be Pluckrose, when you like him because of Pluckrose, when you try to confuse yourself with someone else.

He wrestles up out of his chair with more effort than he needs and brushes his cardigan. "Well, I believe I shall take out the badger hairbrush and clean some upper edges in the dusty stock, get those pages good and spotless." You've made him angry—the shine of it resting just beneath his skin. "Want to join me?" Clipping his words.

"There's only one brush."

"Ah . . ." He pauses, close enough that you can smell him—this vaguely rank, musty scent of a man who lives alone and always will and doesn't much care. You try to do better, keep fresher than that. He leans low to be level with you. "I see it now."

"What?"

"A bit of guilt."

"None of that."

"No, I definitely saw it. Passing like a tiny cloud. Definite guilt."

"I have none." You don't know if he means about your friendship—that it's really built out of a dead man he never met. "I've none." Or maybe he wants you to think of the other thing, the bombs.

"Of course, of course. No reason for anything other than innocence. No need to be guilty." He nudges your shoulder and winks again. "You got away with it."

He's a fucker sometimes, Ivor. Sometimes he's a shit.

"I'm not doing it. I'm a bloody gunner. You want to lose a gunner then you're off your bloody head." The Bastard crouched up in the fuselage of B for Beer. "I won't do it. I don't care."

The rest of the crew packed up along with him, crushed in the space which is no space at all, between the main hatch and the first-aid kit and the oxygen bottles and the spare parachutes and the Thermos stowage and the evil bumps and angles of your fuselage: above and below and port and starboard sides.

Things are even more cramped than usual because of the secret bundles loaded in beside the catwalk.

The secret brown-paper bundles are why they're here.

Molloy sits with his back to the others, legs hanging down from the doorway. Alfred has perched up on the slope that takes him to his turret, where he belongs. Nothing to bang his head on that he doesn't know about.

Times like this, you'd think—how would we ever get out, really? If we had to. She never would let us leave her. All of our Lancs, they love their airmen, keep a tight hold of us right down and into the ground.

The skipper is staring out beyond Molloy at the sun which is low now, dropping into evening, into the run-up to the op. "Well, I agree."

"I won't fu—" The Bastard eyeing the skip, then the rest of the crew. "Then why . . . ?"

"I only said that was the suggestion. They've never used this stuff before. But I think it's a stupid suggestion. We need all the guns we can get."

The Bastard tries catching Molloy's eye, but Molloy won't turn his head, only offers stiffened shoulders and a drift of cigarette smoke. Parks, because he always states the obvious, heaves in with, "I'd do it, guys. I would. But somebody has to let loose with a bundle every minute. That's what they say. Try taking a star shot and doing that—I mean, it won't wash, right?"

"We know." Molloy apparently talking to the doorway more than the crew, glancing up very slightly and murmuring. "We all know that."

"I couldn't navigate . . . Boss is no use."

"Thanks a lot."

"I mean, you've got to be where you always are, bud. And we can't mess around with Miles."

"I should say not."

"Torrington's not an option—we have to let fly on the bomb run, too, drop this stuff all the way. And Skip's . . . the skipper."

"I'll do it." Molloy sways round and in, leans one knee against the edge of the hatch. He sighs, hamming it up. "I'll throw the bloody stuff. I'm the only one who can. But should you happen to need an engineer during your trip—I would point out, you'll be taking a shit."

The skipper watching him, playing the innocent. "If we have any trouble you can chuck the whole lot out at once . . . I suppose." In his hands, he folds and unfolds a black paper strip, it is backed with aluminium, shines and then hides its shining. "Or you could deal with things and then get back to this." Bundles of God knows how many strips stacked at their side, all ready for Molloy to unwrap them, push them out.

"Not that I would ever presume to suggest what you should do." Their new secret—just paper and foil.

"Oh, and I've never known you to . . . you keep clear of that nonsense, don't you . . . you being just the skipper and our humble servant." Molloy nodding, content to be the centre of attention.

"Absolutely. I would never think to try."

"All of that giving orders carry-on . . ."

"Not important to a modern air force."

"I see." Molloy sucks his teeth, almost giving in and chuckling, "Well, on the whole, I should say we'd be better off not having trouble, or else we'll be dead on our hole." He gives the crew his most solemn face, frowns the black of his eyebrows down so far it's a wonder he can see. "So keep all your gen boxes working, you bastards—and I hereby commend the engine to St. Rita. Let nothing go on fire and catch any shrapnel you see, just put it in your pocket for later, because I shall be unavailable: shoving their mystery bundles down the flare chute—and they'd better work, so. Or I'll be back and haunt the boffins to their graves." He draws on his cigarette as if it's offended him badly again and then snaps his head back and grants them a huge, rattly laugh. "I could sit on your lap, Miles, and pitch them through your window. Would that suit you? However I do it, I'll end up bloody frozen." He raises his huge, clever mitts and turns them in front if his face. "And these were magic hands . . . appreciated by so many in so many lovely ways."

Miles grips hold of both Molloy's magical wrists and gazes at him fondly. "You can sit on my lap any time. But I'll want nylons and a fish tea and all of your Horlicks tablets in return."

"You're a shocking demanding bastard."

The skipper adjusts his flying cap—the one that was pristine once, respectable, the one that makes him seem an old sweat now, because he is. "And we appreciate the sacrifice." Every man of you old sweats now, even Parks.

"And it is good to be appreciated, Pilot Officer Gibbs."

"Yes, but enough of the bollocks for now. Thank you, Dickie."

"Didn't expect any better."

"Shut up." The skipper kicks Molloy gently. "Anyway, it's the only solution. And possibly they'll sort themselves out better for the next time."

"Have you ever known it?"

"Boys." Skip giving the crew his slightly crooked, pleased grin. "This is what we've always wanted—a lovely new secret weapon of our very own." He punches Alfred's foot. "Can't complain when you've got a secret weapon."

Alfred grins back, doesn't have to say they will be safe because they have the skipper and no more could be required. "Let's see if it works first."

Molloy lets out a high bark of amusement. "Now when were we ever supplied with a thing that didn't work? The very thought . . ."

Skip makes to go and Alfred echoes the move—he likes to keep his safety in sight, likes to check that all is well. On flying days nothing should bother the skip, which means Alfred keeps an eye on him when he can, gives himself this new gunnery duty, to see no one pesters his captain.

"There you go, Boss." And the skipper folds their secret weapon in half one last time and then hands it to Alfred. "For luck."

And for luck, when the time comes, Alfred will bring out the gramophone and their record and his captain and his crew will stand with him and ready themselves for the trip.

"Come on then, lads. Work to be done. Can't precisely remember what, but I'm sure that we have an appointment of some kind tonight."

But Hanson, of course, interrupts. "Hang about, hang about. While we're here, we might as well." He prods both of his gunner's thumbs into his waistband, wriggles his fingers with significance. "Mightn't we."

"God, you're a filthy hound." But the skipper nods and, Molloy leading, they jog themselves down the ladder and out to the tailwheel.

The shock of sunlight leaves them squinting at each other.

"Home and no trouble every time we've done it." Hanson unbuttoning his fly. "You can't argue with that."

So they set to and duly watered the rubber of the tyre. Which still made Alfred blush—it was discourteous. He'd rather speak to B for Beer the way Molloy did, the way they maybe all did—or sing to her, or kiss her, God knew what would please her most.

As he'd run down the ladder he'd patted her skin, felt it warm and living.

Hamburg tonight. Hamburg and a secret weapon and the skipper and B for Beer. No one could argue with that.

The camp was getting edgy, out of trim.

End of next week and we'll be gone.

There was no cause for alarm, no reason to think there'd be trouble of any kind, but the place was unhappy nonetheless. This morning some bod had been crying in the mess tent. Gad—Alfred thought it had been Gad—had ambled up and intervened, but whatever was wrong had stayed wrong. There was bickering in the showers, in most places. Part of it was waiting, just the old, old chilly friction, the lick of it in your chest.

> "We fucking hate to fucking wait,
> For fucking night to fucking fight
> The fucking Huns with fucking guns,
> H fucking Es, in-cen-dia-rees
> Can't fucking wait to fucking fly
> Can't fucking wait to fucking die."

Behind Alfred an evening cricket game was turning pettish. He was wandering over to the fence, daring himself to lean right up against it, to not even sweat a little or think of guard towers—of goons watching, firing—of bods watching and thinking he was cracked.

A squawk of irritation rose from the game at his back and he half turned to it, only realised he'd caught the ball when he saw it in his hand.

"Well done, that man."

Alfred liking the familiar, night-time ache where the leather had hit his palm. He smiled.

Didn't know you still had it in you, did you, our kid? Smart hands—like Cardini.

A sweating type was trotting up to him, extending his arm. "I say . . . well done, that man." He wanted the ball back.

Alfred wanted to keep it. "If you say so." He tipped his head to the side and carried on smiling. "I wouldn't know." He folded his arms.

"Splendid catch . . ." The man was in front of him, tubby and puffing, unused to exercise. "But we do need to go on with our game." Must have a soft job somewhere, desk work.

"Do you." A kind of laugh knocking about next to Alfred's spine and him thinking of how soft his job was these days, too, and thinking he wouldn't go back to it, that he didn't have to. "That's nice."

And the man darting in as if he would snatch the ball, but only holding fast to Alfred's shoulder and whispering close to his cheek, "We'd like to take your picture. Just a harmless snap. Civilian clothes. Could come in handy. Hut 4. Let us know."

"You what?"

The man hopped back, smoothed his hair. "Good show." He nodded, a drop of sweat falling from his nose.

Alfred took the ball and threw it as hard and as far as he could, watched it clatter the slant of a hut roof and disappear. The cricket team grumbled at him, but only mildly—as if they were glad of something clear they could all be annoyed by. The man only stood and nodded again before starting up a heavy trot, heading off along the line of Alfred's aim.

It had been a good throw—and a good catch, the kind he'd have made six years ago—and there was a logic in that—with the waiting, you knew, there would always come this speed, this depth, this terrible growth in your life until you could barely hold it any more.

Colours—they'd be so sharp and loud they'd spread into each other, until you'd be glad of the dark—and stepping out among civilians, away from your crew, you wouldn't quite believe that anyone could be so flat, so sleepy—and the taste of the Sally Army sandwiches, the bread and jam— it would be like music—and music, that would make you cry, the way it slipped over you, threaded through your fingers and raised your hair—and Joyce.

"Do you put this in your mass observations?" Standing beside her bed when you say this.

And she is almost shy when she tells you, "You're meant to make a record of everything," and doesn't look at you, but the shape of her mouth is flirting, "I try to do my bit," and when her eyes do find you, your hands tremble.

"But you don't, do you . . . ? not everything. Would you?"

Joyce lying on the golden quilt because you asked—on the spare bed on the golden quilt, although you shouldn't be here in her flat, not at all, not together, not even in the day because someone may notice your calling or leaving and may talk—the whole city is nothing but talk—only you don't care and the gold is flaring up around her so that she seems to be lying in bright grass, in fur, sunk into a glimmering fur.

"What I'd, that is . . . Who reads it?"

"I'm not sure." The whole of her so close and you've never seen her like this before, never will again—she's never shown you—the way she's shining and naked and naked and shining, the way she is alight. One ankle tucked beneath the other, her right knee bending out towards you, open. "But I just tell them . . ." She takes your hand and holds it, watches you standing while you wonder what to do, what she'd like best. "I say how I feel and not names and not anything—not anything terribly much, really." There's a tremor in her grip, this shake of pressure she may not mean.

"Are you cold?"

"No."

"Do you . . ." You rub your thumb in the curve of her palm and start again. "I would . . ." Hands and her forearms brown with the sun, but everywhere else so pale, so more naked and she may want you to be this way, too, but you maybe can't, can't undress in daylight, because of being not an oil painting by any means, not a handsome man—but then her mouth makes that shape again and you kneel on the bed and you bend and you bow to her and hide your face in kissing her breasts, the one and the other and back and forth—little breasts, an upward tilt in them and pretty enough to make you cry, although you don't: you kiss and lick which you never dared till now—had only heard about it, nodded while Dickie Molloy said the ladies enjoyed it, told you this often in several bars—and this is her nipple in your mouth and it tastes of her smiling and makes you have to bite while she cups your head in both her hands and she does seem to enjoy it, does breathe and live and shiver underneath you, hot skin at your hands, and her legs rise in, hug in, around you so that you die of her nicely, you go away.

My Best Blue covered with her.

And then me. My best me.

Pretty enough to make you cry.

Keeping still for the thoughts to hit him, letting them find his range. Sometimes he'd do it for company—let in just enough hurt to make himself seem alive.

And then it's very easy to run and press against the wire links of the fence, hook in his fingers clear above his head and hang.

Asking for it, you are, cocker.

Ar, but I won't get it—never do.

But it wasn't his fault, not entirely, this lack of evasive action. He'd started the day badly with a dream of the crew bus: hearing it draw to a halt outside the hut and then the footfalls, the heavy, messy sound of his boys quite unmistakable: his crew walking up in their flying boots, climbing the steps and then pausing.

Cold in his sleep, he'd watched himself slip from his bunk and listen, ease forward, listen again until he was beside the door, no more than a half-inch of wood between him and his proper family, his dear friends. But he couldn't hear another sound from them. He couldn't hear their breath.

They'd scared him.

Nothing to it, of course, when you were awake, back in reality. Not that reality wasn't a funny word: that which exists and is real, but also that which underlies appearances, that which is true. So that which you see, but also that which hides inside it.

This made things slippery, meant you could take a while to shake your dreams—even once you were stood on your steps and awake in the daylight and your bare feet warm on the wood and the usual bods binding off towards the showers and everything as it should be, or as near as you could hope.

Alfred supposed bits of dream would always work out through him now—the way that tiny shrapnel splinters would sometimes break up through his skin, finally leave him.

He shook himself, rattling the fence, and then let go, sat in the dust with his back against a post and the camp growing quieter ahead of him, preparing for another night.

So *think yourself lucky while you're awake and remember a happy crew.*

Think of Hamburg on the Magic Night.

22:50 and they went out neatly, just as they should—you couldn't fault Parks, he was always on his route.

"Burton Coggles, Carlton Scroop, Sloothby . . ." But he never tired of reeling off place names as they drove for the coast. "Mavis Enderby—it's great that you guys really would call anywhere Mavis Enderby. Sounds like a librarian . . ."

Skipper let him run for a while and then closed him down. "You get two more and then you shut up." It was all part of how Alfred started—checking RT and oxygen, pressing the cheek piece on his reflector sight, the comfort of it—feeling the wool of Joyce's hat comfy on his head and thinking of her, just the once, before he hides her all away—and hearing random offerings from the map.

"Worlaby Carrs."

"And this from a man born in Nanaimo—wherever the bloody hell that is. One more. Then it's business."

Lincolnshire a still, dark fabric sweeping back from Alfred and B for Beer singing out well, lively as she twitched and sprang in the busy air—

her squadron up with her· her wing and her group and those beyond hers: maximum effort. Other Lancs and Stirlings, Halifaxes, Wimpies— the thought of them rising with Alfred: silhouettes that made him faintly homesick, more distant gleams and shades, everyone turning, finding their ways.

"Thorpe in the Fallows and Spital in the Street."

"That was two. Now shut up."

And the idea of being watched, expected. All day they'd tested radios, flown circuits—squadron upon squadron, giving their game away. And now the higher they climbed, the quicker they'd be seen. Twenty-three ops completed: that could tend to make you feel anxious for your thirty.

Then came the long moment—Alfred knew it every time—when the Lanc drew herself out and over the coast, crossed the line—it shivered in her spine and rocked him.

The skipper told them, same as always, "Here we go then." Far-off voice, but to Alfred gentle-seeming, sure, and tonight it was Mablethorpe that dwindled out from under Alfred's feet and left him to shrouded water and to air.

"Fuck the lot of you. The whole pack." Molloy breaking in on the RT— the weight of Lancsound receding for a breath.

Alfred quiet in his turret, but smiling while the Skipper asks, "I said, are you ready?"

"On my way. Then five, four, three, two—here goes fucking nothing. Don't thank me."

"Chiefy will give you the nails for your cross when we get back home. Shut up and go."

And nothing more as Molloy heads back along the fuselage and starts his work.

No discernable difference as they jostle on, the enemy coast slicing closer in to meet them and Alfred turning, searching, turning, quartering his sky. This feeling, though, this kind of flurry in his mind.

What if it works?

Light from the route markers tumbling, spilling down yellow-golden—like a tree that grows out from its crown and not the root, like a liquid that is air and fire, like something wonderful against nature. But keep your eyes away, don't want to be night-blinded—and the shimmer of something new, the secret cascading from the shapes of other planes, a storm of metal strips that deepened every minute.

The first Alfred knew about the magic was when he heard laughing— Skip laughing—sounding like somebody else, a boy—and then Hanson and the rest and they're shouting to Molloy and laughing.

Then Alfred sees why—there rolling back from him: this strange, dark channel, searchlights with their beams laid and twitching along the ground, as if they've fallen—others further off that have frozen, tipped straight up: these blue-white columns that cannot harm them, cannot find them. One to port swings and dithers and then drops, exhausted. There is a distant shake of flak, but Alfred can feel there's no sense in it, more a little burst of panic.

Jesus.

He doesn't laugh, is too happy for that.

They leap as the bombs go down, B for Beer feeling giddy, and the job done well tonight, right on the green TIs, slap where they should be. Shorten the war, that's what you want. Hurt them. Hurt them enough and then more than enough, just make an end of it.

The turn for home lets Alfred watch the naked city: small, straight glimmers from canals, shine of the lake, the white scatter of incendiaries as they bite, redden: thick folds of smoke like panels of night, of nothing-ness, and a cookie folding open, hooping itself round with shock and shock, bright and then settling into fire, more smoke. He shouldn't look, but this is Magic Night and so he does.

And for the first time he didn't feel they would come after him for this, because they couldn't. Even dazzled, with dull ghosts in the black wherever he looked, he was sure that nobody was going to hunt up and catch them. Not that he didn't still search, blink, get himself back to nor-mal and concentrate, keep watching his skipper's back. But tonight they could do what they liked, he understood: they could break everything and burn it.

And go home.

"You will light"

Singing as they cross the English coast.

"My way tonight"

Suddenly wishing hard, almost praying, staring so far into the black that his eyes are tearing, because getting careless now would be so stupid, such a waste of their finest raid. Everyone maybe thinking the same and very quiet now as they circle and then make their most delicate landing.

Before they gather up their gear and then come tumbling, scrambling out to the dawn, the sky that's one huge glow, a wide promise of morning that still smells hot and summerish from yesterday, but yesterday he'd done twenty-three and now it's twenty-four.

Hardly one of them making sense in the debriefing and the intelligence bods wanting gen on their secret weapon, on code name *Window*—them and their bloody code names—and questions and questions, but even they were hearty, satisfied, quite patient—and you're hungrier than ever in your life and Molloy is singing—face and hands blacked up like Jolson from the strips he's been chucking about all night and singing something Irish that you don't know, but you love it, you love him, you love the skipper, you love bloody everything.

And when they let you go you got washed, had a good, long swill and fitted down into your bed, clean in your bed and tired, but you couldn't sleep, the light inside yourself too raw to let you rest and so you only lay until you knew it was some kind of a decent hour and the phone box would be unlocked and you ran, you pelted out and called her.

"Hello?"

"God, you'm a good wench."

"Alfie?"

"I was reading this . . . in Shakespeare. I was reading . . . *If then true lovers have been ever crossed* . . . I was thinking . . . You all right?"

"I was up rather late, watching for fires."

"Oh, I'm sorry. I just . . ." You can't talk about what you've done, it's not allowed. "I wanted to hear you." You can't talk about what you're going to do. "That's all. And to say good morning."

Be like Dad, keep mum.

Lousy bloody line.

"Did you have a hard night?" Then checks herself, because that's a bad question and she's sensible, responsible. "I mean . . . bad dreams."

"No. No, I didn't. I didn't." Sick and hot and golden with needing her. "You go back to sleep now. Get your rest."

"Yes, I'm sorry . . . But yes—you, too." Noise of her hand on the receiver. "And I—"

"Yes."

"It was nice to hear from you."

"Good." Sick and sick and sick with needing her. "And I love you."

"I know."

"Wishing will make it so, just keep on wishing and care will go."

They'd been walking home, missed the bus, and Hanson warbling on, *"Dreamers tell us dreams come true, it's no mistake."* Widening his hands and paddling them free in the night, dragging and skipping across the smooth width of the road.

Twenty-five.

Window keeping things sweet.

Twenty-five done.

You could see it in the crew: all of you starting to brace against that final five and trying not to mither about Window and when the Jerry boffins would work their way out to a cure.

Twenty-five. Essen not so easy, not so wonderful—but easier than Essen should be. Landing with a little ventilation knocked through the port vertical fin. You'd seen the line of that: the thick glow of the fragment sniping in to hit.

Landing with a lot more ventilation knocked into the Krupps works—because we're good at what we do—we know our business.

Twenty-five.

The thought of those other five woke with you, was ready and rubbing your mind before you could even think of Joyce.

Molloy not himself about it. He'd got this blank, stiff grin most evenings and you could almost hear something hinging in his mind. "Shut up with that fucking nonsense, willya?" Molloy yelling at Hanson, but his eyes finding Alfred: wet and large, bewildered.

And maybe he saw the same in me — all right when we didn't have a hope. But then we did. We genuinely had a chance. There's nothing more unbearable than knowing you might have a chance.

Molloy swinging his boot at the wall, giving it his weight. "It never made anything so."

"Very clever, I'm shewer. Fuck you."

"You can fucking wish yourself . . . you can wish yourself . . ."

Alfred could see that Molloy was limping, had hurt his foot, but still he was off running.

"And wishes are the dreams we dream when we're awake."

Molloy seeming taller as he leaves them, thinning into the grey light.

Alfred wanting to follow, but Skip catching his arm, telling Hanson, quite sharp, "Hanson, that isn't a song that we like. And don't try another, please, old man. Let's get some peace."

"Skip?" The country round about them busy with sounds in a way that troubled Alfred.

"Yes, Boss?"

"I was . . ." Beyond their footfalls there was scurrying in the ditches by the road and a cry that might be a fox or an owl, might be something hurt, he didn't know — too much going on, so you couldn't relax. "The way things are now — it's safer, ay it — with Window?" Beer making his tongue unreasonable. "I mean."

The skipper clasped an arm round his shoulder. "I know."

"I was —"

"I know — we need to be quick about it. Really bloody quick." Skip nodded heavily and his hand reached round and tugged at Alfred's hair, dropped back to his collarbone again. "Get the ops in. I know. Doing the best I can, Boss."

" 'Course you are."

"Tell you another thing." He broke away from Alfred and looked at him, stood and made him stand while the others straggled past them. "I tell you this." And he took off his cap, reached out his hand. "That one more you've got to do. That one. I'll fly you."

"No, you—"

"I'm twenty-six, you're twenty-five. I remember." He waited. "I'll fly you."

And Alfred removed his own cap, "You're the skipper," and shook hands.

"You're the boss."

The road shifting slightly under Alfred with how late it was and how strange and how good, how difficult to look at his captain now without acting soft. "That's if we'm both still here."

"Naturally." Skip started walking. "Otherwise, we'll be resting and no more they'll ask us to do. You never know, though, about heaven, what with it being up—Air Council Instructions, they might still operate . . . you never know."

Alfred wasn't in love with the concert party: it was getting to be hard work—the director looking for something they couldn't provide and too many technical problems and delays. All morning, they'd sat in rows and watched the same little dance routine, the same fragment of singing, the same bit of patter with three actors messing it up, dressed in frocks and tits and mophead wigs. And over and over, Alfred had clapped and clamoured and yelled as he was ordered, because he was in the audience and the audience was to enjoy itself and laugh. The audience was not to feel stifled, was not to wipe sweat from its face so often that it started to imagine itself raw: skinned, bleeding from its collar to its hair.

And the more he laughed, the more it sounded queer to him—and the voices round him, they were splintering into something that seemed fearful, or hungry, or in pain. After a while, he didn't want to look at the other men, in case they were altered in some way that would come to be dangerous.

Funny: when you're a kid you're scared of all sorts—noises at night and the Hand of Glory and the rats in the back of the coal-hole and the brewer's old Sentinel steam wagon, how it rattles and screams like the boiler might burst. But you're wrong.

It's only people who can harm you. You can never be scared enough of them.

So there'd been days back in London when the shop would have to hide him: when he could barely get there, hardly leave. He couldn't tolerate a bus, the tube, a tram, even the busier pavements—and his evenings would mostly be spent in the back room with Ivor, the street door locked and bolted against people—the only way of leaving to be in the dark, tucked against walls in the still of darkness and trying to remember that he could see well, that he was used to being ready, that he would take care of himself. Then he'd dash for his lodgings, get in, tiptoe up the boarding-house stairs and into his rooms—hope that he'd be tired enough to sleep, that no one would cough, or drop their shoes on the floor above, or stumble at the uneven landing, or pull the chain too loud—hope nobody would do something to claw him up awake and leave him staring at nowhere, clinging to his bed.

People, they got everywhere: the heave of them and their eyes and hands and teeth and a mind that you couldn't predict, something terrible inside their clothes, their blood.

Not now, cocker. You'm among friends here. Or not enemies, anyway. Easy with yourself, go easy.

Alfred's scalp was constricting and a dizziness was sinking in him. The concert stage—with suitably homespun backdrops—was empty. He wanted to think this meant the whole nonsense was over, but no one had said so and the mob on the benches around him was staying put.

Forcing the movement, Alfred turned to the lad on his left and made himself find the boy human, civilised. And the chap did seem a nice kid: polite, only twenty or so, less. He was dressed as a naval flyer and intent on supporting the show, giving out hoots and whistles at quite arbitrary points. The kid's face, the line of his back—they made it very clear that he was monstrously relaxed.

Of course, the kid could feel Alfred's look—we all can feel when we're under somebody's attention. "Something up?"

"No, no."

The lad studied him. "You all right? Seem a bit green, old man. If you don't mind my saying."

"It's the heat."

Up on the stage, a proper entertainer sidled across and settled himself with his ukulele, twiddled a few chords. The kid gave a viciously approving whistle. "Corklino, that's a bit more like it." He nodded to Alfred with a reassuring grin, "This'll take you out of yourself."

Alfred hadn't heard anyone say *corklino* in years. "Yes." Obviously, the lad was trying to get himself into the part—because it was only a part and so he could, like, not take it personally.

"It's a bit old hat, of course." The kid who had never really met the war—you could see this in him—but here he is looking battle-stained but triumphant like a snap from *The War Illustrated* and he's using the word *old* far too often. "But I don't think we'll get any better." He whistled again, one of the soundmen flinching in response.

"No. I don't suppose we shall."

The entertainer cranked out a familiar number about the Maginot Line and Alfred tried not to remember Formby singing it better when the Maginot Line had still mattered and tried not to seem an older and older man with every breath.

You're not thirty yet, cocker—buck up. Years to go, yet.

And is that a threat, or a promise?

Haven't a clue, just slap your hands together like you're meant to, there's a good boy.

And he did manage clapping in time with the others, even stamped a bit, although it jarred his knees.

Twenty-five, going on fifty—however I look. However fit I get.

And then something jammed, or snapped, or otherwise went US with one of the cameras and the pack of them were ordered out to have their tea break early.

It was, naturally, no cooler outside, but there was a half-hearted breeze and the possibility of dispersal, of shade and relative peace. Alfred gathered his mug of tea as fast as he decently could and then sat in the sand at the dark side of Hut 21.

Which is where Vasyl found him.

"Ah, yes."

The toes of Jerry boots messing up the quiet sand that Alfred had been studying, smoothing in his mind. Probably they were real Jerry boots. War surplus. The whole bloody world, up to its ugly neck in surplus.

"Ah, yes. So here is where you hide, Mr. Alfred."

"No. This is where I sit. If I was hiding, you wouldn't find me."

One of the boots scuffled a touch to the right and then both rocked back on their heels with a creak Alfred didn't want to recognise.

"Have you thought any further—"

"I won't sell you the gun."

"Not to worry, old man. There will be plenty of time to discuss this. When I am in London."

This intended to make Alfred look up, which he did. "You won't be in London." That uniform leaning over him, Vasyl's grin drawing the heat from the day, putting a dirty chill on Alfred's skin, so he had to rub his face with his sleeve. "You're a liar." Staring straight ahead now, keeping steady.

"If you weren't my friend, Mr. Alfred, I would be very angry to hear that you say so." Vasyl fanned his hands out ahead of himself, acting harmless, and then moved round to crouch beside Alfred, to lean against him. "I have suffered a long delay, but now everything will be quite fine."

"Anyway, I'm never in London." Alfred concentrating on the sand, the idea of sand.

"Now I think you are perhaps not telling the truth. Everyone here has an address, a record of their address. This is only practical. Very easy to check where somebody lives."

"They won't let you in."

"I will be a good citizen. Obedient. A good citizen is obedient."

"They won't let you in."

"To your house?"

"To my country. They won't let you in to my country."

"Whyever not?"

"Because you're—" And Alfred intending for a moment to be cautious here, but then remembering a knife in the ribs would solve any number of his problems, perhaps all. "Because you're not who you say you are."

Vasyl only made a breathy type of laugh that shook through Alfred's mind, turned him slightly nauseous. "It doesn't matter who I say I am. You know two years ago, your government accepted a whole division." The pressure on Alfred's side increased as Vasyl fitted close, whispered, "A Waffen SS division—all waiting in Italy and then all declared very good immigrants. From the Ukraine. What do I worry? You like us now. We are much better than the Russians, the Communists. And we are very healthy, very intelligent. We are ideal."

Alfred tried to stand, be elsewhere, but Vasyl threw an arm around his shoulder.

"Do you want to know?" There was a surprising strength in Vasyl's grip, a meat smell from his breath. "Do you want to know who I am? The truth. I think you do. I think you have wanted to know for a long time and so I will tell you, because you are my friend."

"I don't care." Alfred had no energy for a fight, somehow—at least not while Vasyl had the height, the advantage. He let himself be pressed down into his place. "I really don't care, Vasyl. Be whoever you like."

Vasyl softly knocked his head against Alfred's, then eased back. "They came in the summer. In '41. When it is hot this way, I remember. You never knew this—the way it is when they come—in the Nazi time. It is like being born. In my home, this was in my real home town—not in the Ukraine—I am from Latvia, but I think it is better now to be from the Ukraine—in my home they come with trucks and tanks and then everything is different and simply only walking about is wonderful because you are so light. When the Nazis come, they take away everything that stopped you moving—it is almost possible you might fly." Vasyl pausing and smiling at Alfred, as if this were bearable, a story, something sentimental and lovely—but also smiling as if he would like to see Alfred opened, emptied out. "A lot of us feel it, this being light, and we try and see what it means. We can tell it means something. So we say what we want to say now, what we want to be, and they are . . . the Germans, they are like fathers—they watch us: how we grow. It's many years since they have been born, but I think some of them like to watch it happening to us.

"And after that we *do* what we like. We find out what we like—and we like what the Germans like. It is very special to obey them and be a part of such a thing. I took . . ." He chuckles and rubs in the dirt with his forefinger. "I took this woman's basket of food—eggs, some bread, sausage. I took it from her, because my mother needed it rather more and because I wanted to and because the Germans were happy to see me do it, they watched me and they were happy."

"Who did you take it from?"

"Nobody."

"Who did you take it from?"

"You know." He smiles. "Nobody." He pushes how fine he's feeling into the silence between them. "You know. Windows, I broke. A little chicken house, I set on fire. You would never believe you would do such things, but then you realise your town is spread out for you now, smooth as a tablecloth—the first time—your town is really yours and this is what you always wanted—to take it."

The earth under Alfred seeming to thin until it is a tissue, a weak thought stretched across a place the dark has burrowed out, a place with no words.

"Then one morning I don't go to work. A lot of us, we don't go. I'm in my shirtsleeves, it's a warm morning—and our baker and our postman, the grain merchant, the station master—very many men also that I didn't know—and we are all in our old clothes, or in overalls—the station master is dressed for a country walk—we had each one separately decided that our worn clothes might be most suitable. Some of our women they come, too, but they don't help much. It is us, the men: we are here and we are going to prove we are new and finished with being born and growing very fast to be true men and our fathers are watching and we have our sticks—our fathers have guns, but we don't need them yet—our sticks are better, they let us understand.

"I hit a female first. Only because of the noise she was making. I didn't know her well: but her husband, he worked making baskets, I think, and sold them, travelled with them. Someone else was killing him. I hit her six, seven times and then some more, because in the beginning you can't stop. But others were coming, they were being driven out, and so I left her then and took a boy I hated. He had been in my class at school for a while. You always knew he thought he was better, thought he was a little bit disgusted with us. But he was still a boy and I was a man now. He was easy. He pissed himself. Partly, he was easy because he was trying to cover up where he was wet and not covering up his head—still wanted to seem better than everyone around him.

"He's almost the last one that I can remember properly. I thought I would remember all of everything, but you don't. It becomes incomplete and then you do more and forget more and then it is very, very long ago and you are different."

Vasyl rubbing the heels of his hand together with a small, dry sound, but he keeps talking, he keeps on.

"We did that first killing almost until sunset. Mainly in the square. I fell once, because of the blood, and I hurt my elbow. I didn't do that again, because it made the Germans laugh at me.

"Of course, then we had to clear the bodies up ourselves—we were so stupid, the way we did it. There were only two or three left alive when we thought of this problem and they weren't useful. You should save people to carry the bodies for you, or the best is to take them out alive and make them dig graves—or ditches, or defences, sometimes we would say all types of lie and they want the lie—it doesn't matter who—I killed all types—they don't expect you will do it, don't really expect, or anticipate? Believe. They don't want to. We are unbelievable for them. Is that a better word? If they don't understand us—sometimes this is why we can kill them. Some, I think, did begin to understand. Some few, they realise—turn into us and then you'll live. But you'll be us. But stay as you are. You don't live. There's no other choice. Maybe not even such a choice. We decide. Mr. Alfred, you think maybe there is another way, but that's not so. When there's no war, you don't see it, but it always has been this way.

"So they dig their graves and then when they're finished, you can begin. Or you take them to the Umschlagplatz, or you do whatever must happen—and whatever happens, it happens to them. And you watch how they cry and how they are so nice to each other and polite—as if it matters, as if it ever matters.

"It's like this—you kiss your wife, I take away her face—which one of us is more sensible? You hold on to her hand when she can't feel and then I stop you feeling—which one of us is more sensible? You care about your daughter—I train my dog to fuck your daughter—you still care—which one of us is more sensible?

"I understand people—they hold blood. That's all they are: they're things to hold blood.

"The first time, I was covered in them when I went home. They splash up on you when you hit them and then I had to lift them into the carts—that rotten stink—shit and piss—and the fear—sweetish smell, a little like the way they'll be when they rot—clings—you only get it when they're terrified, like they sweat themselves out through their skin. Escape. And then the blood. I was—"

"Cunt." Driving your head in hard against Vasyl's. "You cunt." Knocking him on to his side and then punching him, stamping him low. "You cunt." The bloodsmell everywhere, the old slither and clog in your breathing, over your tongue. "You cunt." Holding Vasyl's one arm bent behind his back. "Cunt." Your other hand keeping the grip under Vasyl's chin, ready to twist, break the neck, very ready. Only the ghost of blood is slippy inside your hands, is making you doubt them.

And Vasyl reads you and bucks, writhes, a nasty desperation in him. He gets loose just enough to tilt his face and catch your eye, upset the rhythm you were trained to. You both breathe hard. Both warm and still alive and fighting. He moves with your force on his arm, gives quickly, pushing with his feet, and rolls hard away from you and now he's almost free and you're snatching at each other in the dust. He doesn't seem to be reaching for his knife and you wish he would because then you could use it on him. Self-defence.

"Two types."

You break fast, stand up before Vasyl can manage to and then you rush a kick, clip him in the balls and like the way he twitches after that and whines in the sand. You try for his head, but he's hedgehogged round now, elbows beside his ears and you can't get him. You dodge left and try for his spine.

"Two types."

But he's quick, rolling again, grabs for your feet.

"Two types."

And he won't shut up. "Two types." And he catches you, makes you fall.

"Two types. Of cunt. Their type. Our type."

But he doesn't move on you, so you have the chance to scramble up. And there he is, standing too—holding himself steady against the hut wall, leaning, blood on his mouth—real blood, not a memory—real, out-loud blood—and he's looking at you. "Our type. We kill their type."

This makes you start a lunge in again, but there are hands that pull you back—two fellows behind you who are stopping this, the big lads from Gad's hut, wanting to lead you off, tugging you backwards. They are telling you calm things that you can't hear.

Vasyl keeps on looking at you. "This isn't the shit they taught us. This is the real truth—we don't die. People like you and me, Alfred. It's the other ones that die. We kill them."

"There are other things, you know, to consider."

"He's a fucking murderer." The afternoon's heat shutting against Alfred, while he started to ache. "He's a fucking—"

"But we have other matters to discuss." This from the fat man who'd been chasing the cricket ball. He was now holding Alfred's starboard elbow, steering him back to the phoney concert hall.

Gripping his other elbow was Gad. "Johnnie's right. We've other things to talk about, Day. If you're interested. We thought you would maybe get interested when you heard."

"I'm not." Alfred dug back his heel, brought them all to a stop. "I'm not interested. I wasn't even a digger then. You're both—"

"Daft laddie." Gad stepped to the side and was chuckling, shaking his head. "Not the tunnel."

The fat man kept Alfred's arm, but was sniggering, too—the pair of them beyond wire-happy: simply insane.

"Not the tunnel. We've not the time for that." Gad coughed and straightened himself, became more circumspect. "But we do have possibilities. If you were to need them."

"I don't know what you mean . . . and it's nearly time. The break's nearly over—we should get back. And I'm . . ."

Alfred's elbow was gently lifted and the fat man started him walking again. "You're in a bit of a state, old man. I'd go in and take a seat at the back, I should say. And I'd imagine you'll have a fearful black eye tomorrow."

And the need to turn, finish it with Vasyl, but the two men snibbed him in, closed their arms across the small of his back. The other pair, the giants, dawdled watchfully behind. Binns, the huger of the two, winked at Alfred.

Gad murmured, "A new start, Day. Are you telling me you wouldn't like one?"

"This time next week, Day, you could be somebody else."

"Away and free."

The pair of them muttering nonsense at him.

"Would you not like to be somebody else?"

They halted him, then stepped aside, let go of him as scuffles and lines of men began to thicken round them, heading back to the filming. Alfred feeling exposed now, at risk without the press of his escorts against him.

Gad shielded his eyes and pointed to nothing in the sour blue of the sky. "I've wanted it since '45. I've wanted it since I realised the best I'll ever be in civilian life is a clerk in a shipping office in Kilbowie Road. I outrank the manager. I outrank everyone there. They did nothing. I had a good war. And what did I get? Lease Loan up the spout and tatties on the ration." He spoke in the proper, casual tone for a man observing a bird in flight, an interesting cloud formation. "It's either this, Day, or I'll go down to the fucking docks one evening." He spoke as if this was just chatting, was nothing of importance. "And I'll climb up a crane and launch myself off. I've picked the crane already. That's all there is for me back home."

"He's right, Day."

"Right about *what*?"

Stragglers were running by them now, and Alfred knew—was almost interested by knowing—that if they weren't careful they would be late.

"We have the papers, Day. Black market. Europe's still a bloody mess. Nip out of here when the film buggers aren't quite looking . . ."

The fat man nodded. "Start again before it all settles down and we've still a chance that nobody will notice. There's just enough time. We thought you might like that. To be someone else."

"We have a spare set of papers."

"You give it some thought, Day. And let us know. Fast, though. Not long to go."

Alfred stood in the heat. He gave it some thought.

Lignite, phosphorous, carbon, liquid oxygen: these are substances that follow their own nature, that are true. But let, for example, the phosphorous touch you and it would burn you to the bone—its true self is a harmful thing and so you keep it closed away.

Trip twenty-six.

You keep it closed away.

Trip twenty-seven.

You keep it closed away.

Closed, but not hiding—how would you hide yourself from yourself: where could you go, alone inside yourself?—and twenty-six and twenty-seven, they are a part of what owns you, *is* you, of what occupies you now.

So no hiding. It's only a question of cohabitation, of letting the harmful things live in you, move where you are naked, of feeling them look and smile, but never listening when they speak. And you are a brave boy, always tried to be a brave boy, which means you'll manage this, press on regardless.

The Tuesday and the Thursday of that one hot week—you know about them, all about them, but you keep your mind down on the ground, in their beginnings—sticky inside your turret while you prepared, sun finding you through the Perspex, making the metal nervy, talkative around you, forcing a sweat. You wanted the high cool then, the mission reeling on ahead, the man you could be with your crew and nowhere else.

That's simple to remember and allowed.

For the rest of it, if you're pushed, you'll skip to the end of the week and being with Molloy on the Friday evening. He's sitting hunched in the open window of the Duck's Head, leaning his back against the frame, right foot tapping on the seat of an elderly bench, left leg hanging down over the sill and into the little garden where sweet peas are flowering in among the real peas. Which means that the national drive for increased fruit and vegetable production smells of summer and of women and normal life.

By the bar some fellows you don't know, have taken care not to know so terribly well, are singing.

> "We are the Air-Sea rescue, no fucking use are we,
> The only times you'll find us are breakfast, dinner and tea.
> And when we sight a dinghy, we cry with all our might:
> Per Ardua ad Astra—up you, Jack, we're all right."

Molloy has a pint, but isn't drinking: holds a cigarette, but isn't smoking—he's only peering down at his shoe where it's out in the sunlight. You hold his beer hand and tilt it, steal a sip out of his glass. He does grin when you lift your head and swallow, but this seems to leave him weary.

He catches your ear between his forefinger and thumb, nips it vaguely, "Ah, Little Boss, Little Boss. You'll have the shirt off my back."

"Won't."

"And why not, it's a good shirt. Really very close to being almost new."

"Wouldn't fit me."

He nods as if he has a headache. "That's so, that's quite precisely so. I'd forgotten your problem of being a dwarf." He tries to smile again.

And you would not hurt him or insult him by saying he ought to cheer up, because he has a right to be exactly as he is. It's best maybe to stay with him quietly, drink your own pint and listen to the sprogs up by the bar: now they're singing about a blackout tart who'll do anything for butter. You imagine the song might have made you laugh a while ago, when you were younger.

"D'you hope?" Molloy quiet, his face to the garden. "Despair being a sin, so you mustn't indulge it. But what would you hope? Do you?"

Feeling the dark that you have in your spine, that follows you, creeps out when you're not careful. It wakes, blinks. "I don't know." You shouldn't talk in ways that make it spread. "I mean," but you have to help your friend, "I try doing neither. Not the despair and not the hope."

"You prefer to be dead, so."

"When I'm with—"

"I know. It's different then. If you've love. Then you give it all the engines can stand while you're with her. But in this, where we are, where they have us be . . ."

Molloy with two missions left before he can go—one less than you when one less is a large consideration—both of you so near, too near, and you're sure this should not be mentioned: the terrible idea that sometimes mouths inside your head

I might live.

And the way it drives along your muscles and cramps them tight: the way it could crowd in your thinking when you need your space, when you need to watch and keep your crew from harm: the way it makes you feel afraid.

I really could live.

The way it always feels like it's a joke at your expense.

"I don't know with the hope thing." Molloy clearing his throat and facing you. "I supposed that I ought to ignore it. If it was there then it would sustain me, but I wasn't to touch it, or to consider it, or check on it. Because in our position . . ." He doesn't seem worried: more baffled, exhausted. "I supposed I was a person of *this* world and *this* world was what concerned me. But I was all wrong, d'you know?" He smiles very gently and draws on what's left of his cigarette. "I believed—" He flicks the butt outside and takes your hand. "Are we friends?"

"Of course."

"Friends enough that I won't offend you, because I don't mean to offend you."

"Yes." Although you're not sure, you mostly would like him to be quiet and not trouble himself so much and not trouble you.

But Molloy keeps a hold of your fingers. "I'd thought—" He coughs out a type of laugh. "I'd thought that I didn't believe—all of the training, the way they make you think—the training when I was boy, not here: the angels and dispensations and penances . . . they sent me to the Latin School, you know, with expectations . . . ones I didn't share . . . and so much beating, years of it—d'you see the thumb on me? That one."

He held out his right hand and its slightly twisted thumb, grinned at it sourly.

"Miss Mahon—never knew when she should stop. And the whole pack of them at work for gentle Jesus. Gentle Jesus and the proper declension of Irish verbs. There would have been other ways I could have learned." Again the grin and a turn of his hand, examining it. "And I *did* learn—that I didn't believe. But there I'm wrong—I'd only *thought* that I didn't believe any more. But it was always here the idea that if I do what's right, then in the end I shall be forgiven and dwell in the mind of God. Maybe a little Purgatory for a while—and that would be only fair." He shook his head. "I thought I was past all of that, but truly I'd only changed my mind about what it was right to do, made myself a little room to breathe. The rest, it was still there—the hope of heaven. And that's a hope you don't even notice, because of it being so old. It's really almost as old as yourself and however you happen to think and the mercy of the way your mother smelled when she used to hold you and you were small enough to be good. You don't notice while it's still there—the old hope. Oh, but when it's gone."

And then you cup your own hand around his, around that thumb, because he is lonely in this and loneliness is never good for crew and shouldn't catch them. And also the slide of what you can't face is roaring towards you and you know he sees it, too. So you tell him quick, "But you shouldn't say. Yo cor say. Not about this."

"But am I right?"

"Our kid—"

"Am I right?" Puzzled like a boy and soft when he asks you. "When we did what we did this week—that was the end of heaven."

"Dickie—"

"It's all right." He squeezes your hand to comfort you. "I know it. I understand. I'll have to go to hell now, that's all."

And then it bares your teeth and licks them, holds you so you smell how glad it is you've let it out. The harmful thing. And it makes you forget Molloy and everything else but the way it was, the way it still is, repeating itself against your bones.

Such a good job you did, such a perfect, perfect job—back over Hamburg and the target indicators had gone down so tight, backed up so tight, and then every stick of bombs—it didn't seem that anyone could miss, did miss.

Its hand in your throat and pushing up, filling your mouth and the fist pressing on, cracking you, having your skull, fingers in your skull, digging this out of your brain to show you.

A light you'd never known, a red day swelling up ahead. Made everyone quiet on the intercom. You could feel it: you could tell it was thinking of you. And you're doing your job and you're keeping your eyes on the black, saving them—but the black isn't black any more—it's smoke and ash at 20,000 feet and a life in it, shifting, glowing—bombs go down and you buck higher, rattle over something like a prop wash, an odd turbulence, a fat, high writhe of air.

Never known it before, the way it touched you, batted at the Lanc as if she were paper, a foolish thought.

And slowly, slowly as you arc there is the shape of what you've done— a twist of fire—a whole new kind of fire—one solid flame that sees you and gives you a name that is no name, no word—christens you outside words.

Has to be a mile wide, wider—colours in it that aren't colours, that rise from somewhere human beings cannot be, that fatten and swell—and there's a howl in it, you could swear, the sound of a monster.

Imagining the war must be over tomorrow. It must surely be done after this. Who could stand this?

And the howl dogging you home: screaming beneath the Merlins, raging, and you think

This is death.

This is the edge of the real face of death, its size—we burned the sky open today and now death will come in.

Trip twenty-six.

Never knew another like it.

But twenty-seven was the worst. It was our ruination. When they ordered us back two days later and we went.

"Jesus, you can see it from here."

"Shut up."

"Still hot."

"Shut up."

"Still burning."

"Poor fucking bastards."

We went back and we bombed them again.

At the end of the concert party filming things went peculiar—and it was Alfred's fault. He was very happy to admit that it was entirely his fault.

They'd worked past dinner and into the evening and then the night, everyone tired and the actors seeming nervous of their audience—which struck Alfred as a queer thing: actors not wanting to be watched. Then again, the hall was growing less and less sympathetic. Of course, every time somebody made a mistake, it meant the whole squad of them had to stay longer, had to repeat themselves—but actually inducing another balls-up, that had turned out to be fun: staring, clapping a shade too slowly, turning the tone just a little vicious—that did satisfy, you couldn't deny it. The film wasn't quite in charge any more and neither were its stars, the chaps that you'd seen at the pictures—they didn't altogether cut it here.

The last bod the audience sent packing seemed nearly tearful, said a mouthful to his mates when he'd got off—didn't care who saw him, creating on the sidelines, scrubbing at his make-up with one hand and flapping about with the other.

So the director picked this point to have a sing-song, boost morale. And he wasn't completely wrong. After they'd had a couple of goes at "Run Rabbit Run" and then "Lili Marlene" they did all feel sweeter. Beyond that was the usual Vera Lynn finale and the usual handful kicking off by singing "Whale Meat Again" instead of the proper words. But then the proper words won through while everyone was laughing, not keeping watch: the thick, wide emptiness of them pushed in and made it plain each man here was alone and far from home and far from the time that hurt him and held him and let him live.

Which was no way to finish anything, in Alfred's opinion—and really shouldn't be borne. The day had been bloody enough as it was and needed changing, shaking up.

Not that he'd thought it would work, had thought there would be enough Kriegies about to catch on and help him—not that he'd truly thought at all. He'd only broken out into howling because he had to.

That was how you started it up and running—the orchestra, the old, old orchestra. Open your throat and crank your jaws back and let out the sound of an air-raid siren, that particular climb of warning.

And the others heard him, maybe were half waiting for him: piled straight in with more of the siren, louder and broader—they understood. Soon about half the hall was winding up and down through the siren wails, new voices joining just because they recognised the noise, yelling away in it for the joy of letting go, doing what they liked.

The film people were mainly staying still, Alfred thought, but he mainly paid them no attention, closed his eyes while the whole place lifted into the scream of a raid—the scream they'd made to bait the goons—and old Kriegies started in with the whistles of fluted tail fins, the whistles of falling bombs: battered their feet down in the pantomime of bombing, of Chopper Harris sending up his boys to knock seven shades of shit out of the Fatherland.

Never felt bad about the orchestra—never had, never would—there was no confusion, no guilt in shaping up the sound of the work you hadn't finished, the war you were locked away from. You were in the bag, but you were still noisy, bolshy. You had things to be proud of.

By the time the orchestra was done, most of the film crew were packing up or gone, the actors had dispersed and that meant the phoney prisoners could pretty much order themselves off towards lights-out and sleep, stump cheerfully enough away with small reminders of when they should wake and what would be needed tomorrow, their obligations.

Alfred went and got himself ready, donned his pyjamas, but couldn't quite consign himself to bed. Instead he stood by an open hut window and looked out. The night air was tender, full of grasses and heat and a mindless calm, a little taste of autumn there as well, just a clue that the year was spinning and the big plane leaves would soon start pitching down when he got back to London.

If he ever did.

No need to decide now, though—this was more a night to look for something good, to uncover your happiness.

I don't have to read it any more; I remember.

The first of the letters I still have.

From the camp.

To the camp.

No idea if they'd sent her mine, or what would get through, or what she'd heard, been able to find out. No idea of anything.

And then a letter.

When you'd given up.

My Dearest Alfie

That in itself almost too heavy, too wonderful for the paper, and the other chaps leaving you be, but paying attention all the same and nowhere private enough, or clean enough for this. Warming the paper with your breath and finding the scent of her house, her dressing gown, her kitchen table.

I did sort of know that you hadn't truly gone and then sometimes I was afraid it was just shock and I shouldn't be so stupid. But I did know. I hope you could tell I was here and being terribly solid about it all. Always. And then your wonderful letter and everything all right. As long as you really are well and being treated decently.

Her voice in your hands: her mouth, lips, tongue.

I should say that I dreamed of us being together at this strange kind of party. You were wearing a mask, but I knew it was you. And we sat together and you showed me your face and you looked a little ill, but very handsome and yourself and then someone gave you a medal and you were happy and I was happy for you. Funny dream to have, but it won't annoy the censor, I suppose. Or amuse him. It was like seeing you. Which I want to.

The start of whispering to each other, dreaming, playing in and out of each other's minds: a closeness you hadn't quite reached with her before. The sole mercy your prison gave you, this near, new Joyce.

My Dearest Alfie

That somehow you were curled whole in her palm and resting.

You really should remember that I always sleep with you. I think from the start I may have. Now it's sure. When I lie down under the quilt and I know you are lying somewhere, too, then I think we are almost touching, we are not far. That will be always.

That one person knew you in the world and loved what they knew.

Do please take care.

Not just your crew self—the man you might become, she'd known all that: she'd understood the way you'd be complete.

My Dearest Alfie

Which meant that you might sleep for one more night, pretending you were a real person and had a future and no cause to run away.

And you stepped back from the window comfortable, walked carefully so as not to break the dream that already thinned the air around you, adjusted it to be a gentle fit while you climbed into your phoney bunk and covered up and closed your eyes.

But she didn't come for you, not when the dark spilled in and took you to sleep. The boys came and found you instead, because they could tell you were ready and this would be their time.

Thick din of boots on the concrete and you're with them, clumping along through rain to the blood wagon and a blinded night above you—low, solid cloud—and somewhere inside it a bird singing, a trail of fine, metallic notes across the engines and engines and engines.

"Poor little bugger. We've woken him up." Molloy sniffing, then rubbing his face now he's settled in the truck, tapping his fingers against the canvas sides the way he always does. "Still, I've to be awake, so why not. And aren't we doing it for him, anyway? He'd not want to be a Nazi bird, I'm certain." The weather taps at the cloth in reply and then a bluster of wind elbows it for a moment, pushes then tugs.

The Bastard loading himself inside, last as usual. "You don't half talk bollocks, Paddy."

"And I'd say I was glad you could join us, but there's some bollocks I won't talk."

And the first jolt of motion shaking you all, rocking you shoulder to shoulder as you head out along the peri track. Feel the lean of your skipper beside you, feel the seams in the concrete as the truck goes on, feel the wet, fenland breeze changing to something hungry with so many Merlins ripping it open, waking.

Other bods riding out with you—seem fairly new, but you keep your eyes away from them. Torrington lights his pipe and you concentrate on the red disc of his breathing while the wagon halts at T for Tommy and unloads a crew. Don't watch the sprogs as they leave, because they are dead, it's clear to you: they're smoky and fading and you don't want them to see that in your face. They give you a cool type of sadness that lasts until you jump down at the side of B for Beer.

"After you."

"No, after *you*."

"No, after *you*."

Parks and Torrington mucking about, dim at the foot of the steps.

"Now, boys." Skip whacking at shoulders, arms. "Let's do the job."

He starts to climb, shouts back to them, "And have the sense to get out of the bloody rain." A buffet of wind loosens his cap—always wears his cap out to the plane—sets it rolling and Miles jogs after it, scoops it up and brings it back.

For some reason, Alfred takes it from him and hurries up the ladder.

"Thanks, Boss." Skip nodding as he turns to go forward.

"No trouble." And Alfred starts the usual scramble for his turret as the others come aboard—spin, slide, swing out and drop and that means you're home.

Trip twenty-eight.

Checking: intercom, oxygen, feed belts, breeches, door locks, check the electrics for your suit.

Check everything twice. Then check again.

Passes the time, this bloody bit of time.

Her hat on your head, her work, her care.

Sandwiches and Thermos, get them stowed.

Set your feet in right, set them where you want them, then you won't have to think.

And she speaks then, your other girl, your Lanc—that first tumble into ignition and the port inner fires up, drums in your bones.

Port outer and she's raging already but you want more of her, while you try to sink into your place, to soften as she rattles you from skull to boots.

Starboard inner starts and this isn't sound any more: it's touch, it's your breath matching her breath and the push of her behind you, her need to leap, to spring.

Starboard outer finally turning and she has to go, she couldn't not, and so many noises in her great, hard, beautiful voice: the cycle of shivers and clatters inside her roar and something like the canter of horses—a dash of animals—and your hands feeling blurred but comfortable, resting on the bicycle grip, just so—yourself in your gunner's shape and herself aching, twitching to run and drag you up—first off the ground, you'll always be first off the ground—off it now, chasing, keen as fuck—tailwheel clear and her spine flexing—flesh and metal and crew and her and your blood and the new thing that she makes you, red and new.

Hamburg again.

Longer route.

You didn't want a longer route.

Hamburg again.

Good to get up and over the cloud, look down at the broad moon coun-
try it makes. And watch for snappers dipping up out of it, watch for the bas-
tards everywhere while B for Beer flicks and switches her tail and you keep
hold.

Think of it sometimes like sitting out over the end of a plank, swinging
your feet loose in the sky—gets you happy, that: gets a smile inside the oxy-
gen mask.

"And what the bloody hell is that, d'you think?" It's Skip. But he's not
worried, only asking. You think he's not worried. He doesn't sound it—
difficult to tell with the words so thin by the time they reach you.

"Flak?" Torrington chipping in. "New kind of flak."

The Bastard, "If that's fucking flak . . ."

Catches of light. Revolve your turret hard to starboard and glance for-
ward. More light. Can't be flak—too pale. Too huge.

"Skip?" You have to ask him. "What's up?" Don't want to trouble
him, but you have to ask. "Anything?"

"It's, ah . . . It's a bloody great storm, Boss."

"Don't you fret, Little Boss." Molloy, you think it's Molloy—the
intercom very ropy tonight. "I'll bring along your cocoa when we're
done."

Colder. Check the connections to your suit, but they're fine.

"We'll go in and see how we manage, boys. Then it's another trip.
Any sign of icing, any sign of anything . . . tell me. Cunimbus aren't my
favourite . . . but . . . we go."

Colder.

Feeling her taken in—the first slam down, as if she's dropped a step,
before the cloud grinds by your turret, a cliff to either side, so much higher
than you, so far to the ground when the lightning fires, shows you the
chasm you're chinked inside.

"Jesus."

It throws you, as if you are nothing—because you are nothing—
pounds and slams, slaps until you don't think, can't.

"Fuck."

"Can't turn her."

Hands on the grips, as if they could help you, help anyone.

Walls closing, sealing.

My poor little Lanc, she's moving in ways that she can't, she's kicked sideways, backwards.

And the cloud is something more again—it has a mind that sucks away your breath—and its light only uncovers what you shouldn't look at, spaces you couldn't survive in, vaults that leap to 30,000 feet.

Our fault, this—we burned up the sky and now it's come for us.

"Jesus."

No.

Just a storm. Yo'm norra babby. It's only weather.

"Jesus."

Blue flame starting from your muzzles, your turret blinding—don't know if the ammo will go up—and anyone could see you from miles off, props shining like bloody fireworks while you hurt with the cold—and there's a bright knock to port and you breathe the fresh smell of a lightning strike.

"Miles? Miles? . . . Skip . . . a shock . . . I don't . . . through his set. Skip? I'll . . . back . . . His head, I think."

Youwilllightmywaytonightyouwilllightmywaytonightyouwilllightmy-waytonightyouwill

Only weather.

And its heart looking out at you and laughing.

You

Will

Light

My

Way

Tonight

Until it spits you free.

Merlins so quiet without the thunder.

A miracle.

When you don't believe in them.

But you get one, anyway.

"Fires over there, Skip."

"I see them. That Hamburg?"

"It'll do."

Someone got through, then. And we got through. Dead reckoning and we've something to hit.

And then home.

Get the fucking bombs down and get home.

You can feel her relaxing, tender.

Get fucking on with it, put them down.

"Steady, steady."

Left leg shaking for some reason. Can't stop it, so leave it be.

"Bombs gone."

And keep on north and outrun the bastard weather, jink across when we can, when it's clear. Feel the skipper sink you into the usual, normal bed of cloud cover, trying to hide you, because you are clearly alone now and bombers should never be alone.

That's why it isn't fair when it happens—because everybody is doing their very best.

And because it makes you be alone.

Flak you know what it is when it hits and that it hasn't ruined you because you are still thinking and when it hits it's faster than you think and then it comes again you smell its skin before it blows up stink of smoke and sneaked in the cloud and got you and yo hear the skipper yo can tell it's him and there's other things yo hear like hurt babbies and somebody callin out Molloy and your poor lickle Lanc she seems so sad around yo and wallowing and Perspex to yer right yer winder there's a big ole in it which seems daft and abracadabrajumpjumpjump yo hear that in Skip's voice and someone blartin for their ma and hard to breathe with stuff in your air and abracadabrajumpjumpjump and yo'm tryin but yo cor turret jammed cor get it round enough and yo bay frit but yo do seem away far off and slow and yo try and crank again and it's hard and she's dyin on yer yo can feel how she cries and three engines is all that's gooin and yo gerrout through the doors yo do gerrout and clomber and drap and yo see there's no more Bastard and no more turret where he would have been all shattered and pummellin wind about yo and ash and Window magic Window flying all about and the flak's stopped which is good and why yo'm alive and there's no people yo cor find any people and yo go forward and there's no one yo'm

alone legs rattlin under yo everything rattlin apart and remember portable
oxygen remember yo'll die otherwise only yo'm breathin already without it
and so yo'm low flyin now and doe need it and yo breathe more panicky
with the taste of fuel and glycol and that other thing on the floor that bad
thing that might be the Bastard part of the Bastard and goo forward and
now there's Miles there's this creature they made of Miles and its arms moving but he doe mean them to they're only moving with the Lanc and yo cor
look at it and it's like a poor wammell a poor lickle dog that's crouched with
no chest and yo've got to see your skipper soon you need him or Dickie Molloy or anybody to not be alone and my how she's weeping and singing and
slipping down your lovely Lanc only gliding now she can't manage better
and there's all red on the floor and clip on your chute and make yerands do
it make sure they do it and the astrodome is gone blown out and no Parks
and no sign of Parks and forward yo'm gooin on and she makes a stagger
down but she's brave a brave wench and here he is yer skipper yer safety yer
best yer gaffer and white white in his face doesn't see when yo shout and yo
mun get him to listen because jeth is set by him atein him up yo can see it
and his mouth sayin abracadabra again and his mask off and lollin and
wet and he's took poorly took terrible badly and his cap is gone again and
yo cor find it and his flying helmet tore open and red in his hair not sandy
as it should be and yo want to find his cap but yo cor because maybe it
jumped out the hatch like Torrington must have and Parks is gone and
Molloy and they've left their red behind and yo behind and yo cor jump
because yo look down through the hatch and yo just cor and so yo goo back
and the skipper is still there and still flyin and now he turns awful slow and
different to how he is and he does see yo now he sees.

"Alongin a moment, Boss. On you go."

Bad smile he gives you horrible.

"To pleaseme onyougo."

Yo can tell he's weary with holdin her and wants to go home and yo'd
like to goo wum with him and he has such blue eyes the skipper like he's got
all the morning sky inside his head.

There never is any memory of leaving, nor of pulling the cord to open the parachute. You only tumble into thinking again when your harness yanks you up so hard you feel you've been split in half, or your balls knocked up into you somewhere and no chance of getting them back.

And this is just you now—you and infinity and the cold, deep silence it's made for you to sway about in. For a while you think something will reach down and touch you, something you can't understand and this is the first time you've truly been frightened all night.

Which unhinges everything and you don't know if this is a silence or you are deaf and if this is a mist or you are blind, or maybe this is dying— one last joke to get your hopes up before you get the final drop.

But then you notice you've lost your boots and your Type D linings and your socks and your feet are aching—there they are, your sore naked feet—and a dead person wouldn't be bothered with that and here is some sound, hissing and pressing back in, of the silk above you and the harness and your racing breath and you can understand that seeing will be tricky because you are in a cloud which is why you are wet and freezing, but there is some light, a type of glow which means that day is coming in an overcast dawn.

You wish for a moment that Sweden will be beneath you—the skipper would have tried for Sweden if he could, if he'd thought they wouldn't make it home.

The skipper.

There's no Lancsound. So he's gone. But no fire, no sign of fire, so you can believe that he hasn't crashed, that maybe he's still flying. Or he could have jumped. You want to think that he'll make it to Sweden. Or you don't want to think at all.

Except maybe your hearing's not so hot as you'd thought because there's this rush now, a terrible racket, keeps getting louder, and the mist thinning while your chute starts to buffet a bit more.

And then you see—the whole thing clearing, the whole bloody mess—that you're coming down over water, over a coast, some thin bit of coast—Jesus, a tiny strip of land, island, something, and if you don't make it you'll be in the fucking ocean, you'll be fucking dead.

Tugging and hauling to steer yourself and the wind impossible, can't tell if it's set to take you out or save you—maybe both. Dropping faster now, or it seems that way, and you are—fuckit—you are going to hit the water, but not on the ocean side, you think not on the ocean side, you hope—unless you've got it all wrong—remember to release the harness, hit the release before you're in the water, get away from the fucking 'chute.

Much nearer now, much too near—it will be the water—can't bloody swim—get out of the harness, get out of it now, get the bloody thing, get it away before it drowns you.

And then suddenly it's your business to live, fight for it.

Landing in a way you don't completely feel and the canopy coming down after like a wet skin, like your shroud, and you're breathing water, but it's all queer—your legs are wrong, make no sense of your being in water—and your hands caught for a moment in this soft stuff, warm—before it comes clear in your head how you are and where you are and that you have Joyce to be alive for, maybe nothing else, but she is enough—and you are dragging and dragging and dragging the silk from your back, your head, but also standing, toes sunk in cream-feeling mud—almost—because the water here is up just to your waist and now you're free, open, and it's raining—there's a cold and beautiful thin rain falling on you, washing your face, and this warmish water that you're thick in, that you can walk through—alive—a living man who has fallen from a plane and hasn't died—shove down the 'chute, sink it as best you can—and work your way up to the shore from this lagoon that's bright with the threat of sunrise, that's sparking as it sinks to your thighs and then your knees.

Not too hard to keep on wading along this sort of channel—whistly little birds stirring away from you, but no other disturbance, no shouts, no alarms. Then the channel dries and rises to some kind of springy soil and then there is scrub and then woods, pine smelling—too sparse to hide you.

You keep walking and here is a little road to crouch across and run to its other side until you are on grass—horrible fierce stuff that hurts your feet, so you move to a path and it's getting very light—no houses, no sign of shelter, but that's maybe good—no people, quiet still, but a silver shine everywhere that makes your head ache—you ache a good deal—but you keep on trotting—sand now, more gentle—and you go further, you're in dunes—ocean sound coming at you and tussles of wind, the last of the storm leaving as the rain fades and there's this wonderful smell of roses and bushes: a high, thick mass of bushes, a hill that seems it is roses and nothing else and it pains you, but you tuck yourself in under it—this grey coming when you look and you have to sleep now, you really do have to sleep.

And when you wake there is a kind of heaven with you.

Cloudless sky and warm and the smell of your ma's garden—so many roses—and a calm tide breathing in and out somewhere at the edge of the white sand where you're lying.

Dog roses.

And a tiny blue flower by your face, trembling.

So comfortable here.

Except for your shoulder and your feet.

And they'll know now, back at home—that you're too late to be anything but gone.

And you realise you're thirsty, taste of clay and salt in your mouth.

And you roll yourself over, which causes you this long, tugging pain and you look up and see three faces, three men standing over you, peaked caps elegantly tilted and pencil moustaches—makes you think of a movie, the comic-opera type of thing—gleaming boots and dapper greatcoats.

Fucking Germans, of course.

You understand. Whatever they do, it can't surprise you: you'll always understand.

Dulag Luft: that should be where you're taken, but you don't think you're there. This wouldn't happen there. They don't say where you are and you can't see. There's only this room and the other.

You haven't been processed, or given a number, or given shoes. There's only this room and the other.

You haven't told anyone you've lost your hat, the one Joyce made you and there's no time to cry about it. There's only this room and the other.

They say you're not a *terror Flieger*—because nobody heard your plane—because nobody saw your plane—because nobody found your parachute—because you are not in full uniform—because they were expecting someone who is not a *terror Flieger* and what they expect has to be right. Which only means they're stupid, but you can't tell them that. They don't think you're really aircrew and they don't believe your name, or you serial number, or your rank. You tell them all three, in any case. Whenever they ask. Whatever they ask. But you do not stop them believing that you are something else, something wrong.

It took a long time to get here and people were not kind and did not ever believe you and so you stay here—back in what you understand. There's only this room and the other.

I always was wrong. And nothing my father liked better than the ways I could be wrong: sayin things I shouldn't, lookin arrim funny, actin daft, actin saft—I was made inside me to be wrong. And yo knock that out, yo fuckin knock that out of a boy, yo bate him till he doe feel it and yo knock im right.

Tastes of salt, my fuckin father. Tastes of fuck you. Tastes of I'll fuckin watchyer, I'll watchyer fuckin die and hear yo squeal.

There's only this room and the other. Here is where you get it wrong, in this little space, like a box, and damp brick walls with whitewash on them. You have to stand here. This is the room where you stand. Until they tell you not to. Sometimes with your hands above your head. Shoulder hurts, something bad with your shoulder. Sometimes with your hands down by your sides. Shoulder hurts, either way. It doesn't matter, the important thing is to stand and never lean, never brush the walls, never touch them so the whitewash comes off, because then when they come back to check you they see how you've done wrong and then they take you to the other room.

The other room is where it's your fault you get a beating.

And when I'd hit him, when I tried to hit him, keep her safe, that's when I was a bad boy, made him hurt her. I'd hit him and he'd bate her. Then he'd bate me.

But I knew better than him what I deserve.

I know better than them.

Sometimes rubber truncheons, sometimes leather with a sting in them, a kind of echo once they've hit. Sometimes you don't see. Not interested.

Fucker with a ring, he punched me, cut me—my lip's all swole and bad now.

But I understand. It ay that I doe understand.

If there's no whitewash on you, they beat you, anyway. That's your fault, too, because you can't tell them what they'd like.

Fucker with the ring calls me Alfred, like no one ever does—except her sometimes, except her—an he has a officer's voice an he says he wants to help me, but he wants to help hisself.

I understand.

I'm wrong, so he has to bate me.

He's wrong, so he has to bate me.

They'm wrong, so they have to bate me.

I unnerstan.

I'm running this. I own it. I'm getting what I deserve.

There's only this room and the other, which is why it's hard to tell the time. You don't how many hours or days you've been here, how long you have to stand until you fall now and then and they come and lift you up and beat you or give you a cigarette you can't smoke but you try to and the fucker talks about cricket which you never follow and then you don't please him and sometimes they don't have to hit you at all before you make sounds these noises and curl up and want to be asleep only a tiny piece in the space it takes for them to pick you up you could rest a while stretch the seconds.

Stretch a second with your hand.

They're starting to think you're maybe soft, honest—which makes them beat you differently.

Showing cheek, trying to prove them wrong, when I'm the one who's wrong and that's the way I'll be for ever.

While you stand, there's this crying you do sometimes—when you think you won't look nice for her any more. Don't think her name and then they won't have it. They see names in your face and then they try to smack them out.

Yo cor ave em, though—or me. I was made to be bate. I was made for gunnery and batin. Yo cor find me this way, norrall the way down ere, in where I stop.

I can hear yo. I can feel yo. But yo ay gorra chance to see me. I bin down in the glory hole, I bin, shut in. Yo cor hurt me where I bin. So fuck yo.

There's only this room and the other.

You try to stand the way the air force taught you, be a credit to the service and yourself.

There's only this room and the other.

You don't do it very well.

They threw him back eventually—he was too small a fish. And the Luftwaffe guards came and took him and wouldn't quite meet his eye, because he was embarrassing—the way he had made himself be treated. They gave him a number and a tag, cutlery and a dixie, a blanket and a Red Cross parcel, all of his very own to keep. But the best was getting dressings on his shoulder his face and his feet and then socks and then the chance to scrum in when they threw down a load of boots and he wasn't ashamed to dig and shove to find a pair that fitted and would last— he wasn't ashamed by anything, not even of shuffling into the camp that first evening and seeing men look away from him, just the way the Luftwaffe had.

Because there is a difference between being in a prison and being a prisoner. And, for a while, Alfred had liked to be a prisoner. He was grateful and obedient and quiet and would only look, every now and then, at the Germans—real Germans there, alive and moving about, as if they were people and not what the newspapers had told you, as if they were people and not what had hurt you, as if they were people and not what had hurt your friends. Here they were, the Germans—something to start a flinch in you, although you fought that—chatting and standing guard, sneaking cigarettes, being tired and lazy and officious, angry, jolly, boorish, sly.

You could have worn them away with watching.

You could have gone mad with shaking and not sleeping and needing to weep.

But Ringer saved you.

Yes, our kid—it was Ringer that saved you and not the other way around.

Not the way you seem to remember it, but that's the way it was.

The other chaps had taken to leaving Alfred alone: he was, they could only observe, an almighty bore and his nightmares were trying their patience. And Alfred had taken to watching the Germans, staring at the Germans, in ways that were trying *their* patience. And then Ringer arrived.

Whatever you were watching, you'd see Ringer: the great, bobbing head, the height of him as he shambled about across the sand, that daft helmet perched up above the placid face and the half-soaked smile. There was nothing to fear in Ringer's smile.

"You all right then, boy?" Ringer leaning over Alfred and then crouching to sit a little way off, unhurried, bony knees folded up to his chin. "I'd say you was all right." And there was a rush in Alfred's head that wanted to keep on checking, following the Germans, seeing what they'd do, but something about Ringer tugged at him, slowed his breath and turned it milky and peaceable. Alfred wanted to walk on, but he didn't.

Ringer glanced up at the empty sky and sniffed. "Going to rain." Then he glanced up at Alfred. "Prob'ly." He smiled again and nodded, started tapping with one foot in a way that meant something to him, that made him nod in time.

Alfred stood, kept on standing, until he began to shiver and to think of the whitewash and the room.

"You're all right, you know. I can see in you you're all right."

A tiredness spreading in Alfred when he heard that and a sweet weight bringing him to his knees and setting him with his hands down on the ground, before he could shake his head and laugh, scramble himself round to sit and laugh, reach out to Ringer and shake his long, wide hand and hold on and laugh.

The shivering worse as he let the sound kick out, but Ringer gripped him tight, crushed his palm, "Something knocked the air from you, is all," until Alfred had shaken and squawked to a standstill and the pair of them were left crouching, hand in hand—the idiot and the madman.

Things weren't so bad after that.

It was going to be a long night—and their last. Gad and a few other bods had convinced everyone that a genuine farewell concert was required, a real send-off to close the fake prison and send the fake prisoners home.

The trouble was, they'd got too many volunteers. Almost everyone had a bit of something they'd like to recite—"Boots, Boots, Boots," "The Green Eye of the Little Yellow God," "Albert and the Lion": there was a chap who'd been on destroyers and wanted to play the penny whistle, four would-be pianists, any number of singers with any number of songs, a photographic analyst who blew across the tops of bottles and a chap who'd been something at Myingyan—he did bird calls from home and abroad. Even a few of the Ukrainians had promised unpronounceable offerings. And, of course, there were the Good Germans—one couldn't very well exclude them.

The director, who had lately become rather fond of the older and nicely mysterious lady in charge of costumes, had given the enterprise his blessing, although only Jack from the film types had said he would like to take part.

So at five o'clock, they had settled down to eat, looking about themselves and finding they had almost all made the same decision to change out of their uniforms and make the best they could of their civvies. Shoes had been polished, hair fussed at, shirts ironed—they seemed to have become both less and more military and were quiet with each other, as if they were not quite who they'd thought.

Gad slipped in beside Alfred when they'd reached the pudding—a fine, celebratory treacle tart. "You're sure about this?"

"Yes."

· "Classic distraction, really. I'd never have stooped so low back in the old days . . ." Gad with the old sheen over him, pre-op nerves. "Gives us a twelve-hour start, if not more. I can do a lot with twelve hours."

"Good." Alfred staring at his pudding.

"You don't sound too happy, laddie." Gad sucked at—of all things— a cigar, wanting to have a man-to-man chat. "If you have second thoughts, it's not—"

"I'm fine." Alfred kept his head down. "It'll be fine."

"D'you want that? Because it's a shame to let good treacle tart go to waste, you know." There's a clear smell of drink about him.

"You eat it, cocker. I've got no appetite."

"Nerves, eh?"

"Something like that. And there's someone I want to speak to." He reached and shook Gad's hand, "Nothing to worry you, just a thing I need to do," and then left the table.

Across in a corner sat four guests from the DP camp, here to oversee their charges' cultural activities: two bank-clerk sorts with glasses, a blue-stocking kind of woman and a younger chap with a trimmed beard. They'd been given a tablecloth from who knew where and their own jug of custard to save them from having to walk and ask for more.

"Mr. Fergusson?"

The bearded man glanced up, frowning. "Mm?"

"Might I have a word?" Alfred unsure of how this would go and it was clear now that Fergusson liked his comforts, was thinking mainly of more custard and then the chance of booze. "You are Mr. Fergusson?"

"Yes . . . This isn't exactly—"

"I wanted to talk to you about one of your DPs."

"Well, you can't." A neat purse of the lips after this. "They're under our jurisdiction, no one else's." Fergusson took another mouthful of tart, sighed when Alfred showed no sign of leaving. "Look, old man, if there's been some kind of pilfering, or bad blood, then you really should address your complaints to Mr. Simms there." He jerked his head towards one of the bank clerks. "But you're off tomorrow, as I understand, going home. So there hardly seems any point."

"I don't have a complaint." Keeping the accent RAF, trying to be someone to respect, but knowing your jacket is worn and is cut down from one of Ivor's. "Not that kind of complaint." Leaning closer so you'll make no fuss, because nobody ever wants a fuss. "One of your DPs is a criminal."

At which Fergusson sniggers, wet crumbs on his tongue, in his beard. "Oh, they're all criminals." He frowns, the way one ought to when addressing an idiot. "That's what we expect."

"I mean—"

"I know exactly what you mean. You're talking about ancient history."

"Vasyl." The others at the table not meeting your eye, the woman setting down her spoon. "Vasyl Mishchenko, but he—"

"He's very probably not called anything like that and he's very probably not Ukrainian. We know." As if he's explaining to a child. "But it doesn't matter whether he's a Ukrainian, or some kind of Balt, an Estonian, for example—if we send him back, the Communists will murder him. Do we want that? No, of course we don't. We can't have Communists thinking they can murder people just as they like, now can we."

"He said he was coming to London."

Fergusson drifting his head from side to side, quite thoroughly amused by this time, the others still keeping quiet, the woman blushing. You think he might talk like this often, while they have to listen—agreeing or not, there's no way to tell.

You try again. "He can't come to London."

"London—I wouldn't know. That certainly won't be his point of entry. You have to remember, Mr. . . ."

"Day." And as if this makes any difference, "Formerly of the RAF."

"Good for you. You have to remember, Mr. Day, that Britain lost a great many people in the last war. Almost four hundred thousand dead, hundreds of thousands seriously disabled. We need population. We need a healthy birth rate and good stock. Now either that comes from the colonies and refugees whose cultures are very unlike our own, or we take in lads like your Vasyl, who were misled in their youth, and we live in a country which stays Christian and white. The Yanks have snapped up most of what territory we haven't given away . . . prices in dollars anywhere there's a hope of visitors . . . you know how it is. You surely want our homeland to survive, if nothing more—after all your efforts."

Alfred saying nothing because there is nothing to say.

"And no need to look at me like that. I follow the line which is the government line. We must think to the future, not the past."

"Fuck you."

"Yes, well, we'd already guessed your rank, but thank you for the confirmation. Good evening, Mr. Day. Perhaps we might finish our meal now without further disturbance."

"Fuck you." Not shouting, only disciplined and mild and standing to attention and giving a crisp salute, all of the table watching you now—studying this animal they do not understand. "Fuck you."

Adding no lustre to the service in any way.

Walking clear outside into the start of evening, the heat green and gentle and crickets busy in the grass beyond the wire and the moor growing over its corpses and the bones of its other camps—only this joke, this game left.

Maybe I never did exactly know what I was fighting for, but it fucking wasn't that.

Grass should grow across the whole damn pack of us, clear us away.

"Ready?" Gad tapping him on the left shoulder, but standing by his right—bloody silly trick, Ringer used to play it all the time and Alfred really could have done without it: remembering the wink he'd give when you spun you head round to him after turning the wrong way.

Gad nodded, merrily sympathetic. "You did your best."

More and more of the boys leaving the mess and heading out. "I did nothing." A few of them jogging, even running, to the hall and raising the taste that Alfred can't help knowing: will running alongside will, intention, men deciding they'll do something, preparing. Alfred trotting himself now and Gad beside him, grinning, younger, flushed.

"We'll be waiting for your song, Alf. Bound to get a big response."

"I wouldn't guarantee it."

"Don't sell yourself short, laddie. And dinna fash about the other thing." He seems he is drunk enough to be unsteady. Although this may be an act.

"What?"

"Thon Vasyl. We know him. First job we do once we're out—we'll slide by the DP camp and see to him. As a favour to you."

The men around them in a press, rushing for no particular reason, but rushing all the same.

"See to—"

"The war's only over when we say so. Nice to get some action again. We've friends there—how d'you think we got the papers?"

"But I didn't mean—"

Gad drifting back from him, giving Alfred a thumbs up as he's pushed to the hut steps. "Happens all the time in these places."

Being bumped towards the door. "No. The war's over. I don't want that." Having to shout.

"Oh, your face . . . I wis only kidding. We'll no have the time."

"What?" And Alfred's through the door, half stumbles.

Gad still with his thumbs up, nodding. "I wis kidding. Sing away good and loud, now. Sing away."

The crowd propelling Alfred forward and on to a bench before he can turn again or say anything more and Gad out of sight—just this mass of men filling up what used to be the phoney theatre hut, but now it's a real theatre, operational for the night, because they want it to be and this is when they get what they want.

"Now, then, yes. Simmer down. Simmer down."

A former CSM on stage and the usual whistles and calls from the audience, Alfred stamping his feet without even noticing much, clapping: the performance about to begin.

"Because they have to be back before curfew, our Ukrainian

friends—" A small burst of applause. "Our Ukrainian friends will be singing first. And I do have what they're singing written down, but I can't say it, so I'll just ask you to give them a very warm welcome."

So this is it, then.

And the Ukrainians have made themselves into a choir: two mildly awkward rows of solid men, flesh scrubbed pink: wrists and necks and ankles extending from clothes provided by various donors.

Our show, the one we wanted. Ours.

A moment or two of confusion and then this heavy-headed one starts up the tune and the rest go in after—a deep, cosy spread of sound—and it turns out their songs aren't foreign, only Ukrainian pronunciations of Robert Burns—"My Love Is Like a Red, Red Rose" and some others Alfred half recognises.

Who's to say that Gad wouldn't have killed him? And I minded, but I wouldn't have stopped them. They could have gone ahead and it wouldn't have been my fault, so that would have been all right. I wouldn't have done a thing about it.

Along the row comes a dixie of moderately appalling punch. Alfred has a couple of mouthfuls, because he hopes it will take the bite away from what's bound to be a concert full of love songs and dirty jokes—how could it be anything else.

My love is like a room with nothing in it, only whitewash.

She did care, though.

I have it in writing.

There was a piece in the paper about them landing repatriated prisoners at Leith—an awful lot about bands and "Roll out the Barrel," but they didn't seem to be in too bad shape and said the Germans were being kind. I do hope that's true.

I have it in months of letters I could go and show her and they would prove she must still be that person.

I saw a chap with your hair the other evening. He was sitting in a café window and the way he was turned meant that he looked exactly like you. I can't say how that was, how terribly happy it made me, thinking

*maybe you'd got back somehow and were here. Of course, when he turned
back, he was someone else entirely with really rather piggish eyes. Not
like you at all.*

Because I'm still the man who read them.

*Like in that Keats thing when he melts into her dream. You do that a
lot, my darling.*

The Ukrainians gone by this time, wet-eyed and waving and hugging
chaps at the end of rows as they're marched away. Fergusson and his
crowd perhaps sneaking off after, but probably tucked in a corner somewhere, enjoying a night out, making the most of the drink. A weedy lad
up next, doing his best Max Miller.

"See these eyes, ain't I got big, eyes, ain't I? I do, don't I? Ain't they .
big? Got them from me mother—spent so many years looking all over for
me father."

I'm still the man.

No point in looking all over. What would there be to find?

*Jesus Christ, there's days when you shouldn't wake up and everything
bloody hits you, everything bloody hurts. And it feels like her, like she's
doing it and yo'm still connected, but yo ay. You're not. You're nothing to
do with each other. The pain's your own.*

*February '44. That's how far I made it, until February '44. In the bag
nearly six months and that was it.*

When you say go, I go.

But I was already gone.

I know this will hurt you and I wish it wouldn't.

Such a stupid fucking thing to write.

*And I cor think of the rest. Honest. It's not in my head any more. Oh, I
read the letter often enough that I should know it off by heart like all the
others, but it didn't make sense and you can't remember things that make
no sense—going on about the news from the East and there's terrible things
going on there and she is married, after all, and she doesn't know what's*

what any more and waiting for two people when she only wants the one and what if he ever comes home and she doesn't want to hurt me.

Bloke next to you chuckling away and the chap onstage is getting louder, "And I says, I says, he paid for the new carpet and the new wallpaper and the new piano in parlour?—bloody hell, then shut window— he'll catch his death of cold."

And this noise coming out of your head, again and again, the same fucking stinking noise, like a fucking dog that knows no better than to howl and one day you fucking wish you'll laugh because you're happy, just one time, one fucking day you fucking wish.

As had been planned, Alfred didn't get up to sing until it was almost ten o'clock. Hovering in the wings while "Yours" and "That Lovely Weekend" got hooted briskly across a table full of more and less empty bottles. The audience, he could feel, was admiring, but not exactly entertained. And by now they were fairly drunk.

And he was as close to nervous as he could get.

There's a thing, then. Life somewhere in that old dog, yet.

The bottle blower finished and got his applause—slightly wild—as the stagehands clunked off with his table of props.

"Don't drink them all at once, mate." Someone at the back yelling out and so the room unsettled as Alfred walked out, his feet seeming very big and slightly far out ahead of him. But that's fine.

Can't shoot me. Not any more. Can't even hurt me.

And he stands towards the front of the little stage and he waits and he smiles at them, the rows of men he doesn't much know and will very soon not meet again.

Can't do me a single bit of harm.

And he breathes in as deep as deep and he shuts his eyes and he starts to sing, just the way he did back at his school in the assembly hall—he gives them "Jerusalem," sweet and straight as he can make it.

For a line or two there seems a numb space ahead of him and then a few voices join him in the music as it stretches on forward and up, in the ache it raises out and doesn't fill, only rolls out further.

As the verse widens, strengthens, more and more singers go along with it and, Alfred knows without having to look, Gad and his bods slip outside to lose themselves, to run away.

Alfred standing and the sound like a love in him now and round him, tilting his head and wrapping him with a light he only touches, cannot see.

And he can believe that he hears Pluckrose singing, that lovely awful voice, and they are here together again and yelling the England that will never be.

And he can believe that he hears the Bastard and Molloy and Torrington and Miles and Parks and they are back and didn't die.

And he can believe that he hears his skipper. His skipper.

And he can believe that if he opens up his eyes the benches will be full of all the boys lost to the sky and his friends the closest, his crew the closest, so near that he can take their hands and know they are well and never were harmed and never were frightened, never lost.

And he can believe that he is forgiven.

He can believe so much, the truth of it makes him weep.

A Lanc took them back. He hadn't expected that.

The director gave them a little farewell speech early in the morning and everyone made a quiet effort at three cheers, heads delicate after the night before—the raisin gin and Ukrainian gut rot and the bottles of more conventional booze all having done their work. No mention was made of the six men who'd disappeared, only a thought that they might be sleeping it off in a field somewhere and would turn up soon—their bad luck if they missed the free trip back to England. Or maybe they'd paired themselves off with some local girls. Alfred dutifully passed along every rumour he heard, content that he'd be long gone before the real questions were asked. If they ever were. Nobody seemed much concerned with the past: yesterday was probably too far away already and only drifting further as the hours passed—well beyond the twelve that Gad had wanted.

Alfred waited by the truck and swung up last so that he could look out as the huts shrank away with the guard towers and the wire, the gate wide open behind them and dipping and dwindling as they pulled up across the moor while the sun and the dust rose higher.

All over with. All done.

For the second time, he hadn't expected to be going home and for the second time he'd been wrong.

Walking so long with Ringer, so very long and the war very tired and not pretending any more—all of it there and its true self finally: our men and their men, uniforms almost alike with the rags we'd tied round us for warmth, with whatever we could get round us for warmth, and the civilians the same, only children crying sometimes, or a woman would scream, but some of us would do that, too—and the other poor bastards in their stripes, what was left of them—and if we were still we were dead and if we could move we were on our way to dying and the ones with guns would kill us until they couldn't believe in their guns any more and they left us be, or killed themselves. Rags and blood and guns and moving, that's everything we were.

As they approached the airfield, Alfred shivered, a high pass of Lancsound skimming above them, tickling him in his neck like a kiss. Then there were engines, clearer and clearer, until the truck bumped in past the guardhouse and across the concrete to that fine, high, sculpted shape that was a Lancaster. He stood close beneath a propeller: one blade a smooth hanging force of grey, slabbed up, stretching over his head, the other two winged out above it, each of them waiting to be alive. He wandered by the tailwheel, kicked it gently for luck. He reached the usual doorway in the starboard side, the metal ladder leading inside.

"All right?" A sergeant with W/Op sparks on his trade badge. "Are you all right?"

Alfred stared at him slightly too long, somehow expecting to recognise his face. "I'm . . . I'm fine."

"Not a nervous flyer?" The man smiled, as if he knew the answer he'd get.

Alfred smiled back, sleepy suddenly. "No. No more than the usual, anyway." He began climbing the ladder.

The sergeant followed him up into the dim body, the riveted skin. The others were sitting about, having fixed themselves up as comfortably as they could—some of them very still, thoughtful at being here—but Alfred didn't pay them much attention, because he was turning left and heading for the turret.

"Hang about . . ."

The shock of the sergeant's hand on his arm and then a moment when they didn't speak and came to understand each other.

The man nodded. "I take it you know your way."

"I think I'll remember, yes."

"No forgetting to lock the doors and falling out. That would upset us." He winked.

"I won't forget." Alfred thought they must be about the same age and wondered if that might mean they'd seen about the same things. "In fact, I won't revolve the turret, so there'll be no chance of that."

"Your captain today would prefer that."

"Fair enough."

They shook hands.

And Alfred fed himself back to the place where he belonged and felt the engines start behind him and checked nothing, did nothing, only remembered the last time—ferried back with a bunch of other half-starved Kriegies, taking turns to peer out of whatever windows they could reach as they flew low and level above the bombed thing that was Germany, above their work.

As if the cities had been eaten, as if something unnatural had fed on them until they were gashes and shells and staring spaces, as if it was still down there like a plague in the dust.

It's past eight in the evening before you reach the shop. Walking up the street towards it, the passers-by with no idea of where you've been, the smell of somewhere else on your skin: it makes you feel younger and excitable for about as long as it takes to rap and then batter on the door, stir up Ivor from his wireless in the back room.

"Oh." Ivor with crumbs on his pullover and not well shaved.

"Oh, yourself."

"Didn't think I'd see *you* again."

The city quiet behind you and as summery as it can manage. "Couldn't tear myself away." The shop not untidy and the scent of books very welcome, almost moving. "I see the place has gone to rack and ruin."

"I sold your things." He holds out his hand for your bag and closes the door softly after you. "Ages ago."

"No, you didn't."

"I was going to. Didn't have the time."

"Rush on, was there?"

"A flood of interest in the metaphysical poets, I could hardly keep up. Do you want some toast?"

And he takes you into the back room and you sit in the chair you always take and he puts a new slice of bread in his toasting frame and you think that you cannot stay like this, you do not quite fit any more.

You give him the tin coffee pot and he frowns at it, then puts it on the mantelpiece.

"Handmade."

"I should bloody well hope so. I'd hate to think you'd paid out money for it." He frowns at the pot again. "You look well. Prison life must suit you." It's taken him less than five minutes to start in at you.

"Did me the world of good. Of course, this time they didn't beat me as much as I'd have liked."

"I could always oblige." He smiles.

"You could fucking try." You smile.

And you go to the stove and set the kettle on the gas, because you can't have toast without a cup of tea.

Ivor's brandy is finished and it's so late that it's actually early before you remember that you have nowhere to live.

Ivor waves his arm at this, shaking his head. "Oh, but I know that and it's not true, anyway." He stamps down a foot for emphasis and breaks a saucer. "Fuck."

"What?"

"Your cases and your . . . that . . . your books. They're downstairs with me. Where I live. Which has enough room. Has an extra room."

"You live here." You wave your arm at the fuggy little room.

"No bed." Ivor leans across and pokes you in the chest, quiet delicately. "Where would I sleep? I don't *sleep* here. I have another life elsewhere."

"You don't have another life."

"I *could* have another life." He needs a haircut, you think. "And fuck you. And I have a bath and three small rooms in the basement. One room with your things in, could also have you in."

"We'd murder each other—within days, hours."

"S'OK. You're better at all that than me." Light over his shoulder from the window that faces the yard—blue-grey dawn starting up. "You'd kill me and then you'd hang and I'd know that and die happy."

"Nobody dies happy."

He gives you a frown and then rubs his hairline. "S'OK."

"It's not a happy thing to do."

You sit for a while after that and neither one of you speaks and you think of Ringer being with you in the snow when the Germans had gone and you could go where you liked and there was nowhere to like, except being near to a hedge because that would give you shelter. And it seemed that you wouldn't be shot and maybe in a while you could find food— you guessed there were fields here and maybe underneath the snow there would be something, there would be the leavings of some crop, only you needed a rest, Ringer needed a rest, wouldn't walk any more.

But you should have made him walk, you should have looked after him and saved him the way he'd saved you. You shouldn't have let him sleep.

And then you shouldn't have left him lying—out in the open on ground you couldn't dig.

Nothing about him marked, not a sign on him of death except his colour and the worst death you'd seen because it had crept so gentle and still been a bastard and taken him away.

He'd have wanted a grave in a churchyard, to be near bells, but now you don't know where he is.

Known only to God.

Which sounded as if it would scare him—so far away and nothing with him but the God that watched him die, knew all about it. What's the comfort in that?

"They think we're scum." Ivor not angry, but grabbing for you, catching your wrist and holding it. "That's what they think—I wanted to tell someone . . . but you weren't here to tell." His good eye fixes you.

"Hm?"

"They think we're scum. All the rubbish my mother used to talk about this and that class—it doesn't matter. It's only that whoever crawls to the top of the heap will always think the rest of us are scum. That's the only law. So people like you go off and die and people like me go off and get burned and all of us get bombed, because they think bombing will scare us and make us give up. But it doesn't. They bomb us and we don't give up. They have us bomb other people and the other people don't give up. Because people aren't scum. And we've nowhere to go. We can't give up. All the fuckers in charge, they don't understand."

"Ivor . . ." Suddenly wanting to tell him about the Luger, how it's waiting, dozing in your bag.

But he doesn't listen. "At the start, they didn't give us enough shelters, in case we all stayed in them and never came up—because they expected us to be scum."

"Ivor—"

"And your type—they shoot you in the trenches—*pour encourager les autres*—they threaten you with Lack of Moral Fibre, because they expect you to be scum. But we did so well—so many people did so well . . . and all it means is they learn the next time they'll have to kill more and then more again, because maybe we're stupid scum and we don't know when we're beaten." He seems to be crying. "They never learn, the people in charge—as soon as they get in charge, they forget what people are . . ."

And you don't want to hear this. The start of the day is lifting beyond the dirty net curtains and there's unfinished business that needs your attention, a change you have to make.

Ivor sighs. "Sometimes I—" but he breaks off when he sees you stand. "Going somewhere?"

"For a while. Got to get some air."

"Oh." He sinks a touch more into his seat, shrugs.

"I'll come back, if you don't mind, and I'll take that room."

Ivor studies the patchy carpet. "Need someone here anyway—look after the place . . . I was thinking of going in for more surgery. Maybe."

"Well, that's good, then."

"Yes."

"I'll come back later."

"Don't mind me."

"I do mind you—and I'll be back later. I'm just not sure when."

"Today?" And he checks you quickly, wary.

"Yes, it'll be today."

And it will be today, but first you have to walk and see her, go west across the city in the gold shine of the proper morning and the sparrow din and the start of the rush to work, people climbing out and into their lives and used to the gaps now where the bombs fell and the willowherb growing in them and floating its seed along their streets and used to the new buildings, set where the old ones died, and used to the scars in the masonry from shrapnel and used to the brown linoleum and the shabby passing of small hours and the treats under the counter and the petty greed and not minding what they've lost and what they never got.

You remember the address.

You never forgot it.

Still quite early when you get there, but that might be good, because she could have a job and this will mean you catch her in.

You've checked every year in the telephone directory and there's been the same number, the same address, the same name which is *Antrobus, Donald.* Sometimes you've thought she's kept that for the sake of her husband's memory, or to protect herself—a woman living on her own—or that she just forgot to change it and put her own name, because she can be forgetful, scatter-brained. But usually, you've realised that it means he came back.

What were the chances: that both of her men would come back.

Walking round the block once you've got here and the houses seem slightly more worn, unhappy, but it hasn't changed enough—still pitches your stomach with the full, high wonderful fear. And you haven't been alive as much as this in a long, long while—so you could leave, duck away for the shop and safety and you would still have gained, you would have got your ration of new heartbeats, moving blood, but you won't leave, you'll pass the door for the fifth time and think that they haven't painted it since you were here last, not in all these years, and they should have, it's overdue, and that takes you in closer and the sweep of how this used to be takes you closer yet and this is your hand now reaching and ringing the bell which is next to *Antrobus*, a name that you took once in Lincoln and which makes you want her and that isn't what you intended, it's too much and you really should not stay, you ought to run.

"My God." Joyce standing in her opened doorway and saying what you haven't time to think. "My God."

"Yes."

And she stares at you, covers her mouth with both hands and stares and you feel this on your face, the way it washes you, strips you, touches.

"I . . ." All of those words that you know and there are none of them to hand. "I'm sorry."

She keeps her eyes on you, as if when she blinks, when she glances away, you will disappear.

"I'm . . . No, I'm not sorry." You breathe in, which you haven't for a while. "Are you well? How are you? You seem . . ." You swallow. "I grew a moustache."

She almost grins. "So I see."

"How are you?"

"I'm all right." Such eyes she has. "Considering." Wearing this house dress, flowers on it—blue, all different blues and she's lost a little weight and shorter hair, slightly shorter and her hands are beautiful. "I . . ." And she looks bewildered in the way that she might if you had woken her, something gentle about it and slow. "Where have you been?"

And this hits you in your chest: mouth open, but nothing to say, to tell her, and the sunlight is beginning to make you wince and you need to go, but then she takes a small step forward and then pulls the door closed behind her and this is the most wonderful thing, this is exceptionally fine, this is bostin and it makes you, only a very little, cry so that you drop your head for a moment and cough.

When you look again she's still there and you tell her. "I was away." Which twitches in your neck when you hear it and then you smile without entirely knowing why. "I was away."

Which is when she touches you, cups her hands against your cheeks and holds you so that you tremble.

"I was away."

"You seem tired." This seems to be not quite what she wants to tell you.

"I didn't sleep last night. And I have a hangover."

"Is that a habit?" And the question important to her and making you wonder about the lieutenant and how he is with her.

"No. Not the hangover, anyway. Not a good sleeper." And you swallow, but it breaks out anyway. "I missed you."

Her hands drop away from you then and she begins to walk and you follow, you keep beside her. "I'm sorry, but I did."

"And you think that I didn't miss you?" She's angry-sounding and you would like to reach out for her, but you don't and then she grabs your arm, shakes it. "Having to wait for him and then wanting to wait for you and knowing nothing, then almost nothing, then nothing again—the whole of that bloody building full of women waiting for some bloody man or another and every now and then you'd hear so-and-so shouldn't be waited for any more." She stops herself, lets a chap work past you with his little dog. "I always regretted that letter."

"Me too."

"Yes, I deserve that."

But none of this so very important any more, because you are here and she is here and "Are you happy?" because you want to know, very much, "Because you don't look . . . if you looked as if you were happy I would, I would . . . But you don't."

She pushes her hair away from her forehead. "How does a happy person look?" Her voice quiet, dulled in a way that it shouldn't ever be.

"I'm . . . there's . . ." And because love requires the impossible and you love, "I'm not entirely sane any more, but if . . ."

"I have no feelings for him." Joyce talking past you, gazing over to the other side of the street. "Donald. He came home in a state . . . so that I couldn't leave him. It's not so bad now and also it's worse. He doesn't leave the flat, doesn't do anything . . . not anything useful." A dark in the way she says this that sickens you. "I work to help out with the money—we don't have a lot. He hates it. Would never have let me before, but if I didn't get out of the house, I'd . . ."

Scrambling to understand her, what she might like, would allow, could support. "If I could, we could . . ."

A smile from her you haven't seen before, sharp and small. "He imagines that I have affairs." Before she looks at you, clear into you, and this hurts in the finest way and is a kind of question.

So you give a kind of answer. "It will be complicated."

"What isn't."

"Yes, what isn't."

This bringing the old smile back to her, the one that lifts your hair, the one that rattles out your widest, widest grin and there you are together in the street, the pair of you just like happy people. You intend to kiss her with your new moustache. You intend not to bother if people see.

And a little later, you will go back over to Ivor's shop and find it still closed, although—when you check—it's past twelve. You will rap on the glass until he shambles round between the shelves and lets you in.

"You fell asleep?"

"A light doze. Disturbed by . . ." Ivor will trail off at this and make a great play of stepping back, examining you. He will wag his head and seem pleased in a slightly melancholy way. "You went and saw her, didn't you? You finally went and saw her."

You will tell him, "Fuck off, Ivor."

"You did."

As you walk in past him, he will punch your side, politely, and then follow you, chuckling. "You did."

You will go into the back room and empty the old leaves from the teapot, rinse it out.

"You bloody did."

You will go to your bag, take out the Luger and unwrap it, hand it to him.

"And what the fuck would I do with that?"

"I don't care."

"I don't want it."

"Neither do I. I don't need it any more."

And he will put it slowly into his pocket, the weight of it pulling his jacket and he will want to examine your face, but you will go and stand at the window and see the yard and an angle of the afternoon sky, that late-August blue.

Then Ivor will ask you, "So you'll see her again."

And you will tell him, "Yes. I'll see her again."

And you will feel like laughing.

Acknowledgements

With thanks to The Imperial War Museum Reading Room, and Armoury, the Lincolnshire Aviation Heritage Centre and best regards to John Tile.

ALSO BY A. L. KENNEDY

ORIGINAL BLISS

Emotionally numb, crippled with insomnia, and caught in a frightening, abusive marriage, Helen Brindle believes that God has left her. She spends her days performing banal domestic chores in front of a blaring television. On the BBC one day she watches a self-help guru expound on, among other things, the "rules" of masturbation and the importance of "interior lives." Edward G. Gluck, she discovers, has developed a program that guides lost souls toward contentment. Helen seeks him out, hoping to find an answer. Instead she discovers Gluck's own sadomasochistic obsession, and his profound shame and disgust. And what they both encounter, painfully, is the love each fears and both yearn to embrace.

Fiction/Literature/978-0-375-70278-5

PARADISE

Hannah Luckraft sells cardboard boxes for a living. Her family is so frustrated by her behavior they can barely stand to keep in touch with her. Each day is fueled by the promise of annihilation, the promise of a reprieve, the paradise that can only be found in a bottle. When Hannah meets Robert, a kindred spirit, the two become constant companions. Together and alone, Hannah and Robert spiral through the beauty and depravity of a love affair with alcohol. *Paradise* is a spectacular novel of desire and oblivion.

Fiction/Literature/978-1-4000-7945-2

ALSO AVAILABLE
Everything You Need, 978-0-375-70747-6
Indelible Acts, 978-1-4000-3345-4
On Bullfighting, 978-0-385-72081-6
So I Am Glad, 978-0-375-70724-7

VINTAGE BOOKS/ANCHOR BOOKS
Available at your local bookstore, or visit
www.randomhouse.com